# Magical

# Masquerade

First published in 2017 by CreateSpace
222 Old Wire Road, Columbia, SC 29172

ISBN-13: 978-1542398428
ISBN-10: 1542398428

www.clairesavagewriting.wordpress.com
Facebook: Claire Savage - Author
Twitter: @ClaireLSavage

Cover design by Design for Writers

*For Granny Richardson – who loved a good story – and for Reuben, who walks with me every day in fairy land …*

# Contents

1. Finding Fairyland — 3
2. Silvertoes — 15
3. Prophecies and Pebbles — 22
4. Search for the Riddler — 30
5. Tales of the Realm — 37
6. The Goblin Caves — 48
7. Riddle Me This — 59
8. In Pursuit of Potions — 68
9. Goblins — 77
10. Enchanted — 87
11. Solving the First Riddle — 96
12. Mermaids — 108
13. The Banshee — 119
14. The Runaway Steps — 128
15. Dwarves — 138
16. Through the Cairns — 147
17. Forest Fairies — 157
18. Midnight Revelry — 167
19. Oak Magic — 180
20. The Plummeting Pool — 193
21. Mezra — 206
22. Maps and More — 221
23. Moss Magic — 230

24. Witches     241

25. The Witch's Spire     250

26. Carpet Tricks     259

27. Exchanges     267

28. Any-Ware     275

29. Galloping Gallitraps     284

30. Pixies and Pebbles     296

31. Thistle Glen     310

32. Through the Labyrinth     318

33. The Mystical Mansion     329

34. Mansion Magic     341

35. The Enchanter     353

36. Witchery     360

37. Answers and Expectations     369

38. The Causeway of the Giants     378

39. Secrets     384

40. Crossing Over     393

Epilogue     406

# Magical
# Masquerade

*Paint the picture, set the scene –*
*Where are you going, where have you been?*
*Red or speckled, black or white,*
*Give you a treat – give you a fright.*
*What do I speak of – you want to know?*
*Better perhaps then to stay here than go.*
*But be warned, my dear reader, don't be in a hurry –*
*The things in these pages may cause you to worry …*
*With a witch, an enchanter and a riddler who rhymes,*
*There's also a banshee – quite scary at times.*
*Goblins and pixies and fairies and sprites,*
*Some good and some bad, but they'll put you to rights.*
*A mermaid or two and some nymphs of the water,*
*You won't want to leave them but, really, you oughter.*
*For with magic and spells, and tricks and deceptions,*
*Potions and lotions and some misconceptions,*
*These folk of the fairytale down by the sea,*
*The secrets they keep and the places they be,*
*Are not meant for humans to touch or to see –*
*Best hide if you glimpse them, best yet just to flee.*
*But if you, dear reader, ignore this and … stay,*
*If my rhyming has not yet frightened you away,*
*Then keep turning the pages of the story within,*
*It's the tale of a girl, just a little too thin,*
*When she went to the beach one sparkling spring day*
*She picked up a pebble …*

*… and it whisked her away.*

## Chapter One
# Finding Fairyland

Felicity Stone was *not* one to shy away from adventure. In fact, she liked to think adventure was her middle name.

It wasn't.

She had actually been christened Felicity Petronella Mirabella Stone-Montgomery, but the less said about that the better. She simply went by 'Felicity' and 'Stone' – her mother's much nicer maiden name.

The problem was, Felicity always had to create her own adventures, as the exciting escapades she loved to read about just never seemed to happen to her. It wasn't for want of trying either. Felicity explored constantly around her coastal home – she kept her eyes peeled for the extraordinary and the unusual, but it was no use. Her yearning for true adventure – the sort that springs itself unexpectedly and energetically upon you – had never been satisfied, and she was starting to think it never would.

She'd come to the beach a little out of sorts today, as her father was due to visit in the evening and that meant news of her mother, which made Felicity somewhat nervous. It wasn't that she didn't *want* any news – quite the opposite. It was simply that she couldn't bear to hear if her mother had become any more ill, which she always seemed to be since her father had taken her away two years ago.

Felicity preferred to think of her mum as the infectiously happy person of old, who had taken her foraging in the woods where they used to live and explained to her about the magical elements that surrounded them. The trees had their own language, her mother said. If you listened very carefully, you could hear them whispering in the breeze, though you would be a lucky person indeed if you could understand them, as theirs was a secret language and most humans could no longer comprehend it.

The wind, too, carried mystical messages on its breath, she'd added, and Felicity had subsequently tried many times to eavesdrop on what it was saying. The wind, however, seemed to like teasing her and never gave up the messages it carried. Felicity could no longer enjoy those strolls with her mother and she missed their talks of magic and mystery as they spent hours outside searching for hidden treasures. She was still a scavenger at heart, though, and loved nothing better now than cycling down to the beach to pick through the thick belts of seaweed and the rocks, searching for unusually coloured shells and prettily patterned pebbles. There was always something to be found after the tide receded, and you never knew what that might be.

That evening, the sea was like a lagoon. Clouds crested the sky ahead, gathering as if in anticipation, while the water slapped against the hardened, tightly packed sand. Felicity glanced at her watch. She was going to be late.

She grimaced as she thought of what her father would say – or, rather, what he *wouldn't* say. He would simply throw Felicity a look dripping with disapproval and disappointment, tighten his lips and make her feel as important to him as a pebble on the beach.

She remembered how furious he had been when he'd discovered Felicity had seen her mother doing what he called her 'hocus-pocus' and 'devilment' when she was just five years old. Felicity had found her mother squirreled away in the attic and watched as she mixed together some of the things they had collected outdoors in an old, chipped porcelain bowl, muttering strange words as she did so. Ever since, she'd half-wondered if her mum didn't have a bit of magic in her. Felicity had never dared to voice anything of the kind out loud, however, as she had known that to do so would only have fuelled the growing fire burning between her parents. As it turned out, the flames had fanned themselves and the family disintegrated into ash anyway.

She hurtled over a short stretch of sand, the sapphire sea sparkling in the fading rays of the sun. Spring was seeping slowly into every day, each evening a little lighter than the last. A playful wind picked up.

Felicity loved this beach, which was backed by sand dunes, had a river at one end and a stream at the other. Rocks flung up from the ocean's depths by stormy seas cluttered the base of the dunes while others – larger climbing rocks – marked out the shoreline.

To her distant left was the village; to the right, a rugged coastal path that wound round the cliff. At the beginning of this stood The House, which had a tower, huge gates with a 'No Entry' sign and a rather haunted look about it. It had been sliced up into holiday homes, so was very rarely inhabited and suitably intriguing. It dominated the landscape and Felicity longed to explore inside.

The house rose majestically from the headland, almost like a huge pop-up building from a storybook. It was built in bronze-coloured brick and had large airy windows surrounded by white PVC, which looked out onto the beach below, making it appear old and new at the same time. The brickwork framing the roof looked like a gap-toothed smile and a little rectangular wrought-iron balcony perched outside the topmost front room, while tall chimney pots prodded the sky and a row of converted outhouses backed the property. Then, there was the tower.

It was this which most fascinated Felicity, who couldn't help but think of trapped princesses and tales of magic and enchantment when she saw it. The rounded tower overlooked the sea and stood at the curve of the cliff. It had a properly pointed fairytale roof, no visible door and a single window at the top. Felicity often imagined herself inside and the fun she would have there, for what on earth could be more exciting than living in your very own tower?

Grassy lawns, always neatly mowed, sloped down from the tarmac driveway, ending in thick hedges which sprouted plump wild tomatoes in the summer. A long straight lane was lit up at night by strategically placed lights, while a former gate-lodge guarded entry to the main place of residence.

How Felicity would have loved to hop over the gate and run across the garden slope to inspect the grounds and the house for herself, but she never dared. She had always been taught to respect the property of others and it was a rule she, in this instance grudgingly, upheld.

She raced now across the sand, in the shadow of this grand abode, heading towards the end of the beach, where her bicycle waited by the fast-flowing stream that chattered down through the fields, past the cliff and on to the sea. As she went to cross it, however, something unusual caught her eye.

The stream was glowing gold. Or rather, a certain part of the stream was glowing gold, and it seemed to grow brighter the more Felicity looked at it. She recalled her mother telling her that, as well as the wind and the trees conversing in magical languages, all the rivers and streams and seas of the world talked too, in their own mysterious ways, and she wondered now if this stream was talking to *her*.

Felicity's grandmother, it should be said, also liked to tell tales of magic – sending shivers down Felicity's spine with eerie stories of the Other Realm and of the mischievous fairies and creatures who lived there. She often spoke of the dreaded banshee, who haunted the cliffs on stormy nights, seeking souls destined for the underworld. The banshee foretold a death, she said, and was slippery as a shadow and dark as night, with a mourning wail that could chill the skin off your bones.

Yet she could also appear as a great beauty, tricking those she wept and wailed for who expected to see an old hag. Most unsettling of all, her grandmother warned, the banshee could take the form of a hooded crow, or a stoat, hare or weasel, so you could never be too careful.

Felicity much preferred to hear stories of fairies and elves – even witches – and she usually got her grandmother to tell her about those instead. So it was the most natural thing in the world for her to suppose the glowing stream was caused by magic. What else could it be?

She knelt down for a closer look and found that the light, now pulsing rapidly under the water, came from a large golden rock. Her heart hammering with anticipation, she slipped her hand into the cool, clear water and clasped her fingers around it. The rock was oddly warm and felt smaller than she thought it should. Indeed, when she brought it out of the water, Felicity saw that, instead of the large golden stone she had expected, she was holding a small rounded pebble. It was smooth and looked as if it had been dipped in glitter – or speckled with fairy dust …

Somewhere in the distance a bell tolled, and as Felicity wondered whether the pebble might be magic or not – or whether it was real gold – the wind decided enough was enough. It spun around her in a flurry, and if anyone had been there to see it, they would have been startled by the sight of a mini tornado seeming to appear out of nowhere at the end of the beach on this quiet, ordinary evening. It encircled Felicity, and before she had time even to gasp, it had whisked her away.

\*\*\*

Of course, when there's magic in the air, you'll always find there's somebody watching, *somewhere*, and as Felicity disappeared, a flock of crows happened to be dipping and diving overhead before they went home to roost. They watched the magical episode with interest and then, as one, released a torrent of agitated squawks and set off over the dunes, as if intent on conveying the news of what they had just witnessed to someone who should know of it.

\*\*\*

Travelling by wind was a most unusual experience and Felicity, who wasn't a big fan of flying by ordinary means in an aeroplane, was more than a little anxious when she was swept off her feet.

However, like most ten-and-three-quarter-year-old girls, she had a sense of when something extraordinary was happening and she knew at once that this was magic. So, in the midst of the mini tornado, she decided to open her eyes, as she felt strangely secure and didn't have any sensation of falling or of dust whizzing about her face.

Indeed, Felicity found that she was still standing upright in the eye of the tornado – suspended, as if in outer space. Cocooned from the outside world like a butterfly in its chrysalis, all she could hear was a mixture of silvery bells and sighing wind, and all she could see was the cloud of white around her, so she had no idea if she was still on the beach, close to the beach or aeons away from it. She supposed she might, by now, be nowhere near it. Felicity wasn't alone, however.

Floating around her was an odd assortment of objects, which she studied with great interest. There was a blue-painted door with a shiny gold knocker just a little way above her and all sorts of brightly coloured flower heads danced in the silent space. Their lack of stems made them look like strange, bodiless faces, and when one floated quite closely past Felicity, she was sure she spied two curranty eyes peering back at her.

There was also a solemn teddy bear with a patch over one eye, a garden rake with bent, misshapen spokes, a rainbow-coloured umbrella and long strings of ladies' pearls. Felicity spied an empty chair below her but, try as she might, she couldn't move herself near it so she simply watched and waited to see what would happen next.

What happened next was that she felt earth under her feet and the sound of the silvery bells melted into the distance as the tornado unwrapped itself from her and then twisted away into nothing.

The wind had deposited Felicity on a beach which, at first glance, looked similar to the one she had just left but which immediately afterwards appeared to be so different to where she had been that she wondered why she had thought it the same at all. In the sea, wild horses galloped towards the shore with delighted whinnies, their snowy-white manes streaming out behind them in the breeze as they raced each other before heading back out to the depths to do it all again.

Far out on the horizon, Felicity saw a silver ship, which shone like a polished diamond in the strange half-light of wherever she now was. Billowing white sails gave it a proud appearance, and as she watched, the ship sprouted two long white wings on either side of its hull and flew off among the candy-floss-coloured clouds, disappearing from sight.

She was still standing at the end of a beach and at the bottom of a coastal path which wound around a cliff. In the background, a sing-song sighing sound could be heard, while around her grew all manner of sweet-scented flowers. They bordered a stream not unlike the one she'd been trying to cross before, but swimming in the water were curious creatures with green bodies, long, thin legs and hair that looked like seaweed. These had most certainly *not* been in her stream. They weren't quite mer-people, as they clearly had legs instead of tails, but their feet were webbed and there were tiny gills on the cheeks of their pointed faces. A couple of the creatures saw Felicity staring and grinned at her mischievously, popping their heads out of the water to let off bubbling laughs before dipping down beneath the surface again.

Seaweed lay coiled like silver snakes on the shimmering sand, which was speckled with gold and almost looked like fairy dust. Felicity pocketed her own glittering gold pebble, placing it first in a small pouch that she carried for stowing away such treasures, as she knew she would never find it again if she dropped it on this dazzling sand.

She jumped as a large black bird appeared from nowhere and swooped past her with a raucous squawk. Huge, powerful wings took it down the deserted beach – a dark silhouette against a sky oddly streaked with green and yellow and strewn with those plump pink clouds. Far off in the distance, a bell tolled again and Felicity was about to explore a little further when she heard a tinkling much closer to her. She turned to see where the sound was coming from and her eyes fell upon a fairy.

## Chapter Two
# Silvertoes

The little winged creature was peering at Felicity intently and was the most magical and beautiful thing she had ever seen. Thin as a twig and with exquisite gossamer wings, the fairy, who was no bigger than a rag doll, had a heart-shaped face framed with a cloud of silvery hair. It floated around her almost as if she was suspended underwater, long tendrils curling around her wiry body.

Turquoise, almond-shaped eyes blazed back at Felicity's curious stare, while elongated and perfectly pointed ears were just visible underneath her flowing locks. She wore a trailing blue gown streaked with silver thread, the pointed tips of silver shoes peeping out beneath.

Felicity took a deep breath. And then the fairy spoke. Her voice was pure and clear and sounded like an orchestra of tiny bells tinkling in the breeze. 'You have lifted our glamour, human girl. Welcome,' she said. 'Welcome to Fairyland – the land which lies just beyond yours, the land to which you now belong.'

She smiled sweetly at Felicity, who had no idea what a glamour was or how she could possibly have lifted it. Something else bothered her more, however.

'What do you mean, I *belong* here now?' she said.

The fairy gave a musical laugh. 'Questions, questions, human girl. Is that *all* you wish to know?'

'Well, yes – I mean, it would do for a start,' said Felicity, her confidence growing with her curiosity. 'What's a glamour anyway, and how can I lift it when I didn't actually *do* anything?'

The exquisite fairy smiled and fluttered her wings, flying gracefully to the little footbridge which crossed the stream and perching upon one of its wooden posts.

'Of the knowledge you seek, I can only tell you my part,' she said solemnly. 'The rest must come from the Pebble People, for it is surely they who brought you here through the use of the wind and the pebble, and it is they who now seek an audience with you. My elfin senses felt the change when you crossed over and so I came as quickly as I could. Also, I suspected that you, or someone like you, would soon be arriving.'

'Wait, you're an elf?' Felicity interrupted, in awe.

The elf smiled again and gave her shimmering, silvery mane a delicate toss, making it ripple like water. 'Yes,' she said. 'I am an elf. My name is Silvertoes, eldest daughter of the Elves of the Misty Glade – pleased to meet you.'

'Yes, you too,' whispered Felicity.

'But, hark, I must tell you the answers to your questions before the Pebble People come,' said Silvertoes sweetly. 'They cannot move so swiftly as I, but they are on their way here.' She paused. 'They are very excited about you.'

Felicity swallowed nervously. 'Is that a good thing?' she asked. 'Who are the Pebble People and how do you know all this?'

Silvertoes shook her head and frowned, although her features remained as beautiful as before. 'It is not up to me to tell you their story – only the Pebble People can do that and explain why you are here. But I will offer what assistance I can. As for how I know … Well, my parents work at the fairy palace and are trying to get me to join them in their trade.' She screwed up her face.

'Why anyone would want to slave away for the king and queen is a mystery to me, when there is much dancing to be had at the moonlit balls, and festivities aplenty, with elderberry wine and honey cakes and all sorts of wonderful things!

17

'Anyway, one often overhears things when one is pretending to work.' Silvertoes gave Felicity a sly smile. 'When you picked up that pebble – which was, of course, an *enchanted* pebble – you were transported to the Land of the Fairies, or the Fairy Realm as it is better known. It co-exists with your own world, although there are many more strange, exciting and terrible places here and all sorts of magical things.'

Felicity felt goosebumps rise on her skin. Silvertoes continued.

'Our world is hidden from human sight by a magical glamour – a very powerful spell put in place many moons ago by the Olde Fairy Council, which was made up of some of the cleverest and most magical fairies, goblins, enchanters, witches and wizards.'

She stopped, noticing Felicity's confused look. 'What is it, my dear?'

'I just, I just thought all goblins were, well, *bad*,' said Felicity. 'Witches too.'

Silvertoes grimaced. 'Most are, unfortunately, but there are still a few who work on the side of the good and long ago the council enjoyed the benefits of some wonderful goblin minds – unique in itself, as they are not known for their wit. Things changed throughout the years, however, as, sadly, the goblins grew ever greedier for power.

'As for witches …' She shrugged, then flicked her hair back impatiently and continued. 'The glamour protects us, *masks* us from humans and, I imagine, keeps *your* kind safe – on the whole – from us. It is the way it has always been and must always remain. Few humans cross over into our world and even fewer leave it.'

Felicity gulped. What did *that* mean? As if reading her mind, Silvertoes continued.

'Upon entering the Fairy Realm, by whichever means you have used – whether consciously or unconsciously, on purpose or in error, by capture or by choice – here you must remain for evermore.'

'For, for *evermore!*' Felicity spluttered.

Her delight at having reached the fairy kingdom suddenly deflated at Silvertoes' barbed but musical words. The elf looked at Felicity with amusement.

'But surely everyone must know that,' she said innocently. 'To trespass into our world a price must be paid. We rarely enter the Human Realm and those who do risk death, capture or much worse fates than living for all eternity in a beautiful, magical land. Our secrets must remain with us and must not be taken back to enhance human knowledge.'

Felicity couldn't get the words out, but thoughts were spinning frantically in her head. *Eternity?* As in, not *ever* dying? Forced to live literally forever, away from home, from her family, from *humans*? She thought of her grandmother, who would be wondering where she was. Felicity had certainly wanted an adventure, but not being able to go home afterwards hadn't been part of the plan. She swallowed.

'If I wanted to leave, though, how would I do it?' she asked. 'You said that *few* humans leave, so surely there must be *some* way, if others have managed it?'

'A slip of the tongue, my dear.' Silvertoes raised her eyebrows. 'No, you cannot *leave*. You're here to stay!' She spread her wings and flew excitedly up into the air, whirling and spinning so fast that all Felicity could see after a few turns was a shining silver blur.

'It *would* be nice to stay for a while,' she ventured. 'But I would like to at least let my grandmother know where I am.' (*Until I work out how to leave*, she thought.)

Felicity remembered how her Granny Stone had warned her about the tricks and traps fairy folk laid. Even the most innocent-looking and beautiful magical creature was never to be fully trusted, she had said, although Felicity *did* so want to trust Silvertoes.

The elf stopped her twirling and looked her in the eye. 'Our time is different from your time,' she said. 'Your grandmother won't even notice you're missing.'

'*How* different?' said Felicity. 'Does it go slower here – or faster?'

Silvertoes flapped her wings in frustration. 'So many questions, human girl! Come with me and you will see!'

'No, I need to find out how to get home. There must be a way,' Felicity said firmly. 'I can't stay here forever, no way.'

The transformation was startling and quick as lightning. Silvertoes flew right up to Felicity's face, her eyes now flashing with rage. So close was she that Felicity saw, with horror, little lightning bolts zigzagging across them. The elf's silvery hair stood out even more from her tiny face in a wild mass of curls, which frightened Felicity. They seemed to have a life of their own as they writhed away from the elf's body like twisted, angry fingers.

'How dare you insult me? How dare you insult the Fairy Realm!' screeched Silvertoes, her dainty, tinkling voice now more like clashing cymbals and thunderbolts.

She pointed a long, thin finger at Felicity, who stood petrified before her. *Please don't curse me, please don't curse me*, she thought, *or turn me into a mouse*, for she had spied the little star-tipped wand that had appeared in the elf's other hand. However, Silvertoes had started spinning wildly again – it made Felicity dizzy to watch, but she was mesmerised by the blurry elfin mass. It spun and spun – a hurricane of silver – and, in a flash, Silvertoes was gone.

## Chapter Three
# Prophecies and Pebbles

Felicity sat down with a thump on a nearby rock. She closed her eyes and then opened them again. She took a deep breath. She had realised almost as soon as the words were out of her mouth that she had spoken out of turn. Another of her grandmother's warnings, remembered too late – never insult the 'wee folk': they didn't take it well and more often than not would put a spell on you. Felicity had been lucky then. Perhaps Silvertoes thought her fate of being left alone here forever was worse than anything *she* could inflict upon her. Or perhaps, Felicity suddenly thought, the elf was off to find reinforcements.

The sound of distant footsteps made Felicity jump to her feet. The elf had been quicker than she'd thought – but then again, she had magic on her side. As the plodding steps grew closer, she looked for somewhere to hide, but with the beach to her left and the cliff to her right, she was fully exposed, and so all she could do was watch and wait and let whatever was about to happen, happen. She felt the ground tremble and stepped back as the grassy slope of the cliff opened up into a dark, shadowy tunnel and a troupe of little people marched out, each wearing a smart bowler hat.

Felicity counted – five stood before her. How, though, had they made so much noise for people so tiny? She looked more closely. Aha! Their feet. They jutted out from their bodies at an unusual angle and looked suspiciously like smooth, rounded pebbles.

In fact, the more she looked at the little folk, the more their entire bodies looked, well, pebbly. They had little round faces, round grey-blue eyes, round bodies and even their arms and legs looked more oblong than normal. Their feet couldn't be pebbles, though, she thought. They had holes in the top where the ankles peeped out – more like pebble clogs.

Of course! These must be the Pebble People Silvertoes had spoken of. She hoped they weren't dangerous, although they *looked* harmless enough. If they knew powerful magic, though …

The five Pebble People had congregated in front of their magical tunnel, which closed over and disappeared, leaving the cliff-side as it had been but moments before. Felicity really wanted to ask them how they had done that, but right now, she was too afraid.

There were four little men in the assembled party and just one Pebble woman, who caught Felicity staring at her and smiled kindly. Felicity relaxed slightly – they must be friendly then, surely. The woman whispered something to a Pebble man holding a thick book and wearing rounded spectacles. He nodded and then turned to Felicity. All five stood in a solemn line before her. The little man, who she guessed was the leader, spoke in a grave and authoritative voice.

'Human girl – welcome. Welcome to this, the Fairy Realm. We are the Pebble People. I, Cobble, am the Pebble Leader, this is my wife, Tilda, and these,' he indicated the remaining little men, 'are some of our loyal subjects.'

The Pebble People nodded in assent, the Pebble Leader's wife smiling once more at Felicity.

'We knew the one who could help us would find the pebble we planted – we have waited in hope for this very moment.' He tapped his book. 'So the prophecy said.

'Our pebbles possess magic – some of the most powerful in the Fairy Realm. Only the Pebble People truly know the extent of this power and of what each one can do, but even the wisest Pebble Readers are not always knowledgeable about what a pebble is capable of.'

'What – what *can* they do?' asked Felicity.

'Many, many things,' said the Pebble Leader solemnly. 'Like the one which brought you here, they can spirit you away to a far-flung kingdom – to lands beyond this one or to different parts of the Fairy Realm. They can take you to good places, bad places, wonderful magical places and evil torturous places.

'There are pebbles that grant wishes, pebbles that make your dreams come true – or your nightmares reality. Pebbles to make you rich or poor, happy or sad. Oh, so many pebbles!

'We guard them, lest they fall into the wrong hands, but many dare not try their luck and touch them, nor pick them up, for fear something terrible rather than good will befall them. Only one from the Pebble community can attempt to identify any particular pebble's true nature.'

He paused. 'And so, to the reason you, my dear, are here. Up until now, our enchanted pebbles were known by all folk – or most folk – to be found only under the weeping willows, which grow close to water and so are often located near the many streams, rivers and lakes in the realm. There are many names for the sacred willow, which is ruled by the moon and is therefore a Moon Tree and full of ancient magic. To some, it is the Tree of Enchantment, the Tree of Witcheries or Witches' Aspirin – she wears many names.

'But these are dangerous times for us all because someone or *something* has been disturbing the pebbles, snatching them away from the willows. Pebbles are going missing and, what's more, some have been turning up in places they just shouldn't be. Now there is disarray – there is danger where there ought to be none – as enchanted pebbles are being found by unsuspecting fairies, elves, pixies and brownies, who are then whisked away to who knows where. The fairy king and queen have demanded it stop, but to no avail. It is up to us, they say, as the Pebble People, to stop this from happening!'

'And why haven't you?' asked Felicity. 'I mean – isn't that something you can do as, er, Pebble People?'

Cobble shook his head sadly. 'Perhaps once we might have been better equipped to solve this mystery but, you see, our stony magic is directly linked to the pebbles, and without them in their correct locations, we find our strength depleted. We don't know what has happened to them but our community is becoming gradually weaker and so we fear that not only have they been stolen, but some dark magic is being worked over them, as our powers are being drained daily. This would only happen if the pebbles were being tampered with – or destroyed. We believe those stealing the pebbles are doing so for someone else, as only a great and powerful being could perform such magic.

'Anyone outside the Pebble community must work strong spells over the pebbles to take them and transport them, for only we can safely handle the stones. A common pixie or fairy wouldn't know such magic, so they must have obtained the spells from someone more powerful. But such spells are difficult to maintain and won't last for long with the pebbles, so the thieves would have to stop and recast them frequently. Somewhere along the way, the pebbles are obviously being dropped, and perhaps the thieves themselves are being accidentally spirited away.

'Even we don't know what might happen if this continues, but the pebbles are bound to underworlds and other-worlds and darkness has been creeping into the kingdom. There are whisperings about strange shadows flitting about at night that were never there before; of dangerous new creatures skulking in the woods. We fear the boundaries between our realm and these other-worlds are fraying and that unwelcome spirits are filtering through.

'We've even heard reports of harpies – some swear they've heard their shrieks and cackles in the dark hours.

What magic we had left, we used to enchant a pebble – *your* pebble – to summon the one who could help us. And so here you are. We knew not whom it would be, or why that person would be chosen, but it appears that it is you. The prophecy of the one who will save us is fulfilled, for it is written that when the pebbles are attacked, so she will come!'

Felicity's mind was reeling after the Pebble Leader's long speech. There was a lot to take in.

'I have no special powers, though!' she said in alarm. 'I don't even know how to get home. I *can't* get home!'

'Oh, but of course you can, my dear,' said the Pebble Leader's wife gently.

'No, the elf – Silvertoes – said –' Felicity protested.

'Nonsense and mischief, tricks and deceptions, I'm sure,' said Tilda, or Mrs Pebble, as Felicity decided to think of her. The little woman tutted. 'Those elves are not to be trusted. All sweetness and light one minute and sly and deceiving the next.

'No, I'm sure Silvertoes did not tell you the way home. She ought to be learning her spells and doing her lessons up at the palace, but instead she's meddling where she shouldn't be, as usual. She wanted to keep you here, no doubt – to dance with her and the fairies every night. Beware the fairy rings by the way – step into one of *those* and you'll be lucky to escape!

'No, my dear – you *can* return home – there *is* a way. It will not be straightforward or simple, of course, but we will tell you how ... if you help us?'

## Chapter Four
# Search for the Riddler

Upon hearing Tilda's words, Felicity knew then that she had no choice, but the Pebble People seemed harmless enough. Besides, if she found out how to get home, then perhaps she could enjoy a real adventure by helping them, which she could tell her Granny Stone about later. It was what she'd always wanted after all.

'OK,' she said. 'Agreed. I'll help *you* if you help *me* and tell me what I have to do to get home.'

The Pebble People grinned, exposing white pebbly teeth. Apart from Cobble and Tilda, they didn't say very much, Felicity noticed.

'For a human to leave the Fairy Realm, he or she must complete three tasks set by the Rhyming Riddler,' said Cobble. 'Find the Rhyming Riddler, solve the riddles, complete the tasks and, if after that you live to tell the tale, freedom is granted! But you must never then return, as only once is this trio of tasks granted to the human. Enter the Fairy Realm a second time and be certain to stay. Forever.'

'How do I find this Rhyming Riddler?' asked Felicity at once.

The Pebble People looked at one another and then, remarkably, all spoke in unison.

*'We cannot help you. Find the Rhyming Riddler – it must be done by you. Along the way we hope you'll find what you need to help us too!'*

The Pebble Leader clapped two pebbles together and with that, they were gone. People seemed to come and go awfully quickly in the Fairy Realm, Felicity decided. Still, at least she knew what to do now to get home. Find the Rhyming Riddler.

It was time to move.

*** 

*Find the Riddler, find the Riddler, find the Riddler.*

Felicity kept repeating the words over and over in her head. Not *just* a riddler, however, she reminded herself – a *rhyming* riddler no less. So far she had been lucky with people finding *her* but Felicity knew she couldn't just hang around the beach all day. It remained calm and tranquil and she hated to leave that fresh golden sand and glistening blue water behind, but she was in Fairyland and, despite any fears she might still have, Felicity couldn't help but feel excited. She had always wished for adventures, hadn't she, and now one had actually begun it would be ridiculous of her not to seize it with both hands.

She wondered what her best friend, Sophie, would make of all this. She was a kindred spirit in many regards, who also loved exploring the outdoors and who had taught Felicity the names of the local seabirds and plants.

Sophie lived in the village and was much more popular than Felicity at school, but Felicity found that as the two of them had grown closer her classmates had become a little less suspicious of her. They were slowly accepting her quirks and if they looked at her curiously from time to time it was probably because her mother had gone and her father had left her behind and they still wanted to know exactly why.

Of course, Felicity never spoke of that to anyone except her Granny Stone. She hadn't even told Sophie everything in case she thought Felicity would end up the same as her mum – sent away – and she wondered for the same reason if she would be able to share her otherworldly adventures with her friend – if she managed to escape. In the meantime, there was so much she wanted to know.

If only she had a guide to explain everything to her and help her find the Rhyming Riddler. Was he big, small? Short or tall? Was he prone to laugh or more prone to brawl? Did he have bells on his feet and what did he eat? Did he –?

Felicity stopped herself. What was she doing, creating these absurd rhymes? It certainly wasn't how she normally thought about things and the last one didn't even make much sense! Fairyland must be doing something to her head.

She clambered over the last few rocks to the little wooden bridge where Silvertoes had perched before. It was more solid and sturdy than the one in her world, the fairy wood polished and healthy – as if it was still alive. She had almost crossed the L-shaped walkway and was still engrossed in conjuring up a plan of action when she felt a tug on her skirt. She jumped and stepped backwards instinctively.

'Who's there?' she said tentatively, as she could see no one. The bridge was bare.

She had turned to go when the tug came again. Was it some magical invisible person, she wondered, a little scared. Not everyone here was friendly. 'Hel– hello?' she said again. 'Is anyone there? I won't harm you but I can't *see* you. If I could see you it would be very helpful. Please,' she added.

'Hello back at you,' said a sensible-sounding voice below her. 'I'm not invisible, you know, just camouflaged. Look again.'

Felicity looked and looked and then she saw him – a little brown man perfectly disguised against the beautifully burnished wood. How clever!

When he realised she had seen him, the little figure stepped away from the side of the bridge into the centre and looked up at Felicity. He was about the height of a large hare on its hind legs and was wearing a raggedy coat and tunic, trousers and leather boots, all in various shades of brown. A pointed cap covered rust-coloured hair, while two kindly hazelnut eyes shone brightly beneath shaggy eyebrows. He had a broad nose and slightly pointed ears. Really, he was a sight to behold.

'Hi – I'm Felicity,' she said, holding out her hand.

'Bob,' replied the little creature. 'Or rather, I'm Bobbin the Brownie of the Brightstar Brownie Family, but you may *call* me Bob. Pleased, as they say,' he took a bow with a sweep of his hat, 'to meet you.'

Felicity giggled. 'Hi, Bob – nice to meet you too,' she said.

She would have preferred to call him Bobbin than Bob, as it sounded more of the Fairy Realm, but she

34

didn't want to offend the brownie. 'Do you live here?' she asked. 'At the bridge, I mean?'

Bob shook his head. 'I live a bit further away, in a cosy little house near the Vanishing Lake – a great place for fishing, may I say. But I've been on my travels of late and when I heard the Pebble People on the move I thought I'd follow them and see what was up, as all sorts of strange things have been going on in the realm recently. And … seeing as I'm here, I decided there was no harm in introducing myself to you.'

'I'm glad you did,' said Felicity. 'The only other person I've met, besides the Pebble People, was an elf and she wasn't very friendly.'

'Elves and fairies are easily offended,' said Bob. 'As for pixies, well, they're something else altogether!'

Felicity's eyes lit up at the mention of pixies. They had always been her favourite type of magical creature.

'Don't you go thinking pixies are all safe and fun,' warned Bob, sensing her excitement. 'They're just as tricksy as the rest of them and full of cheek to boot. Wouldn't trust one as far as I could kick him! If you watch your step, though, they can be useful in a tight spot, I suppose.'

Felicity interrupted him as an idea unfurled in her head. 'I wish I had someone like you to come with me,' she said. 'Someone who knows the ways of the realm –

the rules and the people in it. Someone who could explain things to me along the way, so I don't get into trouble while I'm trying to help the Pebble People.'

'Bit of a trickster yourself, are you then?' Bob retorted. 'Fit right in here, I think!'

Felicity felt a little hurt at that but soon brightened up when Bob added: 'Well, I suppose I'm already on my travels, so company would be good, and you really wouldn't last very long without any guidance, I think.'

'I might!' said Felicity, indignant.

'Yes, you very well *might*,' said Bob. 'But then again, you very well might *not*. Besides, if I help *you* to help the Pebble People it will help *me* too. Pebbles being moved to the wrong places – dangerous places – people being spirited away … no, no, not good at all!' His eyes took on a faraway look.

'So you'll help me then? Come with me?' asked Felicity.

'I will!'

## Chapter Five
# Tales of the Realm

Felicity smiled at Bob – Bob and his bright brown eyes. Yes, she felt she could trust Bob. Besides, she had no choice. She was alone in the Fairy Realm, she didn't know her way, the dangers which lurked or the people and Bob was only little – she could easily outrun him if needs be. She had no time to waste and a guide would make all the difference.

'Thank you, Bob.' She grinned. 'But before we go, tell me – what *is* that singing sound I keep hearing?'

'Ah, the singing,' said Bob. 'That's simple. It's the sand! It's known as the Singing Sand. The grains of gold – pure gold, may I add – are so fine, so smooth and so perfect that they sing as the water ebbs and flows over them. It's only hushed now because everything is so peaceful but, believe me, in a storm, when waves rage and crash on the shore, the sand screams more than it sings but with notes so pure they pierce your heart. And, if there happen to be any empty shells scattered around or brought in by the tide, the din can be horrific, as they lament the lives lost from their now empty husks. Pick one up and you'll surely hear the faint echo of their sorrowful song …'

'How sad,' said Felicity, although she found it odd to think of shells grieving. 'What about the sand, though? Don't some fairies try to steal it, if it's made of gold?'

'Well, they *have* tried,' Bob said grimly. 'But,' he added, with a twinkle in his eye, 'it doesn't do much good when it turns back into ordinary sand like in your world when they take it from the beach. Spells have been used to try to keep it golden but the magic just drains away from it once it leaves this shore.'

And a good job too, thought Felicity. It would be such a pity if that beautiful sand was stolen. Bob saw that he had captured Felicity's attention, so he continued.

'And in case you're wondering why it's so quiet, it's always so when someone passes either way through the realms. When you crossed over and lifted the glamour it was sensed and things became unsettled – creatures were wary and retreated. But not for long.'

He tapped his own chest. 'See – you have now met me and, already, the Pebble People and the elf you mentioned.

'The Pebble People said I need to find the Rhyming Riddler,' said Felicity. 'Do you know where he might be or how we might find him?'

Bob tapped his chin, looking deep in thought. He took off his hat, rubbed his head and then put his hat back on. 'No one knows exactly where he dwells, although it has been said he hides out in the Mountain of Lore,' he said finally. 'Nobody knows where that is, though, so it makes little difference to those trying to seek him out, few as they usually are. They do say, however, that the Riddler is not far away when you begin to think or speak in rhymes – annoying creature. It's bad enough he tells you *his* rubbishy rhymes, but then he makes those near him speak the same way! It's insufferable!'

Felicity looked at Bob excitedly. 'I began thinking in rhyme just before you tugged on my skirt,' she said. 'He must be close!'

'In that case,' said Bob, 'let's be off!'

'Yes, let's,' agreed Felicity. 'The sooner we find him the sooner I can get home. And find out how to help the Pebble People too, of course,' she added hastily.

They crossed the bridge and began climbing the cliff path, which passed the sprawling house full of holiday homes in Felicity's world. In Fairyland, however, the house looked more wild and neglected and much more like a proper castle.

Instead of a neatly mown lawn, here the garden was an unruly tangle of wildflowers, broken up with bushes and a few scraggly, bare-branched trees, which scraped the sky with forlorn abandon.

The driveway was overgrown, enshrouded by high hedges, and the house itself was a tumbledown structure of red brick, cracked slates and blank, empty windows, which stared vacantly towards the ocean. It stood silent and imposing, its tower an accusing finger pointing upwards into nothingness.

Bob saw her staring at it as they went by. 'Ah,' he said. 'You don't want to be going near that. Best keep to the path and skirt around it.' He shuddered. 'Strange place.'

'Strange?' said Felicity. 'In what way?' She wondered how anything could be considered strange in Fairyland by someone who lived there, considering *everything* here was strange to her but surely normal to them.

'Well,' began Bob. 'That *place* is either possessed or controlled by someone with very powerful magic. Sometimes it's here – or rather, you *think* it's here – and other times it just seems to disappear, leaving a strange haze or illusion of itself behind. You might catch a glimpse of it from the corner of your eye, but nothing more. Very strange indeed.'

'Who do you think lives there?' asked Felicity.

'I don't know but, personally, I think it's haunted and that's that,' said Bob, stopping to stare up at the turreted tower and distressed gothic windows. 'Be it by an enchanter, witch or wizard, or maybe just a ghost, but you mark my words – whoever it is, you don't want to go meddling with them.'

'Well, I can't say I fancy finding out if anyone's there right now,' said Felicity, although her curiosity was piqued. 'Let's keep on and look for this Riddler – before it gets dark.'

She paused, thinking back on what Bob had said. 'Are there many witches here?' she asked uneasily. 'As in … wicked … witches?'

They had started walking again and were now huffing and puffing a little as they climbed the cliff-side.

'Witches? Oh, yes,' said Bob matter-of-factly. 'It's not just fairies and elves you have to worry about in the Fairy Realm, tricking you and creating havoc – the witches are the worst.

'Witches are wicked. It's as simple as that. Oh, yes, you have the odd white witch – or as they're known, the "Cunning People" – but even they must not be trusted. They tell fortunes to suit their own ends, find "lost" items they themselves have stolen and enchant with charms. But the Black Witches are the worst – they who practise the dark arts and ancient witchcraft, who take the form of their familiars, black cats and crows. Oh, the crows! Which is a witch and which just a bird? But beware, for even the true crow is in league with the witches and few of them are to be trusted either. They spy and keep watch on the fairy folk and you must always be on your guard when they're around.

'Witches will capture unsuspecting pixies and brownies like myself, especially brownies, for we are hard workers. Some are kept chained up as prisoners and slaves.

'The chains are tied to the captive's ankle and are sparkling silver and thin as thread, but try cutting them and the broken ends magically re-join, for they are enchanted and won't release you until the witch orders it.'

'Let's not talk about witches anymore,' said Felicity. 'It gives me the chills.'

'Yes.' Bob looked grim again. 'And so it should. Best to be aware of them, though, for you never know when you might run into one!'

Felicity looked at him in unhidden horror. 'Well, I very much hope I do *not* run into one – or one of their crows. Horrid creatures! Why side with the witches?' She knew she was never going to look at another crow in the same way again.

'Why indeed,' said Bob. 'It's just the way things are.'

They had now reached the cliff-top summit and stopped to enjoy the view and catch their breath. There was a warm afternoon glow bathing the beach below, although Felicity had no idea what time it actually was, as her watch, she now noticed, had stopped.

A sharp splash shifted her attention to the rocks. Was that –? No, it was just the waves, surely? The sea was still though. There *were* no waves. She looked intently at the spot which now showed only widening ripples.

'Did you see that?' she asked Bob.

'Yes, a mermaid, I think,' replied the brownie. 'The Mermaids' Cave isn't far from here – it's just a little further along the coast. Beautiful creatures they are – and quite playful too. But, as with most folk in the realm, best not to make them angry!'

'I'll bear that in mind,' said Felicity, although she secretly thought the folk of Fairyland shouldn't be quite so touchy. She would really have loved to meet a mermaid but they had to find the Rhyming Riddler and, besides, the mermaid had disappeared and to go looking for her would mean backtracking down the cliff. No, best to push on. Anyway, this was the Fairy Realm – there was sure to be more excitement around the next corner.

***

Felicity and Bob kept walking, Bob chatting away and pointing things out to Felicity as they went. There was a clump of magical mushrooms – a small sliver of one often a key element in common spells. And there was what looked like a mere rabbit-hole but was actually the entrance to an underground warren frequented more by brownies and fairy folk than their furry friends.

Along the way, Felicity also discovered that Bob was not only 'a very helpful brownie', who used to travel frequently into the human world to assist households there but now rarely did because of their disbelief in brownies, but he was a carpenter by trade, making furniture and mending items for his customers. He also adored books and said his house was piled high with them.

Felicity found it all fascinating and had almost forgotten about the Riddler. She was just about to ask Bob more about what his house looked like inside and quiz him on his inter-realm journeys when she saw the sun spark off something lying on the grass. She stepped off the path to take a closer look.

'Wait!' she said to Bob. 'What's this?'

Felicity crouched down beside an antique glass bottle with a small scroll of paper inside. She picked it up with delight. A message in a bottle! To be fair, found on the cliff and not the shore, which was a little strange, but still, it was a message all the same. She wondered what it said and pulled the cork out excitedly. She had never found anything half as thrilling as this when she and her mother used to go treasure-seeking.

'Wait!' cried Bob, jumping up and down frantically. Felicity looked at him. 'What's wrong?' she asked. 'I'm just going to read what it says. I'll put it back.'

'Be careful,' said the brownie. 'These bottles send magical messages between some of the fairy folk and they don't like others to meddle with them. It could contain instructions for a spell or the answer to an important and secret question.'

'Then they really shouldn't leave the bottles lying about where anyone can pick them up,' said Felicity in a bit of a huff. 'I won't tell anyone's secret, but I've always wanted to read a message in a bottle!'

And with that, she poked her fingers into the bottleneck and pulled out the parchment. As she did so, a small sprinkling of silver stars scattered around her.

'Fairy dust,' muttered Bob. 'Well, read it quick and then let's be moving on before we get into any trouble.'

Felicity unrolled the tiny scroll and read the scrawled words out loud:

*'Rhymes I love,*
*Intrigue fits like a glove,*
*Dark secrets I keep,*

*Destinies from the deep.*
*Learn from me if you will,*
*Except please don't stand still …*
*What am I?*

'Well, that's obvious,' said Felicity. 'It's the Rhyming Riddler, of course! What sort of a ridiculous riddle is that? And the last bit doesn't even make sense! Don't stand still? Why on earth not?'

Bob frowned. 'Once the answer is said, the riddle is dead. From wherever he may be, the Riddler you will see,' he said from memory. 'That's usually the way of it, so why has he not appeared? No, that can't be the answer. His rhymes aren't always the most difficult to work out, though, so I'm sure we'll get it soon! Bring it with you and we'll think on it as we walk.'

Felicity pocketed the little bottle and read the message again, not looking where she was going. She studied the last line in particular. *Except please don't stand still.* What did *that* mean, she wondered, as she took another step forward onto a dark patch of spongy grass.

She jumped as Bob gave a shout, a look of horror flickering across his face.

'Keep walking! Keep walking!' he yelped, hands clutching his little hat. 'Don't stand still!'

'*Don't stand* –' Felicity's thoughts were rudely interrupted as the ground suddenly opened up like a trapdoor beneath her. She heard Bob cry out, 'Wait for me!' before everything went black.

## Chapter Six
# The Goblin Caves

As darkness swallowed her up, Felicity realised she was not falling, as she had feared, but *sliding* and, judging by the sounds above her, it appeared that Bob had made it in just before the gap closed over and was following behind.

Knowing that she was on a bizarre kind of slide in the cliff, Felicity tried to calm down and catch her breath. It was a little difficult, however, considering she was gaining speed all the time – her hair streaming out behind her and her eyes beginning to water. That aside, she was actually starting to enjoy the ride when she shot out into a small, dimly lit cave and bounced off a wall – not, thankfully, of rock, but of spongy cushions. She squinted in the gloom.

The 'cushions' were yellowy-orange and, given that they were a little moist and in a cave, Felicity decided they must be some sort of sea sponges. She was extremely glad they had stopped her instead of hard rock. Bob bounced off them next and then sat, dazed, clutching his hat and blinking his eyes rapidly.

'Where *are* we?' said Felicity, looking around with curiosity.

Bob fixed his hat on his head, jumped up and said simply, 'The goblin caves.' He shuddered and then sighed. 'Your first Fairyland mistake – standing still on a goblin trapdoor.'

'But how was I to know?' Felicity said, indignant. 'It all looked the same to me and I was trying to read the Riddler's rhyme.'

'Well, not to worry,' said Bob. 'I should have warned you about them before. The problem is, the goblins' trapdoors move around, so you never really know where they're going to be. The only way of spotting them is by noticing how the grass is a deeper shade of green and the patch in question is usually circular in shape. But we're here now, so we'd better try to get out. Goblins are notoriously unfriendly and suspicious creatures and I wouldn't be surprised if they knew who's been shifting the pebbles around. Where there's meddling and mischief, goblins usually aren't far away!'

'What will they do if they find us here?' asked Felicity.

'Hmm.' Bob rubbed his chin. 'Capture us, perhaps, use us as servants or try to sell us to the witches for gold. Goblins are incredibly greedy for gold. Also – they have a taste for, er, human flesh, so best we don't stick around.'

Noting the horrified look on Felicity's face, he added hurriedly, 'But these caves run right through the cliff-side, I wager, with many tunnels besides, so with any luck, we might well miss running into any goblins. I also know a little magic, although I'm not sure how well I'd manage without my books …'

Felicity's eyes lit up. She'd love to see some real magic. She only hoped they wouldn't have to use it to avoid being eaten by goblins. She studied their surroundings.

Candles glowed in little hollows in the rock walls, throwing a dim light into the tiny cave. The wall in front of their slide was covered in the soft, squishy sponges and the rest of the circular space was just bare black rock, glistening with moisture. Felicity guessed that no more than twenty bodies could fit in the cave comfortably. A thought struck her.

'There's no door!' she exclaimed. 'How do we get out? There's no way we could go back up the slide!'

'Oh, there's definitely a door,' said Bob. 'It's just a matter of finding it. Feel around the walls – there's sure to be a handle or a lever or something. Best get a move on, though – before a goblin flies down that slide!'

Felicity needed no more encouragement. She began feeling her way along the wet walls, her fingers fumbling over the rock face, searching every crack and crevice. She really had no idea what she was looking for but she had a feeling she'd know when she found it.

'Do you think the Riddler was watching us back there?' she asked Bob as they searched. 'Was it all a trap?' She frowned.

'Well, we weren't talking in rhymes, so I don't know if he was nearby,' said Bob. 'But I have no doubt that he meant for you to fall down here. He won't be expecting you to have a guide though – not that I've been much use to you so far …'

'Well, you did *try* to warn me back there,' said Felicity. 'And I suppose we know now what the last line means. What about the rest of the rhyme, though? Is it the first riddle or just his idea of an introduction?'

'No, I think it's the first riddle,' said Bob. 'He meant for you to come here, so there must be something we, or rather *you*, have to do in the goblin caves. We'll just have to decipher his clue and find out what to do!'

'Wait a minute,' said Felicity. 'You're starting to rhyme – just a bit at a time. Wait, so am I – the Riddler must be nearby!'

Bob stopped searching. They looked at each other. Silence. Felicity still didn't know if she ought to be scared of the Rhyming Riddler, but decided she mustn't be – he was her ticket home, so she had to work out his riddles and fulfil her tasks, whatever they might be.

The gloom of the cave, with its soggy sponge wall and wet, glistening black rock, did now, however, take on an even more spooky quality. It was the unknown which unsettled her, along with thoughts of sneaky goblins and the mysterious Riddler and his rhymes. She reassured herself, however, with the thought that anticipation was always – well, *almost* always – worse than the reality of something.

'What now?' she asked Bob. 'Will he appear if he's near?'

'Don't worry, my dear. I'm near and I'm here and *all ears*!' a voice boomed behind her.

Felicity jumped in surprise and scrambled away from where she had been searching for a hidden lever or button. Bob hastily joined her and they peered into the dark.

At first Felicity couldn't see anything resembling a riddler – or rather, a person, for she had no idea what a riddler should look like.

As she stared intently at the spot where she thought the voice had come from, however, she saw the black there was just a little blacker, and the more she watched, the more it seemed to take shape before her eyes.

'He likes to be theatrical – it's really very impractical,' whispered Bob and then made a disgruntled noise in his throat. 'Really, Riddler, *must* we rhyme all the time?'

The black, shadowy shape now looked more figure-like, but in an odd sort of a way, Felicity thought. As it took form before her, she noted that the Riddler was taller than Bob but still shorter than she was. She might overpower or even outrun him then if she had to. No, don't be ridiculous, she thought: this is the Fairy Realm and he's magic and a trickster – there was no way she could overpower him, was there?

A cool breeze circulated the cave as the Riddler finally appeared in full before them, and Felicity caught the scent of old, stale air – air heavy with anticipation and fear of the unexpected.

She shivered.

The Rhyming Riddler bowed with a flourish, whipping off a black hat which drooped to a point and was tipped with a silver star, revealing tufts of grey hair streaked with a kaleidoscope of colours. He looked every inch the little magic man, with shaggy grey eyebrows, a long, thin nose and two coal-black beady eyes watching all around him. A wide, crooked mouth completed his fantastical features.

Long, thin arms were attached to a rather scrawny, knobbly body and tapered down into long, thin fingers that protruded from the sleeves of an oversized black tunic covered in a dazzling array of stars and rainbows, flowers and fairies. Charcoal pantaloons with ragged bottoms completed the Riddler's attire, along with a pair of pointed red boots, which curled up at the toes in spectacular fashion and were each topped with a small bell, which tinkled softly when he moved.

He held a long, glossy staff of darkened wood, twisted at the top into an elaborate swirl. Around his waist was a golden cord with various small pouches and bags attached, some jingling now and again as the Riddler shifted about. Felicity wondered what could be inside them.

The Riddler glared at Bob. 'No, you shan't now rhyme, for I haven't the time, and besides, your rhymes aren't as good as mine!'

Bob looked indignant. 'Well, it's not as if we can help what we say, usually, when *you're* around,' he said huffily.

The Riddler turned to Felicity. 'I believe you've been looking for me? Well, here I be.'

Felicity thought the Riddler was a little on the rude side but kept her thoughts to herself. She didn't want to annoy him when she so desperately needed his help.

'Yes, I was. I mean, I am,' she said. She took a breath and then it all came out at once. 'I need to get home but it appears that I can't until I find you, work out the three riddles you set and complete the tasks they describe. Oh, and I have to help the Pebble People too and find out who's been stealing their pebbles from under the weeping willows and causing fairy folk to be spirited away.' She paused. 'And we really must get out of here before the goblins come. Can you help us?'

The Riddler smiled a sneaky smile. 'I'm here aren't I, my dear?' he said. 'But you have my first riddle. I don't waste my precious rhymes, and bottled ones at that, for mere pleasantries.

'Haven't you worked it out yet? I've made the first one extremely easy for you. I only came here to formally introduce myself – not quite protocol, but done when I feel so inclined, and it *has* been a while since a human strayed into the realm. Also … I thought I should warn you that – they're here!'

With that, the Riddler clapped his hands and vanished. Felicity started. *Who* were here? Goblins? What were they to do now?

'Quick,' said Bob. 'We need to find a way out – and fast!' He ran his hands over the cave walls with nimble speed but still found nothing. 'That Riddler. He wasted our time when we could have been finding a way out,' he said in exasperation. 'We'll be for it if the goblins catch us here trespassing.'

Felicity stopped searching and listened. She thought she could hear footsteps coming from behind one of the cave walls. 'But surely they won't come in here?' she said. 'It's the way *in*, not the way out. It doesn't lead anywhere!'

'No, you don't understand.' Bob shook his head. 'Goblins can simply whoosh up the slide to the cliff – a little like old Saint Nick. A finger to the side of the nose and up they go!'

Felicity looked at him in dismay. 'But we've searched all the walls and there's nothing here!' she said.

The footsteps were getting louder and closer and Felicity could now hear the murmurings of voices. She looked around, trying to think. Her gaze fell on the wall of sponges.

'Wait!' she said, as a thought came to her. 'We haven't checked *this* wall. We just assumed it would be a lever in the rock but what if it's over here in the sponge?'

Bob looked doubtful. 'I suppose it's worth a try,' he said.

They both dashed to the wall and began pushing and prodding in earnest. The goblin voices were getting clearer and closer by the second, and just when Felicity felt sure they were done for, the sponge she was pushing on, right at the very bottom of the wall, gave way under the pressure.

'Bob!' she said excitedly. 'I think I've found it. Quick!' Her hand had gone through the sponge but, to Felicity's surprise, no door swung open. What now?

'It must be a sort of portal,' said Bob. 'We must just go through the sponge. There's no door to open or wall to remove. Simple, but effective. Come on!'

Not quite sure what he meant, Felicity watched as Bob stuck his hand through the gap she had made and then pulled the sponge apart with the other. Her eyes widened as he made a hole big enough for him to squeeze his entire body through.

He beckoned for her to follow and, with no other choice, she did, widening the hole just a little bit more and pushing her way through the soggy sponge. Once on the other side, the hole sealed over and instead of soft sponge there was now hard black rock.

'Amazing,' said Felicity. 'And not a moment too soon, I think!'

'Indeed not,' replied Bob, adjusting his hat. 'Now, let's get on the move and see if we can't solve this riddle and get out of here!'

Felicity eyed the dimly lit tunnel ahead of them. 'Well, there's only one way to go! Come on – into the goblin caves.

'The sooner we go in, the sooner we can hopefully get out!'

## Chapter Seven
# Riddle Me This

The goblin caves were, on the whole, dark – very dark – yet the soft glow of something – Felicity wasn't sure what – faintly lit their way as they walked. She couldn't see any lamps or candles so could only assume that magic was afoot.

When she glanced back the way they had come, however, velvet darkness was all that remained. It made her a little uneasy so she decided it was best just to keep walking and not think about what might be behind them.

'*Rhymes I love, Intrigue fits like a glove, Dark secrets I keep, Destinies from the deep. Learn from me if you will, Except please don't stand still – What am I?*' Felicity muttered. 'Well, we know what the last line means, so I suppose we can ignore that now. We, sorry, I, stood still on the wrong spot and now we're here in these creepy goblin caves. But as for the rest of it, I can't think what it means at all!'

'Hmm,' said Bob, deep in thought. 'The thing about the Rhyming Riddler's riddles is that they aren't often all *that* difficult to work out in the end, because he's really not as clever as he likes to think he is.'

He scratched his head. The tunnel continued before them – a long, long tunnel of emptiness, thought Felicity. But no twists and turns meant no nasty surprises, she supposed. They could clearly see if any goblins were approaching. The problem was, any goblin would also see *them* and there was nowhere to hide … What if they never found their way out, she suddenly thought in horror. These caves could go on forever – these eerily lit and silent caves under the cliffs, with goblin danger lurking around every corner.

She shook her head. Best to rid her mind of such thoughts: there was no point panicking about that until she had to – *if* she had to.

Bob, who had gone very quiet as Felicity pondered their predicament, now gave a grunt, followed by a loud guffaw.

'Of, course!' he exclaimed. 'I've got it! Stupid Riddler – he's really not that clever at all!'

'Have you cracked it?' said Felicity excitedly. 'What does it mean?'

'Listen,' said the brownie, stopping to explain. 'Take the first letter from the beginning of each sentence and what do you get?'

Felicity frowned. 'Rhymes I love – "R". Intrigue fits like a glove – "I". Dark secrets I keep – "D". Destinies from the deep – "D" again. Learn from me if you will – "L". Except please don't stand still – "E". R-I-D-D-L-E … Riddle?' she asked in disbelief. 'But what sort of sense does *that* make? The answer to the riddle is *riddle*?'

She was annoyed even more now with this Rhyming Riddler. What was he playing at? She would never get home at this rate if all he did was play tricks. Just then, laughter echoed around the rocky tunnel, but the Riddler failed to materialise.

'It appears your first riddle quest is to *find* a riddle – down here, as this is where the Riddler brought us – and solve it,' said Bob. 'That will give you your first answer.'

'But shouldn't that count as my *second* riddle, as we've already solved one?' asked Felicity.

'I would expect not,' said Bob. 'The Riddler isn't overly clever but he *is* tricksy. And I don't suppose this new riddle will be what it seems either, especially if it's down here. Goblins and riddles – dangerous territory if you ask me!'

'Great,' said Felicity. 'Well, we'd better keep walking if we're going to find *another* riddle. It's not fair to trick us like that.' As they continued onwards, Felicity began to blink rapidly. Something strange was happening to the tunnel. The glow which had kept the caves lit up before now dimmed. The tunnel walls also appeared to be moving inwards. She didn't like what was happening – surely the cave walls weren't really *moving*?

'Bob,' she said. 'Are you seeing what I'm seeing?' Felicity cleared her throat nervously. The light had returned to 'normal' again for the time being.

'Don't worry,' said Bob grimly. 'Walls move and I wouldn't expect anything less in the goblin caves. It's meant to make folk like us feel trapped and fearful. Which we're not,' he added. 'Just another one of their tricks – the light too.'

While they had been talking, Felicity and Bob had reached the end of the tunnel. They stopped. It was a dead end. Or so Felicity thought until she looked a little closer. Carved into the hard rock, on either side of her, was a series of strange symbols.

'A riddle!' she exclaimed. 'Look – see these symbols? There are loads of them. They must be some sort of code or riddle – maybe the one we're meant to solve! The Riddler did say he'd made the first one easy. Maybe he meant it was easy to find?'

Bob peered at the symbols. 'Hmm,' he scratched his chin, 'curious indeed, but do you know – I think you might be right. I've never seen anything like these before, but then I can't say I'm ever in the goblin caves.'

Felicity was sure the symbols were the riddle. There was nowhere else for them to go except forward and forward was a solid mass of black rock with bizarre magical inscriptions on it. This had to be it.

'You don't know what it means then?' she said.

'No, I'm afraid not. But,' the brownie grinned, 'I know someone who might!'

'Who?' asked Felicity.

'You'll see,' said Bob. 'Now hush while I summon them.'

Felicity hushed immediately. Who could Bob mean? A fairy? An elf? She frowned. As long as it behaved itself she would be happy to meet anyone who might help them break the riddle's code. She looked at it again. The symbols really were very unusual and meant nothing to her at all. They were just meaningless loops and swirls. How could anyone be expected to decipher it? Was it just another trick to keep her in Fairyland? Well, she wasn't going to let them get the better of her!

She watched Bob, who was now sitting solemnly on the ground, eyes closed and humming in the gloom. She waited patiently, even though she didn't feel very patient inside. Bob stopped muttering and opened his eyes. Felicity couldn't see that anything had changed but the brownie smiled at her and pointed. She looked to her left, where the dark, glistening wall of the sea cave was now glowing with a pale-white light. As she watched, a small opening appeared and with it a whoosh of water and something which moved with such speed she couldn't make out what it was.

A little light darted about the cave before stopping in front of Bob and, for the first time, Felicity could see clearly what it was. Or rather, how it looked, as she had no idea what type of creature was now before her.

It was no bigger than her hand and had a pixie-ish face, with pointed chin and nose and ears, along with a mop of dishevelled white hair. Large aqua eyes peered, unblinking, back at Bob and then Felicity.

It was hard to tell if the creature was male or female, and its clothes consisted of something that resembled mist or vapour. Water droplets dripped steadily from the tiny being, who sported a pair of fine and sharply pointed wings.

Bob grinned. 'Thank you for coming, Aqualine,' he said. 'We're in a bit of a predicament here. We have a puzzle which I think only you might be able to solve and we would dearly like your help with it.' He glanced at Felicity. 'But first – introductions!'

Aqualine looked at Felicity, scrutinising her with those big blue eyes.

'Felicity, this is Aqualine – a sprite of the sea. The sea sprites are great friends with the mermaids. And the brownies too, of course.'

'We are alike,' the sea sprite said in a soft, slippery voice.

'Yes,' said Bob. 'Sea sprites are the helpers from the sea – *of* the sea – and brownies are the helpers on land. Broadly speaking, of course. We share a common cause.'

'Nice to meet you,' said Felicity. 'I'm glad you came and I hope you can help. We really need to solve this riddle if I'm to help the Pebble People and get home.'

Aqualine shook his/her wings, spattering Felicity and Bob with droplets.

'Show me the message,' he said. (Felicity had decided it would be a 'he' until she knew better – she didn't like to refer to another living being as an 'it'.)

'Here,' said Bob, pointing to the symbols. 'What do you make of these? Can you decipher them?'

Aqualine studied the carvings, frowned and then flashed a smile. 'Of course!' he exclaimed.

Felicity couldn't stop herself. 'What does it mean?' she said eagerly.

'I can read it for you, but only you can solve it,' said Aqualine rather solemnly, drops of clear water dripping from his tiny frame onto the rock below. 'It is written in the language of the sea. Whoever put it there has learnt this language, as it is only known to us sea dwellers and changes like the ebb and flow of the tides.'

'Which is why I can't read it,' Bob butted in.

Aqualine continued. 'You, human girl, must listen to this riddle, understand it and then follow it. Good luck!'

With that, the sea sprite fluttered his wings and turned back to the wall.

'*Potions so potent they'll make you explode,*
*Potions for silver, for jewels and for gold.*
*Potions to make you enthralled by the old,*
*Potions for fortune … or so I am told.*'

Rhyme read, Aqualine flew straight at the wall of the sea cave and disappeared through it with a splash. Water droplets landed on Felicity's face and she brushed them away with her hand. She looked at Bob in exasperation.

'Creatures do come and go very quickly around here,' she said. 'And I don't know what that rhyme means either. Potions – are we to find one? And if so, how? This rock is blocking the way!'

'Hmm,' said Bob, deep in thought again. 'Let me think.'

Felicity waited, trying to think herself.

'All the sentences begin with the word "potions", and they all rhyme at the end,' said Bob. 'But before we work out what it means, I think we have to use it somehow to get through this rock. Riddles often have double meanings and multiple uses and can be used to unlock not only secrets, but hidden pathways as well. In this case, I'm quite certain that only magic will get us through here!'

'Potions, potions, potions, potions,' said Felicity. 'What if –?'

She was cut short by a loud cracking sound, which made them both jump.

'Look! The rock!' said Bob. 'Quick, get back!'

A large jagged crack had appeared where the symbols had been, cutting through the wall.

'You must have said the secret code to open the entrance,' said Bob. 'I wonder what's on the other side?'

Felicity wondered too, as she watched the crack slowly widen and a soft glow spilt out into the tunnel. When there was just enough room for someone to squeeze through the gap, without further ado, that's just what Felicity and Bob did.

## Chapter Eight
# In Pursuit of Potions

As they stepped through the crack in the rock, Felicity was struck by the glare on the other side compared to the dark tunnel they had left behind. She blinked and checked to see that Bob was beside her. The little brownie was looking around him. He caught Felicity's eye and smiled.

'Well, we got through,' he said. 'But it seems we're not going back that way either.'

The crack in the rock was sealing itself up as he spoke and Felicity swallowed nervously. The only way was forward.

'We wouldn't have made it back up that slide anyway,' she said, more bravely than she really felt. 'Let's see where we are and decide what to do next.'

Where they were was yet another small cave, lit by a large lantern hanging overhead, which conjured up misshapen shadows in the gloom and made Felicity squint to check they were just hers and Bob's. She was glad to see they were still alone but worried about where the goblins were and just when they might run into them, for surely they couldn't keep avoiding the creatures?

The cave was circular and cut into the rock was a collection of doors – all of varying shapes, sizes and colours and all bearing neat handwritten signs with large looping letters. Felicity went over to an oval emerald door with a golden knocker and a shiny gold handle in the shape of a hand. A sign in ruby-red lettering read 'Spells and Potions'.

'I think this might be the door we need,' she said to Bob with excitement. That had been easy.

Bob read the sign. 'Yes, I think you might be right,' he said. 'But let's check what the others say first – just in case.'

They approached a rectangular blue door and read a sign painted in curly yellow lettering.

'"Potions and Spells",' said Bob. 'Wait a minute – that can't be right!' He ran to the next door – a bright-orange triangle with curvy blue letters declaring its destination. '"Potions",' he said.

Felicity read another sign on a larger yellow door with black lettering. '"Spells",' she said in despair. 'They can't all lead to the same place surely! Which one are we to choose?'

'It must be another trick from the goblins,' said Bob. 'You can be sure they wouldn't so easily reveal the way to their precious potions and spells. I suppose we'll just have to pick a door – any door – and go through it.'

'Yes, but which one?' said Felicity in exasperation. 'It's just trick after trick and I haven't even solved the first riddle yet. This is impossible!' She sat down. 'And I'm hungry as well. I'm hungry and I'm tired and I want to get out of these caves.'

Adventures in Fairyland, as she was quickly finding out, weren't as fun as Felicity had once thought they were going to be.

Bob looked at her kindly. 'It's an adventure and it's *your* adventure,' he said. 'This *is* the Fairy Realm, however, so tricks are just part of the day-to-day life here, I'm afraid. Let's pick a door and see where it takes us. We might find food and somewhere to hide and rest a while. But we really shouldn't hang about for too long. You never know who or what might come out from behind one of those doors!'

'OK,' said Felicity. 'Shall we choose the green door? I like the look of that one I think.'

'Yes, why not,' said Bob. 'It's as good as any I suppose. Try the handle and see.'

Felicity strode over to the little oval door and gripped the golden hand-shaped handle. She turned it but nothing happened.

'Try turning it the other way,' suggested Bob. 'Things have a habit of working back-to-front in Fairyland.'

Felicity tried again and this time the handle moved, although not quite in the way she had expected. Instead of simply turning, the little handle gripped *her* hand right back and shook it! She was too astonished to feel any fear and just stood there in shock. The door, however, swung open and she instinctively took a step forward. Bob followed, and once he was through the door slammed shut behind them.

This time, it wasn't silence that greeted them but the hum of distant voices and muffled rattling noises.

'Goblins,' whispered Bob. 'Best be careful!'

The door had led them into a dimly lit tunnel, although, for the first time, there were more obvious signs of goblin life within their rocky surroundings. Small alcoves off the main tunnel held cloaks and curly toed shoes, and here and there stood a small spade or a pickaxe, propped up against the walls. Tiny lanterns lit the way, some swinging overhead, others perched on ledges cut into the tunnel.

Felicity went over to one where the light was flickering more intensely than the rest and peered inside.

She gave a start. 'There's something in there!' she said in horror.

Behind the glass, something was moving, but it was whizzing around too quickly for Felicity to see clearly what it was. She tapped on the lantern with her finger and the flurry of activity ceased. Inside was a small fairy, glowing more faintly now she had stopped her panicked flying.

'Oh, the poor thing,' gasped Felicity. 'She must be a prisoner. How cruel! Don't tell me the goblins have shut her up in there just to get some light for their tunnel? That's awful!'

'That's what they do,' said Bob grimly. 'They don't care about anyone but themselves. They're always capturing fairies and elves, turning them into their slaves or selling them on to witches and enchanters for gold. They're greedy and cruel. Let's get her out shall we?'

'Yes, of course.' Felicity fumbled with the lantern latch and the little door swung open. The fairy flew out at once, raced up the tunnel and then came back.

'Sorry, I just *had* to stretch my wings,' she said in a shimmering, tinkling voice. 'Thank you for releasing me. I am indebted to you. The goblins caught me whilst I was out collecting spider thread for my new dress. I was so busy gathering it that I didn't see them creeping up behind me.

'Then they put a spell on the lantern so I could only escape if someone let me out. Hardly anyone except goblins ever come down here so I thought I would be inside it forever.'

'That's terrible,' said Felicity. 'Goblins do seem to be incredibly nasty creatures. I really hope we don't meet any.'

Bob grunted. 'They probably have an inkling there's someone here already, so we'd better keep moving.'

'Can I come too?' asked the tiny fairy. 'I don't know the way out, but I'll do all I can to help you. And,' she said, fanning her wings, 'my glow can help guide us!'

'I think that's a wonderful idea,' said Felicity. 'What's your name?'

'Twinkle,' said the fairy shyly, bowing her head. Her hair was cherub-like, with tight golden curls bunched together in a boyish bob, and she wore a dress of sunshine silk. She looked sweet and Felicity felt sure they could trust her.

'OK,' said Bob. 'Let's get going then. Loitering around in goblin territory makes me uneasy.'

Felicity looked ahead. The tunnel still glowed faintly and, further on, curved off to the right. There was nothing else for it but to follow the path they had chosen and just hope they didn't run into any goblins along the way. The little party set off again, each one silent as they approached the corner. When they reached it, Felicity decided she, who *had* after all chosen the route, would be brave and go round it first. So, without saying anything to the others and before they could protest, she darted ahead of them.

'Felicity!' hissed Bob. 'Be careful!'

Felicity's grinning head popped back around the corner a few moments later. 'Don't worry,' she said. 'It's OK. See for yourselves – no goblins!'

As Twinkle and Bob joined Felicity, their sense of relief quickly turned to astonishment.

'What *is* this?' said Bob in amazement.

Before them stood another wall, but this was *much* more exciting than any ordinary old wall of rock, as it wasn't black, it wasn't wet and shiny and it wasn't covered in sharp pointy bits. No, *this* wall was alive with iridescent colour and almost blinded the trio with its brilliance as they stood speechless before it. The wall was beautiful.

Like an image viewed through a kaleidoscope, it was a psychedelic jigsaw made for mesmerising, with multiple surfaces like a diamond. Each 'face' of the wall was a different colour, with everything from rich purples and browns to burnt orange, yellows, blues, pinks and more, though all were locked together by a single blood-red rock, which pulsed at the wall's core. There must have been every shade under the sun, thought Felicity, and it was a startling contrast to the rest of the inky-black rock around them.

Twinkle flew up close to the wall for a better look. She shielded her eyes and peered into a blue panel. After a few seconds she gave a small squeal of excitement.

'I can see little people inside!' she exclaimed. 'Come and see. These must be windows or something. Maybe they're prisoners like I was!'

Felicity and Bob each peeked through a coloured pane. Sure enough, Felicity could make out tiny figures behind the rock, which mustn't really *be* rock, she thought, but some sort of glass or gem. She was looking through a purple panel, behind which a cluster of folk seemed to be stirring pots and cauldrons, with smoke rising up in small puffs above some of them.

Felicity crouched down and looked through a pink panel next. She could see floating coral clouds but guessed that could just be the effect of the glass. Tiny figures with long, drooping hats and pointed shoes were seated around a long table, tucking into a mouth-watering spread of sandwiches, cakes and jellies. Felicity felt her stomach growl. She hadn't eaten since she'd arrived in Fairyland and for someone who was *always* hungry that was no mean feat. She knew she was staring but she couldn't help it.

'They're digging down here,' said Bob, who was standing with his nose pressed up against a yellow panel. 'Looks like they're mining something …' His face paled. 'Oh no.'

'I think mine are looking at me,' said Twinkle. 'Shall I wave?'

'Get back – *now*!' hissed Bob, waving them away from the panes. 'They're goblins!'

Twinkle jumped as something hit against the glass she'd been looking through. 'Can they get out? Are they going to capture us?' she said fearfully.

'What'll we do?' said Felicity. 'Bob?'

'I don't know. I'm thinking,' said the brownie.

But it was too late. Twinkle's glass was now glowing more intensely than before and one by one the other panels followed suit, until the whole wall was a blaze of blinding colour.

'I can't see anything!' gasped Felicity. 'It's too bright!'

The wall shook and shuddered and then the first goblin popped out of the red centre. Before they knew it, knobbly, hard hands had grabbed hold of them and Felicity heard Twinkle scream. They'd been captured.

## Chapter Nine
# Goblins

After what seemed like an eternity but which could only in actual fact have been a few minutes, Felicity began to make out shapes – lots of shapes – around her. She wondered if Bob and Twinkle were OK. As the light dimmed to a softer glow and her eyes focused with it, she stared at the mob around her.

A motley assortment of ugly little creatures glared back and amongst them she spotted Bob. Poor Twinkle was already back in a glass prison, as one of the goblins held a jar with a cork firmly pushed down into it to keep her from flying out.

'She won't be able to breathe,' said Felicity in a panic, pointing to the jar when the goblin gave her a confused look.

Her plea came to nothing, however, as he then twisted his mouth into a sinister smile and popped the jar in his pocket.

'You can't do that! She'll die!' Felicity struggled in vain against the knobbly hands that gripped her wrists, prompting sharp, pointed nails to dig into her flesh.

'*Silence!*' roared a particularly tall and thin goblin. He had a long hooked nose and large pointed ears with tufts of hair sticking out of them, which Felicity could quickly see were standard amongst the goblins but far too big for their heads. This one's bulbous and unblinking eyes were also much too large for his head and, with his long ears and nose, made him seem all out of proportion.

Clumsy spade-like hands and feet and a small balloon-like body completed the look of what Felicity assumed was the goblin leader. She drank in his extraordinary appearance while trying hard not to think of poor Twinkle in the jar in the other goblin's pocket. She blinked back tears – these evil creatures would *not* see her cry.

The other goblins shared features similar to their leader but in varying sizes – some being shorter and fatter, some rounder, some pointier, but all just plain ugly, thought Felicity. They wore tunics smeared with dirt and a slime that she hoped was seaweed but rather suspected was snot. Their hats were long and drooping, with mud spattered on most, and they were all bare-footed – their skin so tough and leathery they might as well have been wearing work boots. A few also had beards, while their goggly eyes merely added to their overall frightening appearance. Felicity felt a chill crawl along her spine. What would they do with her and Bob? And Twinkle – what of her?

The head goblin spoke.

'You,' he said, in a croaky, raspy voice, 'have trespassed where you should not. You have entered the goblin caves. You have walked our tunnels, freed our prisoner, spied on our workshops and living quarters and sought our potions.'

He paused and looked round at his crew, who watched him intently, large eyes blinking rapidly in a very unsettling way.

'Now – *you will be punished!*' roared the goblin leader. He pointed a crooked, bony finger at Felicity. '*You* will be our prisoner – until we can fatten you up for the table, that is! Till then, you will serve as our slave and will never see the light of day again. Dare to enter the Fairy Realm and come into our caves? A dangerous game to have played.

'And you,' he pointed at Bob, 'will be sold to the witches – your punishment for bringing the human here and trespassing in our caves.'

'But,' Bob sputtered. 'I didn't –'

He was silenced by the goblin's glare. 'Do. Not. Speak,' he growled. '*I* will speak and I only!'

He glanced at the goblin who had taken Twinkle. 'The fairy prisoner,' he yelled, stretching out his hand for the jar, 'is to be returned to her lantern to serve as light for all eternity. Or perhaps we should sell her as well – double gold for getting shot of a brownie *and* a fairy.'

The goblin with the jar held it out to his leader with a wicked smirk on his face. 'Too late, boss,' he leered. 'Fairy's dead.'

He shook the jar and Felicity, who felt her heart stop with shock and began to feel lightheaded, glimpsed a tiny figure slumped at the bottom. As she began to lose consciousness, she felt a jolt of unimaginable terror and the horrific realisation of where she actually was – what those around her were capable of – and for the first time, she was truly petrified.

***

When she came to, Felicity still felt a little ill. She had never fainted before and decided that she didn't like the experience one bit. She flexed her fingers and moved her feet. At least she wasn't tied up.

She had, however, been transported to some sort of prison cell while she had been out cold and she knew one thing for sure – if she hadn't been lost and out of her depth before, she certainly was now. Was Bob with her?

She heard a groan from the other side of the cave so, thankfully, she assumed so.

'Bob,' she whispered. 'Is that you?'

'Ow … yes,' he answered back. 'My head hurts. Those goblins whacked me so I couldn't see where they were taking us. I have no idea where we are, but it isn't good, Felicity.'

Felicity's heart sank at his words. 'I know,' she said softly. 'And Twinkle …' She blinked back tears. She couldn't quite believe it had happened, but it had. Twinkle was gone and she felt that it was her fault.

As if reading her mind, Bob spoke up. 'We can't help Twinkle now,' he said. 'The goblins don't care who they hurt. They do whatever they want, but it wasn't our fault, Felicity. It's a terrible thing to have happened, but for now, we must focus on trying to escape. It might sound harsh, but if we don't, well, you heard what the goblins said …'

Felicity knew he was right, but it didn't make it any easier. She tried to take in their new surroundings. It was clearly meant for prisoners only and was bare and murky. A single candle struggled to light the space near what she assumed was the entrance – a heavy-looking and huge black rock. Rolled into place by goblins or magic, or both, she supposed. Other than that, it was really like any other cave. Empty and dark.

She sighed. It was almost too unbelievable to be true. She had been trapped in an underground sea cave by angry, evil goblins – with a brownie – while on a quest to solve riddles, help Pebble People and escape the Fairy Realm. A day ago she would never have believed such things could happen to her. She was on the biggest adventure of her life. It just couldn't end here.

'Listen, Bob,' she said. 'There has to be a way out. Don't you know any magic that could help us? Think, please!' She tried to keep the urgency from her voice.

'I know some magic from my books, but I'd need some equipment, and goblin spells are strong,' said Bob. 'They deal with witches and enchanters all the time, bartering and often stealing spells. I'll have to think.'

Time ticked on and Felicity could only sit and wait, hoping the goblins wouldn't land back anytime soon. With nothing else to do, her thoughts strayed to her grandmother and she wondered what she was doing and whether she'd noticed Felicity was missing yet. How quickly – or slowly – was time passing here compared to at home?

Her Granny Stone was a plump, kindly old woman, prone to worrying about her only granddaughter. She was approaching her seventieth year but was still as fit as a fiddle in every other respect. Indeed, her only ailment, if it could be called such, was having to wear reading glasses when she pored over her recipe or gardening books – although what Felicity's Granny Stone didn't know about either of these subjects was surely not worth knowing.

Her grandmother loved to grow flowers and vegetables in her sprawling garden, which had neatly spaced rows of lettuces, carrots and cabbages, as well as a greenhouse for tomatoes, grapes and all sorts of other things Felicity couldn't name. There was a special herb garden where everything looked much the same to Felicity, yet her grandmother could distinguish each and every plant growing there.

The garden also had a small apple tree, some rhubarb and an old, gnarled chestnut tree, which bore sweet chestnuts for roasting in the autumn. The rest of the space was consumed by wildflowers, roses, pansies and, well, every flower that Granny Stone could comfortably fit into her colourful paradise, along with thick rhododendron bushes and a cherry-blossom tree, which fluttered pink petals onto the grass in the summertime.

From this wonderful garden, which buzzed with bees as spring drew in and attracted numerous garden birds, Granny Stone could cook the most mouth-watering meals. Her specialty, however, was bread and, living as they did on the coast of Northern Ireland, both Felicity and her grandmother enjoyed tucking into warm, freshly baked wheaten bread with homemade apple jam, or soda farls with crisp bacon and a soft poached egg on top for a special breakfast. Granny Stone also made a mean chicken soup, served with potatoes pulled straight from the potato patch, and her tangy apple tart and thick custard was absolutely heavenly.

Being a practical sort of a person, Granny Stone always wore her apron. Her face – plump and smooth, with surprisingly few wrinkles – was always powdered, with just a hint of lipstick staining her lips and, despite her daily labour, her hands remained soft and supple, thanks to the large quantities of hand cream she rubbed into them day and night. She had bright, twinkling brown eyes flecked with green and short, curly grey hair, always perfectly coiffed.

Thinking of her now, at home in the kitchen or out tending to her vegetables, made Felicity more than a bit homesick and she swallowed the lump which had sneakily wedged itself in her throat.

A falling pebble jolted her out of her daydreaming, however, and she swung round. Had someone else been in the cave with them all this time? She squinted. Was that something moving? She felt a shimmer of fear.

Without blinking and without alerting Bob, Felicity watched, frozen to the spot. She almost jumped when the wall of rock itself seemed to move towards her.

She couldn't help it. 'Bob!' she hissed. 'What *is* that?'

Before Bob could answer, another voice spoke – a soft, gravelly voice.

'I'm here to help. Don't hurt me,' it said.

Now standing by the flickering candle, the voice, they could see, belonged to a small, rounded little person, with the distinct look of a …

'Pebble! Pebble People! I mean, person,' spluttered Felicity. 'You're a Pebble Person. Thank goodness. And you're here to help.' She sighed. 'But how?'

'I'm a Pebble Reader,' said the little Pebble Person solemnly. 'My name is Clarity, because I bring increased clarity and meaning to the pebbles. Though my powers are weakened now,' he added, 'and weakening daily, since the pebbles have been disappearing. But I was still able to listen to the rocky tunnels and realised you had been captured within them, so I've come here from the Rocky Valley to assist you in your quest. You must escape the goblin caves in order to help us.'

'Yes, we know that,' said Bob gloomily. 'We just don't know how.'

'But we can't leave without finding the potions,' said Felicity. 'The riddle – remember? Sorry, Clarity. I *will* help your people and I thank you so much for coming here to find us, but I need to help myself get home as well and for that I have to solve these dratted riddles.

85

Can you help us find the potions first, before we escape? Please?'

She looked beseechingly at Clarity, who hesitated only a moment before saying, 'Yes, of course. But we must hurry. I overheard the goblins say they were off to meet with the witches, so we may be able to avoid them if we're lucky. Follow me. Speed is of the essence.'

Felicity jumped up. Bob was already on his feet.

Clarity turned back towards the rock wall and Felicity and Bob watched as he gently touched it. The rock shimmered, wobbled and then a dark shadowy doorway appeared. Magic.

## Chapter Ten
# Enchanted

The Pebble Reader stepped into the tunnel and beckoned to Bob and Felicity, who followed gladly. They certainly didn't want to linger in their prison.

They moved quietly as Clarity, who looked exactly like the little Pebble People from before, muttered magic to keep their route clear. They were, after all, walking where there wasn't actually supposed to be a tunnel – Clarity had conjured that up and Felicity couldn't help but think it must be taking a lot out of him.

She glanced behind her once or twice – Bob was between her and Clarity up ahead – and she was fairly sure the tunnel was sealing off behind them as they went. It was good news in one respect – the goblins certainly wouldn't be following them – but Felicity also felt a little claustrophobic and hoped their journey would end soon. When they had walked for what seemed like an incredibly long time, Clarity suddenly stopped, Bob bumping into him with a grunt.

'Here,' said the Pebble Reader. 'The wall feels weak. I think this will take us into one of the main goblin tunnels. Unfortunately, my magic isn't strong enough anymore to keep making tunnels from scratch.'

He pressed his palms against the rock and whispered a few words under his breath. Before their eyes, the wall wobbled and then a small hole appeared in the centre. This grew until it was large enough for a person to slip through. At this point Clarity stopped his spell.

'Right – in we go,' he said. 'Keep quiet, though – we don't want to alert the goblins.'

Felicity and Bob didn't need to be told twice. They slipped through the wall after Clarity, who turned and sealed it up again when they were all on the other side. Back in the goblin tunnel, Felicity felt very vulnerable. She looked at Clarity.

'Which way?' she whispered.

Clarity's eyes were closed and he appeared to be deep in concentration. He rubbed his temples with his fingertips and Felicity was tempted to interrupt him, thinking they were wasting time. She trusted the little Pebble man, however, so decided it was best to wait until he was ready.

Clarity's eyes snapped open. 'This way!'

He pointed in the direction they had roughly been following in their secret tunnel.

'I don't mean to be rude,' said Felicity, as they began walking again, 'but how do you know this is *definitely* the right way?'

'What I was doing back there helped me map out the area,' said Clarity. 'We Pebble People have special connections with all pebbles, rocks and stones – some stronger than others, granted, but as a Pebble Reader, I can read the rocks here if I concentrate hard enough and find out what they protect.

'The Potions Cave isn't too far away, although I'll have to concentrate hard when we get down there to see precisely where it is. The goblin network is like a labyrinth and we don't want to get lost.'

They hadn't walked very much further when the smell of fresh bread came wafting towards them. Felicity's mouth watered and she tried to block out thoughts of her Granny Stone baking wheaten bread at home. Her stomach rumbled.

The tunnel, she noticed, was growing increasingly lighter and had widened somewhat, while more lanterns, thankfully devoid of fairies, swung in alcoves on either side of them.

They rounded a few more corners before reaching a solid oak door with a gold knocker.

'The goblin kitchen,' said Clarity. 'We'll have to go through it to get to the Potion Cave.' He placed his hand on the wall beside him and stepped through.

The goblin kitchen was filled with the most delicious smells Felicity could have imagined. What was more, it was absolutely huge. She gazed upwards. The ceiling was so high it couldn't be seen and she wondered just how deep down they really were.

Bob poked her in the ribs. 'Look – disguises!'

Clarity was holding hats and cloaks – *goblin* hats and cloaks. 'I'm sure they won't miss these,' he said cheerfully. 'But all the same, let's be quick. Follow me, keep your heads down and don't draw attention to yourselves, for pity's sake. Felicity, you're taller so be sure and keep to the shadows – goblins aren't all that clever but they're not completely stupid either. It's not too busy, though, so our luck might just be in.'

It was true – there were very few goblins about and those who *were* there looked incredibly busy. Some stirred frantically over steaming pots and cauldrons, while others ran to and fro fetching ingredients or stood with hands submerged in soapy water, washing dirty crockery. It very much looked as if they were preparing for a feast which, fortunately for Felicity, Bob and Clarity, meant they took absolutely no notice of three extra cloaked and hatted bodies walking around.

Felicity tried to take in as much as she could but was distracted by the aromas around her. She desperately wanted something to eat. In the centre of the cave was a giant spiral, which it soon became clear was actually a table, cleverly saving on space by snaking round the room. Chairs of all shapes and sizes were pushed in underneath it.

The walls of the cave were lined with shelves cut into the rock and were packed with pans, utensils, bags of flour and, really, too many types of food to mention. Meanwhile, meats hung in one corner and herbs in another, with a hoard of exotic fruits also nearby.

Long benches also wound round the cave, with the result that, organised though it was, the overall impression was of chaos and disarray. The space was used wisely but there wasn't much of it left.

It did, however, make it easier for the trio to blend in. As they passed a bench laden with bread, Felicity couldn't help it. She reached out and took two buttered slices. She bit into one ravenously – it was the most delicious bread she had ever tasted: light and airy, with butter rich and creamy. She quickly polished it off, followed by her second slice, and then stopped before a plate of little sandwiches. She tasted one – was that some sort of meat? Whatever it was, it melted in her mouth. The fillings were fresh and flavoursome and she had to resist taking too many in case she left a large gap on the plate.

She caught up with Bob and Clarity, who looked round guiltily from where they'd been tucking into a fruit salad. Felicity, however, was drawn to a basket of strawberries so succulent and juicy she had never tasted the like of them before. She ate some greedily, then took a spoonful of thick white cream from a little silver bowl sitting nearby. Delicious.

She bit into a pear next, the sweet juice quenching her thirst. Spying what looked suspiciously like pastries and pies, however, she left the fruit and looked longingly at the section of bench groaning with steaming food.

Slipping discreetly behind a cauldron being stirred by a red-faced and sweating goblin, she beckoned for Bob and Clarity to follow her. They passed a large oven, standing on clawed feet and glowing very hot, before reaching the pastries, where they all helped themselves. Now feeling quite full, Felicity couldn't help but whisper, 'Could we just try a cake before we go?'

They all shared a glance which said, 'Yes, let's!' Being careful to navigate the various obstacles in their way, the three headed for the bakery section.

Ovens set into the rock were wafting the most wonderful sweet, sugary smells in their direction. Meanwhile, a few scattered tables in front of the ovens were piled high with all sorts of biscuits, cakes and even colourful, wobbly jellies. Feeling full no longer, Felicity was torn as to what she should try first. A clutch of goblins scurried about from the ovens to the tables and back again, occasionally letting out a loud yell when they inevitably got burned on a hot oven door or tray in their haste. One or two barked orders to what Felicity assumed were goblin children and she also spied a couple of fairies sombrely assisting, but with long silver chains running from their ankles to the rock wall. Prisoners.

Despite the risks, something drew Felicity to a table laden with cakes. She beckoned to Clarity and Bob, who were soon at her side. Felicity especially loved chocolate cakes, so her eyes lit up when she saw a simply enormous one perched on a beautiful silver stand in the centre of the table. It was covered in a thick chocolate buttercream, decorated with dark-chocolate drops and looked irresistible. Picking up the knife which lay beside it, Felicity cut large slices for all three of them and they sat under the table to eat them in safety.

The chocolate cake was light and moist and melted in Felicity's mouth. She sighed with satisfaction. Inside were thick rivulets of dark chocolate sauce, sandwiched between layers of springy sponge. The exterior, meanwhile, was luxuriously smothered in that rich chocolate cream and sprinkled, she now noticed, with tiny flakes of milk chocolate as well as the dark-chocolate drops. She devoured every mouthful. She had to admit – fairy food was delicious and very moreish. Even her Granny Stone's chocolate creations didn't come close to this and that was saying something!

Bob had spied biscuits and crept out boldly from under the table, bringing a plate with an assorted selection back with him. He took a thin wafer-type biscuit and popped it in his mouth, where it fizzed and immediately disappeared. He grinned. 'Feisty confectionary!'

Felicity smiled but was beginning to feel a bit strange. The food was gorgeous, but the chocolate cake had reminded her of home and she suddenly realised – wasn't she trying to get *back* there? So why was she wasting time devouring a goblin feast? She looked at her friends. 'We have to go, I think. *Now*,' she said. 'There's an exit just over there. Come on.'

Bob and Clarity looked disappointed but followed her towards it nonetheless, Bob grabbing another biscuit on the way. The goblins were still scurrying about – baking bread, mixing cakes and bringing biscuits out of hot ovens – so they took no notice of them. Once out of the goblin kitchen, they looked at one another, as if snapping out of a dream.

'Enchanted fairy food,' said Bob. 'I should have known. Goblins bake all sorts of magic into their breads and cakes, making it impossible to resist temptation. I just hope we haven't wasted too much time by stopping to feast on it.'

So *that's* what had happened, thought Felicity.

'It's not far to the potions room now, if I'm correct in my navigations,' said Clarity. 'Just follow me, keep to the shadows and keep quiet.'

This tunnel was much wider than the previous ones and Felicity and Bob made sure they hugged the edges of it, where dark shadows danced, keeping them out of the glare of the lanterns hanging down the centre of the passage. They kept the goblin cloaks and hats on – the grubby garments would help them blend in.

Clarity was indeed correct in his calculations, for as they rounded a corner after a fairly short walk, they saw a sign pointing to a right-hand fork in the tunnel. It said, in crooked writing, 'Potions'.

'At last,' said Felicity. 'Now let's get the potion and get out of here!'

## Chapter Eleven
# Solving the First Riddle

Unfortunately, there was one flaw in Felicity's plan. She still had no idea what sort of potion she was supposed to be looking for and she was becoming increasingly convinced that it might all just be another one of the Riddler's tricks and wouldn't be as straightforward as they expected.

She was also rapidly getting sick of the sight of dark tunnels and couldn't wait until they were out in the fresh air again. Unfortunately, the tunnel to the potion room seemed to be spiralling deeper into the ground. It wasn't long before they reached the end, however, and without any sign of the goblins, although Felicity wasn't sure if that was a good thing or a bad thing. What *were* they up to?

Thoughts of goblins were soon put out of her head, though, when an oddly shaped bottle floated past the little party. It was made of coloured glass and bobbed solemnly beside her, the dark liquid inside slopping about but contained by a cork in the bottleneck. 'Potions,' said Bob with a grin. 'We're here!'

They were indeed and 'here' was quite extraordinary. As they got closer to their destination, more and more bottles floated by, although Felicity thought they must be under a spell to keep them close to the potion room, as they weren't bobbing around unchecked through the entire tunnel.

Fat bottles, thin bottles, tapered and compact – clear glass, marbled glass, patterned and plain – they were all so enchantingly different that Bob, Felicity and Clarity had to try hard not to bump into each other as they looked around at them.

Some bottles contained dark swirling liquids of greens, reds and blues, as well as myriad multicoloured mixtures, while others held grains of sparkling gold dust and miniature silver stars, which glittered tantalisingly in their glassy prisons. Powders pressed against the sides of a group of tubular bottles, which looked much more experimental, Felicity thought. So many fantastical concoctions floated around them but as they walked deeper into the cave, which was lined with shelves hewn out of the rock face and all crowded with potions, Bob elbowed Felicity.

'Look up,' he said in awe. She did and saw that the shelves stretched right to the tip of the domed ceiling, covering every possible surface with magic. As in the goblin kitchen, there was a variety of cauldrons and benches scattered here and there, with apparatus Felicity didn't recognise set out upon them. Smoke rose from one or two of the cauldrons and she heard bubbling from another, but they were all unattended.

Each rock shelf was lit by lanterns suspended, it seemed, by nothing. Just magic. The thought made Felicity smile. *Just* magic? She would never have dreamed the day would come when she considered magic 'just' anything. Mesmerising as it all was, however, she realised something.

'How are we ever going to find the potion we need in all of this?' she asked in dismay. 'We don't know what we're looking for and even if we did, how could we possibly know where to find it in here? There must be thousands of potions!'

'OK,' said Bob. 'Let's not panic. We'll sit down and work it out. Come on.'

He sat down on a nearby protruding rock, took off his hat, scratched his head and then put his hat on again. Clarity continued walking around the cave, muttering to himself.

'What's he doing?' Felicity whispered.

'Trying to talk to the rocks and find us a way out, I would think,' said Bob. 'Now, let's see. *Potions so potent they'll make you explode*: exploding potions, right. *Potions for silver, for jewels and for gold*: a potion that creates precious stones and metals – OK. *Potions to make you enthralled by the old*: an age potion, or an *old* potion. *Potions for fortune ... or so I am told.* Hmm. It's old, makes your fortune by creating precious stones and it explodes! That's it!'

Felicity wasn't completely sure what he meant but Bob seemed excited and they really had nothing else to go on so she said, 'That's it?'

'Yes!' said Bob. 'Look for an old, old bottle filled with sparkling powder or liquid – all the colours of the rainbow, as that represents the jewels. If we take some of the powder and use it, I'm sure it should cause some sort of explosion, which might just create a quick way out of here, as well as solve your riddle. I've a feeling the potion we need will somehow draw us to it, hence the *enthralled* part of the riddle. The Riddler's puzzles are never very complex, like I've said before, so this must be it!

'He could come here himself to get the potion, of course, but I don't think there's much that he actually *needs* at this point – it's more a case of making the task as tricky as possible for *you*. Also, he and the goblins don't get along, so he probably doesn't want to risk being captured. Anyway, let's get looking!'

That, however, was still easier said than done. There were so many bottles that Felicity didn't know where she should start. She scoured a shelf in the hope of finding a label or some indication of what it held, and eventually spied a tiny gold-plated sign stuck onto the corner with the letter 'C' etched onto it.

'They must be alphabetised,' she murmured, running her finger along the assorted bottles, none of which, frustratingly, were labelled. Or rather, they had labels but there was no writing on them.

Felicity walked on to where she thought the letter 'J' for jewels might be. Bingo – she saw a swirly 'J' scratched onto another little golden sign. Now – which bottle of the many in this particular section was the one she needed?

She ducked her head as a large black bottle bobbed by and then resumed her search. All of these bottles looked too new and clean, though, if they were meant to be looking for something old. She frowned and scanned the neighbouring shelves, watching the black bottle bob on and then turn left, disappearing out of sight. She was about to start her search again, then hesitated. The bottle had turned left, but surely there was nowhere to go if the shelves ran unbroken?

Felicity hurried over to where she had seen the bottle disappear. She would have missed it except that she knew to look for a gap and there, just as she had hoped, was a thin entryway. She took a breath and squeezed through, just about fitting between the shelves, and came out into what looked like a secret store. Felicity's eyes gleamed. The cave was small and cobwebby and the bottles here looked old and worn. She felt sure *this* was where she would find their potion. The shelves, however, didn't seem to have any letters and she knew this might take a while, so she squeezed out again and called to Bob and Clarity.

'Over here,' she said.

'Marvellous,' said Bob, when he saw the hidden cave. 'Absolutely marvellous. *And* we'll be safely hidden if any goblins come calling!'

'Indeed,' said Clarity. 'But all the same – better hurry. With three of us in this small space it shouldn't take so long.'

They lapsed into silence as each studied the bottles before them. After a few minutes Bob gave a yell. 'Do you think this is it?' he said excitedly. He held an antique cobwebbed bottle filled with bright-gold powder streaked with rainbow colours.

'It looks old, but do you think it's, well, *special* enough to make jewels?' asked Clarity.

'Well, maybe,' said Bob doubtfully. 'Let's each pick a bottle and keep our options open. We can try them all!'

'OK, agreed,' said Clarity and Felicity, resuming their search.

Felicity wanted to find the black bottle, as she now felt sure that was the one they needed. At last, her eyes lit upon it, nestled at the end of a shelf low to the ground and enshrouded with shadows. She reached out for it at once. On closer inspection, she saw the glass was very dusty and grimy, but not actually black. It was the liquid inside which was dark, but throughout it glimmered with an iridescent sparkle, as if it was bewitched by tiny stars.

Clarity chose a small square bottle containing silver and gold-flecked blue powder. Once most of the dust was wiped from them, the bottles and their contents looked quite pretty, Felicity thought – and extremely magical.

Bob spoke first. 'Right, we all have our bottles so I say we see what they can do! I'll go first, shall I?'

Felicity nodded and Clarity looked on in anticipation. The powder in Bob's bottle gleamed brilliantly and Felicity wondered if it was actually real gold dust. The little brownie carefully uncorked it and sprinkled some of the contents in a circle on the ground, reciting the riddle as he did so. They waited, but nothing happened.

'My turn,' said Clarity, his eyes shining with excitement. He recited the rhyme as he uncorked his bottle, again dusting the ground with a tiny circle of powder. He looked expectantly at it. Again, nothing.

'OK, my turn then,' said Felicity, taking a deep breath but expecting more of the same. If this didn't work, they still had a hefty search on their hands. She held the bottleneck tightly with one hand, gripped the cork with the other and then began to recite the rhyme.

'*Potions for silver, for jewels and for gold,*' she began, popping the cork from her bottle.

'Hang on a minute,' said Bob. 'Maybe just say "a potion" – you only have one bottle and I wouldn't put it past the Riddler to trick us like that.'

Felicity nodded and began again.

'*A potion for silver, for jewels and for gold …*'

A little sparkle of powder spilled onto the floor as Felicity shook the bottle gently and it began to glow. All three looked at one another with delight.

Felicity continued. '*A potion to make you enthralled by the old …*'

Every remaining speck of dust instantly vanished from the bottle, which now sparkled and gleamed like new, so clean was the glass.

'*A potion* – oh, wait!' she exclaimed. 'I left out the first line!'

'Don't worry about that now – just keep going,' urged Bob. 'Something's definitely happening!'

'*A potion for fortune or so I am told.*'

The powder now flowed steadily from the bottle in a continuous stream of chameleon colour, changing from shade to shade as it fell.

'*A potion so potent it'll make you explode,*' Felicity finished.

The words had just left her lips when she felt a sharp stone hit her on the arm.

'Ow! Who threw that?' she said in annoyance.

She looked down and, to her surprise, saw a red glassy rock in the centre of her circle. She bent to pick it up. 'It looks like a –'

'Like a ruby!' exclaimed Clarity. 'The spell has worked!'

'Wait – isn't there meant to be an explosion of some sort to come?' said Bob, pushing them back from the circle.

A thought also struck Felicity. What about the goblins – they were bound to come straight to the potion room if there was an explosion! Before she could speak, however, a blast shook the cave, showering them with gems. When the dust settled, Felicity, Bob and Clarity – who had all immediately hunkered down and covered their heads with their arms when the explosion went off – looked up, dazed. A steady stream of precious stones cascaded down from a hole now visible in the black, glistening surface of the cave wall, like a beautiful waterfall of living rainbow.

'Jewels,' breathed Bob. 'And lots of them. It worked, Felicity! It actually worked!'

Worked it most certainly had, for as the three – mesmerised by the jewels – continued watching, they saw the precious gems fall faster and faster until they formed a rather large pointed pile on the cave floor in front of them and trickled to a stop.

Felicity coughed. 'The goblins are bound to have heard that,' she said. 'We need to hurry.'

Something had shifted in the air around them: she could feel it. She had that same feeling of dread that came just before getting caught with your fingers in the biscuit tin or being found out after telling a white lie. The air felt electric and in the distance came the thud of heavy feet – a *lot* of heavy feet.

The goblins were coming.

Bob ran over to inspect the opening, standing on his tip-toes to see what was on the other side.

'I ... can't ... see ... anything,' he grunted.

'Excellent,' said Clarity. 'Cover for an escape. Come on then – time we got going.'

Felicity hesitated.

'Do you think I should bring some of these jewels with me – as proof that we solved the riddle for the

Rhyming Riddler? I don't really know exactly what he was after: the potion or the jewels?'

Bob frowned. Behind them, the footsteps were growing louder by the second.

'Bring the bottle, as I suspect he might want *that* for his own purposes and the riddle *was* all about potions. Best never to take fairy gold or jewels from their source without permission, as the folk here don't take kindly to people stealing their things.'

Felicity pocketed the little bottle, which still had some of the magic potion inside. It would have to do, as they didn't have time to hang about. 'Fine by me,' she said. 'OK – ready.'

Clarity gave Bob a leg-up into the dark hole, then Felicity helped Clarity and she, as the tallest, brought up the rear, hoisting herself up into the space after her friends. She was disoriented for a few seconds, as it was so dark compared to the cave they had left behind. When her eyes adjusted to the inky blackness, she could just make out the shapes of Bob and Clarity in front of her.

The tunnel was small and cramped and Felicity found that, while Bob and Clarity could walk fairly comfortably along it, she, being taller, had to crawl. The goblin footsteps were muffled behind them but they still sounded too close for her liking. Soon, they would surely reach the potion room and find their escape route. She kept looking behind her, even though she couldn't see anything in the dark, expecting any minute to feel a gnarled goblin hand grab her foot.

They'd been on the move for quite some time when Clarity finally stopped.

'What is it?' said Felicity. 'Is it blocked?'

'No,' said Clarity, his voice trembling with either excitement or fear. Felicity hoped excitement. 'It looks like a slide!'

## Chapter Twelve
# Mermaids

A wave of relief washed over Felicity, followed quickly by a feeling of trepidation.

'If it's the only way we can go, then I guess we're going down it,' she said. 'But what if it takes us back into the heart of the goblin caves? How do we know it will lead us outside, and even if it does, surely we'll end up at the bottom of the cliff-side?'

'You're right,' said Bob. 'Is this the only way, Clarity?'

'I'm afraid so,' said the little Pebble Reader.

'Right, well, we'll just have to hope for the best,' said Bob. 'If we land back in the goblin caves then we'll have to deal with whatever comes our way, but if we end up *outside*, then we need a plan for how to get to the top of the cliff.'

'What about the mermaids?' asked Clarity. 'They could guide you round to a safer place to climb or give you refuge for the night in *their* caves if we summon them.' Felicity listened in silence. She secretly thought that would be a brilliant idea. Imagine seeing a mermaid! Although, she remembered her Granny Stone mentioning how they led sailors astray. Well, they weren't sailors, so hopefully that wouldn't happen.

'That could work,' said Bob. 'But we'd better be careful and not tell them too much of what we're up to. Best not to trust anyone until we know what's what.'

Clarity and Felicity nodded.

'OK – down the slide then,' said Bob. He paused. 'Do you hear that?'

Felicity gulped. 'Hear what?'

'Silence,' said Bob. 'The footsteps have stopped.'

It was true. The goblin footsteps could no longer be heard and it filled Felicity with an even greater sense of dread than when she'd heard them behind her. Where had they gone?

'Quick,' said Bob. 'We have to go – now! They could be anywhere. You'd best sit on something going down, or I imagine you'll wear a hole in your clothes.'

He took off his goblin cloak, rolled it up and sat on it, gripping the edges with his fingers. 'See you at the bottom.'

With that, Bob pushed off and slid into the darkness.

'You go next,' said Clarity. Felicity took her own goblin cloak off and folded it beneath her, fingers shaking. She edged towards the mouth of the slide, her heart beating just a little faster as she did so. She took a deep breath and then pushed herself forward.

The slide was not quite what she had expected, which was darkness and eerie silence. Instead, Felicity found herself in a space which glowed with soft hues of ruby and emerald – the long, golden tongue of the slide she was sitting on stretched out clearly before her.

She had thought before that they were already quite far down inside the cliff but the slide, which kept going straight, without nauseating twists and turns, lasted a good few minutes more than she had anticipated. Also, she could hear faint piping music from somewhere. This grew louder as she slid towards the bottom and finally shot out into the welcoming night. She was deposited roughly on a pile of strong-smelling seaweed and she quickly jumped up – aware that Clarity was probably not very far behind her.

It was the dead of night, but Felicity felt a wave of relief and exhilaration wash over her at being out in the fresh air at last. She breathed it in deeply, filling her lungs. Stars stitched into the inky sky winked down at her and she could see the curve of a silver moon smiling in the distance.

'Bob,' she said in a low voice, still wary of lurking goblins. 'Are you there?'

There were a few seconds of uneasy silence before Bob replied, 'Yes, I'm just trying to conjure us up a light.'

Felicity jumped as Clarity whizzed out of the slide behind her.

'Are we all here then?' she heard the Pebble Reader ask.

'Yes, all present and correct,' confirmed Felicity.

A golden glow suddenly appeared and Bob's cheerful face with it. 'We have light!' he said proudly, swinging what looked like a flaming ball of seaweed in front of him.

Catching sight of Felicity's expression, he added, 'I've enchanted it a bit, of course – to make it glow brighter and to keep it burning for as long as we need it. Now, what about summoning up a mermaid or two then? It's not safe to be out here in the open for too long.'

'I'm afraid I will have to leave you here,' said Clarity. 'My mission was to help you escape the goblin caves and now that is done you must continue the quest without my help, Felicity. I have to help my people protect the stones which remain. I have magic just powerful enough now to spirit myself home, but you are following this path for a reason. We are sure you will find the answers to our dilemma by continuing with it. Good luck.'

With that, Clarity took two pebbles from his pocket, tapped them together and disappeared.

'Thank you,' whispered Felicity. She felt a little less safe now that Clarity had gone, but at least she had company in Bob.

'Bob,' she said suddenly. 'Why are *you* helping me? I'm grateful that you are, but why? I mean, I know I asked you to come along with me but with all that's happened, well, it just made me wonder.'

'Like I said before – it's an adventure and I've been travelling around recently anyway,' he said. 'Also, you're here for a special reason and I want to help.'

'But why?' pestered Felicity. 'It's dangerous and I know you said brownies are helpful by nature, but you don't really know me yet you've already risked so much. Is that really the only reason? For an adventure? I don't mean to pry but, well, whatever the reason, I just wanted to say thanks. It's nice to have someone along to help.'

She looked at Bob, who had lowered the burning seaweed ball and cast his eyes downwards.

'I suppose I should tell you,' he said, after a few moments' silence. 'I want an adventure, yes, but I also want to find out who's taking the pebbles and why – and it's because, because ... well, because they took my best friend away.'

He stopped talking, took a breath and then continued angrily. 'My friend Butterkin – he's a boot-maker and collects pebbles and stones to decorate his garden – well, he picked up a pebble one day when we were out in the woods and just disappeared – pebble and all. One minute he was there, the next minute he'd vanished.'

Bob looked up at Felicity with sad brown eyes. 'I've known him all my life and now – he could be anywhere. I didn't even see what the pebble looked like, or I might have asked Clarity what sort of place he was taken to. It could be a place of nightmares or of torture. He could be a prisoner somewhere or … or have been put under an enchantment!'

'He could also be in a good land, though, couldn't he?' said Felicity gently. 'Bob, I'm so sorry. We'll find out what's been going on, I swear, and we'll put a stop to it and get Butterkin back. You know – I still think those goblins have something to do with all of this.'

'Speaking of which,' said Bob, 'we'd better make a move before they come whizzing down that slide after us. We'll summon a mermaid and hopefully get shelter – safe shelter – for the night and then we'll find out what these goblins have been up to!'

'It's a deal,' said Felicity. 'But how exactly do we summon a mermaid?'

'Like this,' said Bob, perking up again and giving her a grin.

He cupped his hands together and let out a long, low moan. It could have sounded quite sad but Felicity decided it was actually rather hauntingly beautiful, as Bob slid into soft singing, the notes quietly reaching a crescendo and then diminishing, like the ebb and flow of the tide. When he stopped, all they could hear was the gentle lapping of waves against rocks. Bob held his seaweed lantern high, pointed seaward and said, 'Look.'

Felicity could see a large cluster of rocks just a little way out from where they stood and there, draped languidly over one, was a silent shape … with a long, elegant tail.

The mermaids had arrived.

*** 

'Come on,' whispered Bob, nudging Felicity's arm as he set off towards the mermaid.

Hesitating for just a second, Felicity followed. The seaweed lantern swayed as the brownie made his way over the rocks, spilling pools of gold as they went and revealing a deep rock pool here, a cluster of slippery seaweed there.

Felicity had always prided herself on being quite a good rock climber and even now in the dark she was fairly sure-footed as she made her way across. As usual, she was half-excited and half-hesitant. On the one hand, meeting mermaids sounded amazing, but then only if they were friendly. She hoped they would be. Clambering over the last large rock in her path, she found herself beside Bob and face-to-face with a mermaid. The creature gazed back, unblinking, forcing Felicity to look away. She didn't want to stare but was itching to get a good look at this mysterious maiden of the waves.

'You called?' said the mermaid. Her voice was clear and crisp – like a cool breeze on a hot summer's day. Felicity looked back and the mermaid flicked her long tail and raised a finely shaped eyebrow.

Bob spoke up. 'Yes, we need your help, my mermaid friend. We require shelter for the night and need to find our way back to the top of the cliff. Can you help us?'

The mermaid, who had held Bob's gaze the entire time he was speaking, now blinked her quite startlingly violet eyes. 'I will,' she said.

Bob opened his mouth to speak again but the mermaid cut him off.

'I can show you the way out and lead you to shelter,' she said. 'But I must warn you – this is goblin territory and you stay here at your own risk. Although, my sisters and I saw a vast number of them steal away from their caves tonight, so you might be in luck.'

Bob glanced at Felicity, who remained silent, as agreed.

The mermaid studied them both. 'Perhaps we should move now before they return, for then, well – I could not help you.'

'Perfect,' said Bob. 'Where are we going and, er, how are we getting there?'

The mermaid smiled. 'Somewhere safe – and by boat, of course. The goblins seem to have one going spare.'

As if on cue, Felicity heard a slapping sound and turned to see a round shell-shaped boat bob up against the rocks. Inside sat another mermaid.

'It's so much more relaxing than swimming,' she said coyly, thumping her tail – dark green and streaked with silver – on the base of the boat. She arched her body and then plunged gracefully over the side into the dark water, before re-emerging. Her hair was fiery red and her skin as white as marble.

The mermaid on the rock had long trailing hair as black as the night around them, with violet fish-like eyes which gave her an ethereal, dangerous look. The tail was what held Felicity's attention, with its shimmering scales of silver and violet.

It was very long – longer than legs would have been if the mermaid had been a person – and ended in two beautifully tapered fins which curved in towards one another and looked very powerful indeed. Both mermaids had webbed hands and Felicity thought she could see delicate gills at the sides of their slim necks. Although they resembled women, it was surprisingly difficult to view them in that way.

To Felicity, they were more like beautiful wild animals – free to roam the ocean and sing sweetly to unsuspecting sailors.

'Come on then,' said Bob. 'Let's not hang about.' He jumped over the rocks and into the boat. Felicity followed suit, though she couldn't help but feel she was trespassing.

'Um, are there oars or do the mermaids push us?' she asked Bob. She had never rowed a boat before and didn't know what she should be doing.

The brownie grinned. 'No, it's magic! The boat can steer itself. Goblins aren't just evil – they're incredibly lazy as well. Why row when you can let sorcery do all the work!'

The mermaids laughed at this as they swam away from the boat.

'This way ...' Their voices bubbled faintly through the water as they quickly created distance between them and the goblin craft.

'Quick, make it go faster,' said Felicity. 'We'll lose them otherwise!'

'Don't worry, they won't abandon us,' Bob reassured her.

Sure enough, the two mermaids soon swam swiftly back to the boat and then they were off again, frolicking to and fro in the deep moonlit ocean. It was an incredible sight.

The little boat floated along the water at a moderate pace, the sea still as calm as Felicity remembered it from her world. She trailed her fingers over the side of the vessel – the water was refreshingly cold to the touch and sent shivers through her body. It lapped against the wood, playing in perfect harmony with the murmuring voices of the mermaids as they cut through their liquid landscape like a scythe through soft spring grass.

Felicity tried to pick out all the different sounds around her in an attempt to differentiate the magical from the natural.

'What's that noise?' she asked, as a mournful wail picked up amid the night-time melody. 'Can you hear it? It sounds so sad, but beautiful too. Is it another mermaid?'

Bob, who had been tinkering with something in the boat, turned to Felicity and listened. Against the glow of his lantern she saw his face turn ghost-white.

'That's no mermaid,' he stammered. 'It's – it's a banshee!'

## Chapter Thirteen
# The Banshee

Face frozen with fear, Bob stood like stone in the goblin boat, seemingly unable or unwilling to move. Felicity felt the colour drain from her own face. She remembered what her grandmother had told her about the banshee, whose melancholy wailing – or keening – warned of an imminent death. For whom was she crying tonight?

The banshee's mournful lament slid over the cliffs and across the sea, cloaking their boat in a ghostly chill. Felicity shivered, her spine tingling, and felt goosebumps rise on her skin. Never had she understood the expression 'somebody walking over your grave' more truly than at that very moment. The wail was the saddest sound she had ever heard. It poured over them in waves, a crescendo of a cry which ebbed away to a murmuring moan – a moan which steadily grew into a heart-wrenching shriek before dissolving into soft sobs.

There was a jolt as the goblin boat struck a rock. In their distraction, they hadn't noticed the mermaids guiding them back towards the shore and just caught a glimpse of their tails as the sea maidens disappeared into the depths. Felicity looked at Bob anxiously.

'What do we do now?' she said.

The wailing was getting closer by the second and, with it, the fairy woman it belonged to. At first, she looked like a speck of moon, but as the silvery shape grew steadily larger, Felicity could see the outline of a woman with long silver-white hair streaming out behind her. She felt her ears ringing as the banshee approached, her shrieks becoming almost unbearable.

Bob grabbed her arm.

'Quick, we have to move!' he said. 'I doubt she's coming for us, but it's best not to get caught in her path and that lament will only get more ear-splitting the closer she gets. Hurry!'

Felicity didn't need telling again. She swung her leg over the side of the boat and picked her way across the slimy, seaweed-covered rocks as quickly as she could, feet slipping and sliding in her haste.

By now, her eyes had adjusted to the moonlit darkness and with the aid of Bob's seaweed lantern, of course, things were a little clearer in the gloom. Bob was making a beeline for a cave up ahead, the banshee getting closer and louder behind them all the time. Just as they reached the yawning black mouth of the rocky haven, however, Felicity stopped. She could bear it no longer. The wailing was sharp and pointed as glass and yet she felt compelled to turn and face the banshee, hands pressed tightly over her ears in an attempt to muffle the sound.

Moving swiftly through the sky, the fairy woman was almost level with them. Rooted to the spot, Felicity stared up at the silvery mass as it flew closer to the cave, unable to look away. Then the banshee looked straight at her.

Like a flash of lightning, the spirit spun off course and sped across the remaining space until she was hovering above Felicity, almost close enough to touch. She wore a shimmering silver gown and began to brush her long silver-white hair with a comb of the same colour. Her face was that of a young woman and she was beautiful, though her eyes were red-raw from crying.

As Felicity watched, the banshee shook her head, slowly, then opened her mouth even wider, releasing an ear-splitting cry. Her youthful features began to crumble into those of an old crone and a black veil fell across her face as her gown faded to a sooty shade, her hair now grey and lifeless. Then she turned away and, before Felicity could blink, was swallowed up by the night.

*** 

Inside the cave it was dark and gloomy and it took Felicity a few moments to get her bearings, as her ears continued to ring after the banshee's wailing. She wasn't keen at the thought of navigating yet more caves and dank dreary tunnels, especially with the goblins still unaccounted for, but it seemed as though they had little choice.

'I'm glad *that's* over,' said Bob. He shivered. 'Are you OK?'

Felicity nodded. 'Yes,' she said. 'I'll – I'll be fine.' She was trembling, but took some strength from the fact that she'd stood her ground before a banshee (whatever would her Granny Stone say!) and they were back on land once more.

'Let's go,' she said. 'I just want to see daylight again – and get out of these caves. Who knows where we are now!'

The pair moved quietly through the cave and into a dark tunnel, feeling their way along the damp rock, as Bob's seaweed lantern dimmed to a faint glow. Felicity grew more and more nervous the further in they went. What if they got lost down here forever? Who would find them – or know to look for them? They continued to walk in silence and then, without warning, she bumped into Bob as he stopped abruptly.

'I think I've found something,' he said. 'A door.'

Felicity swallowed. 'A *goblin* door?' she asked nervously.

'Perhaps,' said her friend. 'I hope not, but I fear we must try it nonetheless, as the tunnel has come to a dead end. The mermaids travel quickly, so if they were guiding our boat for that last bit of the journey, then we may have travelled further than we realised. So it might be a goblin door – or it could be something else entirely.'

He paused. 'There is a legend – though I'm not perhaps the best to tell it – of the Fisher Folk, a race that kept to itself and used to trade fish with the fairy folk. This was years and years ago, but it was said they started over-fishing, before the stock had a chance to replenish its numbers, and were over-charging into the bargain.

'They were finally forbidden to trade unless they treated both their customers and their livelihood fairly, which they refused to do. Some thought they had taken a leaf out of the goblins' rule book and were becoming as unreasonable and ruthless as their neighbours – out for gold and silver above all else. They were finally banished and retreated to their caves, never to be seen since.' He paused. 'So it could be one of *their* doors.'

'I'm not sure they're the sort of people I'd really like to meet,' said Felicity. 'Do you think they might have something to do with the missing pebbles?'

'It's an idea,' said Bob. 'For who would suspect a race of Fisher Folk who have supposedly long disappeared – those who most of us believed had fled the kingdom in disgrace? They could be working with the goblins down here. And yet, it seems unlikely, as they disappeared so very long ago.'

The door was cut roughly into the rock and had a stone handle, but no knocker. It looked solid and disused and not very welcoming. Bob grasped the handle and pushed. It swung open with surprising ease to reveal a flight of stone steps stretching upwards into yet more darkness.

'Well,' he said. 'I suppose we'd better get climbing and see what's at the top. Hopefully it might lead us out into fresh air again.'

'Here's hoping,' said Felicity.

***

She had half-expected something to happen as soon as she stepped onto the staircase – up until now nothing had been ordinary as far as Felicity was concerned. To her relief, however, the stairs were just stairs and they began to climb them easily enough. It was tough going, though, and the way was gloomily paved with just step after monotonous step.

'I should have counted them,' she said after a while. 'How many do you think we've climbed now?'

'It feels like hundreds,' puffed Bob. 'I'm not as fit as I thought I was! But we just have to keep going. *Per aspera ad astra* – "through hardship to the stars". We'll get there!'

But where was 'there', Felicity wondered.

'Maybe we could stop for a minute or two for a rest,' she suggested finally, when it seemed the steps would never end. Without waiting for Bob's reply, she sank down onto a cold stone step. Thankfully, it was dry. She propped her arms on her knees and sighed.

'It all seems so impossible,' she said. 'I just want to get home and get out of these caves and, so far, I feel as if I've done nothing to help with that at all! I was stupid to think I could solve the pebble mystery and three magic riddles. How can I, when I'm stuck down here? I always thought coming to Fairyland would be a brilliant adventure, but right now I wish I was at home reading about someone else's!'

'We'll get there,' said Bob. 'I'm sure we can't be far from the top now and once we're above ground again we'll find that ridiculous Riddler and get your second riddle. You'll be out of here before you know it! There *is* still the problem of the pebbles, of course, but something tells me we'll sort that out too – things have a habit of turning out all right in the end.'

'I hope you're right,' said Felicity. She smiled at the little brownie.

'Right then!' he said, jumping to his feet. 'Best get a move on. No time like the present to get cracking!'

Felicity got to her feet and turned to face the steps once more. They still loomed ominously before her, challenging her with their seemingly never-ending ascent, but she knew Bob was right and, buoyed by his words, she knew that this *would* come to an end, as all things surely must eventually, and then she would look back on it and wonder why she had almost lost hope.

The pair began their steady climb again – in comfortable silence so as to preserve their energy and keep their focus. Their footsteps echoed up and down the staircase of stone – a staircase upon which others had previously travelled, but who? Goblins? Elves? Fisher Folk?

As they progressed, the oily black gradually lightened and Felicity and Bob instinctively quickened their pace until it was evident that light was trickling in from somewhere up above. Soon, they could make each other out quite clearly and no longer needed Bob's lantern.

Felicity couldn't hold her relief in any longer. 'Bob,' she said excitedly. 'I think we're at the top!'

## Chapter Fourteen
# The Runaway Steps

Fairyland sparkled as Felicity and Bob bounded back above ground after what seemed like an eternity in the underground caves. It was daylight again and there was sky, birds and, most of all, fresh air and freedom. They must have spent most of the night climbing, thought Felicity in surprise.

She looked around with undisguised pleasure, though the area didn't look familiar to her. The scenery before had seemed to mirror the world she had left behind, but this didn't quite fit. They had emerged among sand dunes, but she didn't recognise the beach ahead of her when she ran to the top of the sloping sand to have a look.

This wasn't the little horseshoe-shaped cove she knew and loved.

For a start, this beach was much bigger and it had a wild, untamed look about it. Instead of soft golden sand, there was a carpet of white, as if the shore had been washed clean by the crashing surf which beat relentlessly upon it.

To the left was a scattering of scraggy rocks further down the beach, which led to a part of the cliff with a huge hole in the middle. To the right, more rocky outcrops invaded the sea. Felicity couldn't see what was around either headland, so she had no idea which could possibly be the safer way to go – or the right way to go. The dunes, where she and Bob had appeared, were like mini mountains stretching down to the sea and were dressed in swathes of marram grass, wildflowers and shrubs, backed by a spine of cliff and fringed with sand. Felicity walked back to Bob, who seemed to be having the same problem she was.

'This isn't right,' she heard him muttering. He looked up at her as she approached. 'This,' he gesticulated impatiently at their surroundings, 'is *not* right.'

'That's what I was just about to ask you,' said Felicity. 'I don't recognise it and wondered if you did. But if you don't either then where is it and how on earth did we get here?'

'Something tells me that staircase was more than it appeared,' said Bob. 'We climbed to the top and emerged somewhere completely new, so I suspect it's enchanted. It must be fixed with some sort of travelling spell so it opens into different parts of the realm each time you climb it. Perhaps that's why the Fisher Folk disappeared – they just took themselves up it and went off to find somewhere else to live. I've heard of such things but have never come across them – until now.'

Felicity glanced back to where the staircase had emerged amid the dunes, but it had disappeared.

'Well, let's just hope that wherever we are is somewhere that will help with the riddles and the pebble mystery,' she said. 'I don't particularly want to go back underground again, but it looks as if we don't have that option now anyway. So, which way should we go?'

'I'm afraid I have absolutely no idea where we are, so it's up to you,' said Bob. 'Looking around, though, we'd probably be better to work our way through these dunes – it's less exposed than the beach.'

'Yes, that makes sense,' agreed Felicity. 'Maybe we'll find someone who can give us directions.' She turned 360 degrees and then said, 'Let's go left.'

'Fine by me,' said Bob cheerfully.

Direction decided, they set off once more. White-spotted mushrooms were dotted about the landscape, interspersed with pink and blue wildflowers, bright-yellow buttercups and purple heather, the air lightly scented with their sweet perfume. Felicity was so absorbed by it all that she wasn't really watching where she was going and so she didn't see the chimney until it was too late. She tripped as her foot caught on the little structure and she flung her hands out to break her fall, taking the chimney with her. Stunned and surprised, she turned to see what it was and stared open-mouthed when she saw what she had broken.

'Where on earth did that come from?' she said incredulously. 'Is that a *chimney*?'

'Yes, but whose?' said Bob. 'It was sticking out of the ground. Wait a minute – I think I hear something. Footsteps ...'

Felicity could hear them as well. They came from underneath the soil and were quickly getting louder. She could do nothing but wait with Bob, as there was no time to run and hide. They could only hope that whoever was approaching would be the friendly sort.

A sharp tap on her back almost made her jump out of her skin and she whirled round to see who, or what, was there.

'Did you break my chimney?'

The voice came from what appeared to be a dwarf, though he certainly wasn't as friendly as the seven Felicity had in mind. She smiled at the little man, hoping she looked apologetic.

'Yes, I must have tripped over it,' she said. 'I'm really sorry, but I didn't see it. It's my first time in the Fairy Realm, you see, and I wasn't expecting –'

'Well, I should like to think you didn't see it, otherwise you wouldn't have damaged it, I hope!' interrupted the dwarf, an annoyed look on his face. 'If you *did* see it then you did it on purpose, which is altogether an entirely different matter.'

'She really didn't see it,' said Bob, stepping forward and proffering his hand in greeting. 'My name is Bobbin the Brownie – I go by the preferred name of Bob – and this is Felicity. She's here on a quest to help the Pebble People and at the moment we're lost, so we're terribly sorry about your chimney, really we are, but can you please help us and perhaps also tell us where we are?'

Felicity was once again glad to have Bob by her side. She had wanted to say all that as well but the dwarf, small as he was, intimidated her. The little man studied her intently, then looked at Bob and then back at Felicity again, obviously sizing them up.

'A quest you say, eh? Well, someone had certainly better sort out this nonsense and calamity, with pebbles popping up here and there, there and here, everywhere and anywhere, over here and over there … terrible, terrible.'

'You're rhyming!' said Felicity. 'Which means –'

The Rhyming Riddler faded into view behind the dwarf, startling him so much he fell over with a grunt onto the ground. He scrambled to his feet and darted off to the nearest hillock, where he promptly disappeared from view.

'Wait!' called Felicity. 'Please wait!'

She glared at the Riddler, who arched his eyebrows and smirked.

'What have we here, Felicity, dear? Taking time to roam, when I thought you sought home?' He gave her a sly smile. 'And you *did* take your time in solving my rhyme ... Perhaps I was wrong and you want to stay gone?'

'You tricked us and trapped us!' said Felicity indignantly. 'And you left not *one* rhyme, but two at a time. So it's no great wonder we were so long under.' She knew she shouldn't risk making him angry but she couldn't help it – he made *her* angry.

The Riddler took a step forward, the tiny bells on the curled tips of his red boots tinkling softly as he did so. In the strong sun, his tunic rippled with colour, and if Felicity hadn't known better, she would have sworn the swirling shades and fabric fairies sewn onto the garment were twirling and dancing. She squinted at them but was distracted by the Riddler pointing a thin, bony finger in her face.

'*One* riddle so far, I think you'll agree,' he said. 'You'd better be careful, Felicity. Don't make me angry – don't disagree.' He peered at her from under his bushy eyebrows. 'Now, I believe you have something quite special for me?'

He held out a knobbly hand. Felicity looked at it for a few seconds before deciding the best thing would probably be to cooperate, so she fished the potion from her pocket.

'Here, take it.' She dropped the bottle into the Rhyming Riddler's outstretched hand.

He grinned greedily at his new-found treasure and then quickly opened a pouch hanging from the gold cord about his waist, dropped the magic potion inside and tied the pouch up again.

'First riddle completed, the goblins defeated,' he confirmed. 'Now for riddle number two. Listen up, both of you!'

Bob rolled his eyes but said nothing.

The Riddler looked directly at Felicity, who was determined not to let him see how nervous she was. In fact, apart from Bob, everyone she had met so far in the Fairy Realm had unnerved her in one way or another.

'Please tell me the next riddle,' she said.

*'When the Riddler next sees you, let me tell you this,*
*In your hand you should hold something she'll miss.*
*Fashioned from fire – clear and bright,*
*It's a teller of tales, with the gift of sight.*
*Where will you find it? Go low, then higher …*

*Through the whispering woods – there you will spy her!'*

The Riddler clicked his fingers and disappeared.

Felicity was about to say she couldn't possibly remember all he had just said when she saw strips of yellowed paper float down around her. She picked a piece from the air as it fell.

*'It's a teller of tales,'* she read aloud. 'It's the riddle, but we need to catch it all and put it in the correct order. Quick, Bob, make sure we get them before they disappear and we forget which way it goes!'

They carefully and quickly collected all the scraps of paper and laid them out on the grass. Felicity then read each one and arranged them accordingly.

'I think that's the right order,' she said.

Apparently she was correct, because the slivers of paper began to writhe and wriggle like panicked worms in freshly turned soil, until they were firmly sealed together in one complete scroll. Thin, silvery lines below each sentence were all that remained to show where the pieces had joined.

'Good, that's that done at least,' said Felicity with relief. 'I have no idea what it means but at least we can start trying to work it out. Now, I wonder where that dwarf went to. We still need his help.'

As she spoke, the dwarf stepped out from behind the small hillock where he had been watching them the entire time. He held his hand out to Felicity. 'My name is Drundle – Drundle of the Dune Dwarves,' he said. 'I will help you if I can.'

Felicity shook his hand. 'Thank you, Drundle. As Bob said before, I'm Felicity. It's nice to meet you and I'm sorry again about your chimney. I really didn't see it.'

'Yes, yes, well, come now. Come to my home and we will talk,' said Drundle. 'I don't want that rainbow-bright Riddler interrupting again.'

Felicity suppressed a smile. The Riddler did look slightly ridiculous but then so did Drundle. He was short, as all dwarves were, with shovel-like hands, huge feet, a small squat body and a craggy face with a rather big nose. His feet were encased in large brown, scruffy boots, his tunic and trousers were mossy green, as was his hat, his belt was red with a shiny gold buckle and his eyes were coal-black, but looking at her more warmly than before.

Felicity and Bob followed Drundle round the hillock and over to a mossy piece of ground that looked a shade darker than everywhere else. Drundle mumbled a few words and then jumped into the moss and disappeared.

'Follow me!' he called back.

'Does he mean we have to go through there as well?' said Felicity, although she had a feeling she already knew the answer to her question. 'Will that work for us?'

Bob grinned and jumped in, whooping as he did so. There was nothing for it – Felicity followed.

## Chapter Fifteen
# Dwarves

Despite her trepidation at going underground again, Felicity actually found it quite thrilling to jump into the springy patch of moss and drop down onto the pile of cushions below. Even so, she sat dazed for a few seconds before looking up for Bob and Drundle. She found them watching her patiently, which prompted her to jump to her feet. The underground space accommodated her height easily, and her surprise at this must have shown on her face, as Drundle spoke up.

'We don't get a lot of visitors down here but when we do we can't expect them all to stoop. This way!'

They followed him out of the cavern which, Felicity noted, completely crammed with cushions of all colours, shapes and sizes to break the fall most magnificently of anyone entering through the little mossy drop-hole. She thought it would be a lovely place to lie down and rest. She hadn't realised how tired she was until now, but suddenly all that step-climbing, running from the banshee, dodging goblins and dealing with the Rhyming Riddler had caught up with her and she longed for a night of deep sleep.

In the meantime, however, she followed Bob, who followed Drundle down a short, brightly lit passageway to a little circular reception area with doors set into its curved shape.

So far, this underground experience was the complete opposite of the dank, dismal and dreary goblin caves. The tunnel was made of warm brown earth for a start, instead of cold, thick rock, and had a comforting earthy smell rather than one of salt and slimy, decaying seaweed.

The dwarf tunnel was also well lit with oil-burning lanterns and was wide and well kept. The doors now surrounding them were all round in shape – like portals on a ship – and were made of dark-brown wood, blending perfectly into the soil. Each had a coloured handle – flower-shaped, Felicity realised – along with a letterbox and a brass bell, which hung beside each door, long chains dangling down for the visitor to ring. Felicity was tempted to pull one but thought she had better not.

Drundle walked straight up to a door with a purple handle. He turned the flower, which Felicity saw now was made of china, and swung the door open.

He beckoned to Bob and Felicity. 'After you.'

This time, Felicity went first. She stepped over the threshold and into a large round room. It was filled with shabby but comfortable-looking furniture, with bright rugs on the floor and a round table in the centre. More lanterns burned in alcoves scattered around the room's perimeter and the earthy walls were covered with pretty wall hangings.

Bookshelves had been carefully constructed within one particular wall, with wooden panels set inside for the books to rest on. A door directly ahead of Felicity suggested another room beyond.

Bob and Drundle joined her inside, Drundle closing the door behind them.

'Have a seat, have a seat,' he said, his generous hands pointing to the various armchairs scattered about the room.

Felicity obligingly sank into a big, squishy dark-blue chair, while Bob chose a smaller red one opposite.

'Make yourselves comfortable. Back in a tick!' said Drundle, disappearing through the door Felicity had spotted. It closed again behind him and she took the opportunity to shut her eyes for a few minutes.

When she heard the door open again Felicity forced herself awake and looked up to see Drundle emerge with a tray of refreshments.

'Food first, then talk,' said the dwarf. He placed the tray on the wooden table at the centre of the room. 'Pull up your chairs!'

Felicity and Bob dragged their chairs closer and Drundle did the same, pulling up a three-legged wooden stool which he somehow managed to perch on cross-legged.

'Help yourselves,' he urged. 'It's all from my own kitchen and very nice too, if I say so myself.'

Felicity reached for the jug and poured everyone a glass of sparkling yellow liquid. She sipped it, the fresh tangy taste of lemons immediately quenching her thirst. The drink was cool and sweet and delicious.

'Homemade lemonade,' said Drundle proudly. 'My own recipe – with extra zest!'

He offered Felicity a plate laden with tiny pies. She bit into one and her mouth filled with the flavour of meat and gooey gravy. After the miniature pies was a plate of pineapple sandwiches, which Felicity adored, followed by sugar-snap biscuits. Feeling full and relaxed, Felicity watched as Drundle darted back into the kitchen and emerged with a cake covered in strawberries and cream.

The dwarf cut them each a generous slice and then finally asked, 'So, what can I do to help?'

Felicity swallowed her cake – it melted in the mouth – and turned to Drundle.

'First of all, thank you so much for all of this already,' she said. 'We really appreciate it and it has all tasted delicious.'

Drundle smiled with obvious pleasure and nodded at her.

'If you could tell us exactly where we are, though, and help point us in the right direction, we'd be really indebted to you,' Felicity added. 'We need to solve this riddle and we have to find out who has been taking the enchanted pebbles. Do you have any idea who might be behind it?'

'Start at the beginning,' said Drundle, 'and I'll see if I can help. But as to where you are – this is Whitewater Bay and here is where the Dune Dwarves live.'

Between them, Felicity and Bob recounted their adventures so far, Drundle listening intently throughout. When they had finished, he took the riddle scroll from Felicity and read it through a few times. He frowned and then looked up at them.

'Well, it looks as if you've strayed far – very far – from where you began,' he said. 'Whitewater Bay is at least half a realm away from the Golden Sands, where you,' he pointed at Felicity, 'entered the kingdom. The Runaway Steps really did run away with you, it would seem.' Felicity and Bob glanced at one another. So that's what they had climbed – the Runaway Steps!

Drundle saw their surprised looks. 'You didn't know? Well, the Runaway Steps are a sort of portal – like the cairns we guard here.

'They're located not far from the goblin caves where you were and can be used for travelling to other parts of the realm, though they'll do whatever they like if you don't know how to control them ... As soon as you mentioned steps I knew it must have been those that brought you here.

'But I'm afraid you won't find much of anything in these parts. We Dune Dwarves are a solitary breed and live simply, away from the rest of the fairy folk. We do not often court unknown or unexpected visitors. That,' he looked bashful, 'is perhaps why I reacted as I did before.'

'Where are the rest of the dwarves?' asked Felicity curiously.

'Oh, they come and go,' said Drundle. 'There's an entire warren of tunnels and underground dwellings around here – my home is only on the outskirts of that. During the day many of us fish, while the others guard the cairns.'

Bob broke in. 'You keep mentioning the cairns,' he said. 'Do you mean the old gateways to the rest of the realm? I didn't know those were still in use.'

'Yes,' said Drundle, nodding at the brownie.

Felicity's ears pricked up. Weren't cairns just piles of rocks people piled on top of one another as markers for fellow travellers, or just for fun? What did they mean 'gateways'? She voiced her question.

'The cairns, if arranged in a circular pattern, can open magical gateways or portals to other parts of the Fairy Realm,' said Drundle. 'But they only stay open for a short period of time – mere minutes – and one can never be one hundred percent certain of where they will take you. Of course, the traveller or travellers generally use magic to try to control their destination but, even so, that is easier for some than others.

'However, a portal left open for too long and which opens into an evil or dangerous place can let unwelcome sorts through – those who should never cross the gateway or indeed leave their place of origin. If this happens, it throws the kingdom out of kilter, as most of these creatures have designs to wreak havoc or cause mayhem. Kobolds or trolls, imps and ogres, blacker than black witches, harpies and dark elves …'

'The stones that make up the cairns are similar to the pebbles guarded by the Pebble People,' added Bob. 'Stone magic is very old and unpredictable, and there are much easier and safer ways of travelling, so the cairns were put out of action years ago, from what I heard?' He looked at Drundle.

'That's correct,' said the dwarf. 'Though, perhaps the Runaway Steps did you a favour, for the cairns and the pebbles are surely connected in their magic, so perhaps you will find answers here. We are permitted to use the cairns on rare occasions or in emergencies, as long as it's under full supervision, so that might be the solution.

'But first – the riddle. I have studied it and I have solved it, but I wager you won't like what it says.' He shook his head. 'No, not one bit.'

'You've solved it already?' Felicity was impressed.

'It wasn't hard,' said Drundle. 'The Rhyming Riddler's reputation is more for the dangerous quests he makes the unfortunate one who attempts to solve his puzzles undertake. You said he sent you to the goblin caves first? It's a good job they were distracted. You had a *very* lucky escape there!

'And a banshee encounter as well?' The dwarf shook his head. 'The Riddler will put plenty of peril in your path. You might just have one riddle to solve but you will generally have to battle more than your fair share of hardship as a consequence. No, it isn't the riddles themselves which are meant to cause you worry – not the first two anyway. He *wants* you to solve them so he can watch you squirm, face certain death and ultimately fail at the final hurdle, so you will stay in Fairyland forever.'

Felicity was chilled to the bone by the dwarf's words. She knew she couldn't trust the Riddler but still – it left her with a distinctly sick feeling in the pit of her stomach.

'What does it mean then, the riddle?' she asked Drundle worriedly.

He spread the scroll on the table and looked up at them both.

'The specifics aside, one thing is clear,' he said slowly. '*You* are going to Witch Wood.'

## Chapter Sixteen
# Through the Cairns

Felicity gulped. Witch Wood. Witches were eerie and evil. Woods could be impenetrable and dark and were dense with trees – trees which hid and were hidden behind, with leaves that whispered and rustled and dappled the sunlight with shadows. Up until now she had always regarded woods as places of adventure, where she looked for treasures with her mother. Being told she had to seek out a wood with real live *witches* in it, however, was an altogether different matter.

'Are you sure?' she asked Drundle.

'It's quite clear, I'm afraid,' said the dwarf. 'The second part of the riddle refers to whispering woods and, while all trees talk in some way or another, Witch Wood – home to many witches – is where you will find an old, old witch who, it is said, lives in a tall stone spire surrounded by whispering trees. It must surely be this witch the Riddler wants you to seek out, as he mentions

that you must *go low, then higher* before you will *spy her* –
rhymes with "spire", see? Anyway, that's how it's said
you access the witch's spire – you must go down,
underground, before you go up into it, for it has no front
door. I would imagine the way in is well concealed – by
trees and by magic – so you must be vigilant at all times.'

Felicity gulped again.

'The rest of the riddle is about what you must take
from her, but I can't work out what that is, I'm afraid,'
said the dwarf. 'Hopefully it will become clear once you
find her. A word of warning, though. Familiars, the
witches' magical companions, are commonly cats, owls,
crows or even toads, but in Witch Wood, it's the crows
you would do best to look out for. Beware if you see
them, for the witches can glamour themselves and
appear as crows too.'

Her next quest was sounding more dangerous by the
minute and Felicity looked nervously at Bob.

'I don't like the sound of this at all,' said her friend.
'But if that's where we need to go, then that's where we
*shall* go – right, Felicity?'

She nodded, hoping she looked more confident than
she felt. 'How do we get there, Drundle? The cairns?'

The dwarf nodded. 'Yes. But first, we'll have to make
sure you're fit for the journey ahead, for even the cairns
are unlikely to take you straight to Witch Wood because

of the magic around it. We will try instead to send you to the Enchanted Forest, which has its own risks, and from there you must journey to Witch Wood, which is buried somewhere deep within the forest.

'How about having some rest, and when you wake, I'll take you to the cairns? It will be nightfall by then, which is a safer time to use them than in broad daylight. I'll meet with the other dwarves while you sleep and make preparations.'

With tiredness creeping steadily through their bodies, Bob and Felicity nodded their agreement. Drundle pointed to a door, which Felicity was sure hadn't been there before, tucked into the far left-hand corner of the room. It was made of brown oak and had a brass handle shaped like a little bird.

'You will find beds through there,' said the dwarf.

'Thank you, Drundle,' said Felicity, hoisting herself out of her comfy chair and making her way over to the door. Bob followed suit.

The room behind the oak door contained lots of oddly shaped little beds, which Felicity assumed must be for other dwarves.

She chose one with fat blue cushions strewn across a prettily patterned floral quilt and a dark wooden headboard shaped like a pointed hat. It looked quite comical and very inviting.

Bob rolled into a smaller bed, which bulged out at the sides and had a blue and green patchwork quilt and comfy pale-green cushions. The pillows on both beds were snow white and when their heads sunk into the welcoming softness, Felicity and Bob fell fast asleep.

***

When they awoke, it was dark.

A lantern was burning in the bedroom, casting a warm golden glow around the little space and painting dark shadows across the walls, which changed shape as the light flickered.

Now that she was more alert, Felicity counted six beds in total, spread in a circle around the earthen walls. In the centre of the room was a low wooden table with little stumpy legs, a lamp on top and a circular carpet decorating the floor beneath. Vibrant colours swirled together on the fabric, spiralling into the middle and making Felicity feel dizzy just looking at it. Shelves were cut into the hard earth beside a few of the beds and held books, candles and other odds and ends. Besides that, there was no further furniture – the décor was simple and modest.

Bob threw back the covers from his bed. 'Best see if it's time to go,' he said briskly.

'I wonder how the cairns work,' said Felicity, as she tidied up her bedcovers. 'And will it take long to go through them, do you think?'

Bob looked grim. 'That I don't know,' he said. 'I've never travelled this way before but I can't imagine it will be a long journey, no. Magic tends to work quickly.'

Beds remade, Felicity and Bob returned to the living room, where they found Drundle and three other dwarves deep in conversation. Drundle looked up as they came in.

'Ah, just in time,' he said. 'I have here with me fellow Keepers of the Cairns – Brindle,' he beckoned to a squat, thick-set dwarf with meaty arms and a barrel body, 'Mendle,' he indicated a larger lankier dwarf with an absurdly big nose, 'and Grandle.' A dwarf of average height with ropey, muscled arms grunted at them. All wore solemn expressions and offered no small talk, but Felicity thought they certainly looked capable enough of protection.

'Here's what we're going to do,' said Drundle. 'Felicity – you and Bob must enter the cairns separately, as travellers must go one at a time for the magic to work best. However ...' He paused. 'There's a small chance you may not end up in the exact same location because of it. That's the thing about cairns – they're unpredictable and this is one of many reasons they're no longer in use.' 'Do you think that will happen?' asked Felicity.

'There's a possibility,' said Drundle. 'But the problem is that you won't know until you're on the other side. There's no way around it, I'm afraid. Do you still want to go ahead with the plan?'

Before Felicity could answer, Bob spoke up. 'I think we should do it,' he said. 'If it's the best way to get you closer to Witch Wood, then we must take the chance, Felicity. I'm sure I'll be right behind you and, if not, well, I'll be sure to find you again. Trust me.'

Felicity looked into the brownie's hazel eyes. She knew he was right, but it didn't make the decision any easier. Imagine if she ended up in the Enchanted Forest – and Witch Wood – by herself!

'OK,' she said. 'Let's do it.'

'Good,' said Drundle. 'Right then – it would be best to get going. The moon is full – a good omen – and it is a still night so far. Time we were off.'

And so Drundle, followed by his three dwarf companions, followed by Bob, followed by Felicity, left the underground room, went through the earthen tunnel and emerged into the cool, quiet night.

The moon was indeed full and shone brightly in the darkened sky, casting a ghostly pale glow upon the ground and cloaking the grass with silver – the blades like tiny swords piercing the earth. The beach was bathed in the luminous light, which was bright enough to allow walking without lanterns. They travelled in silence, following the dwarves down to the white sand and along the shore. They stopped about halfway.

'Here,' said Drundle.

Felicity saw five small piles of rocks arranged to form a rough circle. Each rock was carefully balanced upon the other, larger ones at the bottom giving way to gradually smaller stones on top. There was just enough room inside the circle of stones for a person to stand or sit down.

'Felicity, you had better go first,' said Drundle.

Felicity nodded and stepped into the circle. She looked at Bob. 'You *will* come straight after, won't you?'

'I will,' said Bob confidently. 'Straight after. You don't get rid of me that easily.' He gave her a smile and Felicity felt a little more reassured. She trusted Bob.

'Right,' said Drundle briskly. Brindle, Mendle and Grandle had taken up position and with Drundle moving into place they formed a square around the outside of the cairns.

'Stay close, brownie,' said Drundle. 'As soon as the girl disappears you must jump in the circle yourself. Now, we will begin the spell that activates the cairns and instruct them to deliver you to the Enchanted Forest.

Good luck!' The dwarves closed their eyes and after a few moments began a low chant.

They each stood still as statues – solemn little men at their four corners. Their chant rose and fell, growing steadily louder and then sliding off into a soft whisper. They were speaking a strange language Felicity had never heard before and as she listened, their chants became faster and faster, until she wondered how on earth they could speak so quickly.

She stood in the circle, aware that something was about to happen at any moment, and looked nervously at Bob. The little brownie was staring, transfixed, at the cairns, however, so Felicity turned her attention to the stones. Having done nothing yet of significance, she saw they were now beginning to glow. They were white rocks, so the glowing made it difficult to look directly at them as they grew brighter. An ominous ringing sound seeped into the stillness of the night. Clear and steady, it was nevertheless a sinister accompaniment to the dwarves' chanting.

Felicity felt herself getting dizzy and sat down in the middle of the circle. As she did so, she realised something was spinning. Was it the stones? Was it her? The ground? She didn't know. The bright-white light from the cairns was dazzling her, the scenery suddenly a blur, the ringing loud in her ears, the chanting a steady stream of confusing, foreign sounds which hurt her head.

She put her hand out on the sand to steady herself, even though she was already sitting on the ground. Nausea washed over her as the spinning continued, white stones and sand and moonlight blurred together, the chants and ringing a clash of noise in her ears. Her head was buzzing, so she lowered it to the ground and closed her eyes, shutting out the craziness around her. It was too much – this was really too much. She felt she couldn't breathe now and opened her mouth to call for help. Nothing came out.

And then, it stopped. From chaos came calm and Felicity opened her eyes as soon as she sensed it.

The moonlit beach had gone so the spell had obviously worked. She had come through the cairns to – somewhere. It was dark, much darker than the beach had been, with only small patches of silver filtering through whatever was blocking out the moonlight.

Felicity looked up and saw the faint outline of knobbly, crooked arms, which rustled gently at her in the breeze. Trees. They towered above her, their leafy branches barriers to the moon and the visibility it would otherwise have provided.

The grass felt damp so she got to her feet, brushing down her clothes. She hoped Bob would be here soon, as the darkness was thick with unsettling silence. Only the trees whispered to each other in the breeze, but who knew what lurked in the black depths of the forest and its murky foliage, for she was surely in the Enchanted Forest, as planned. Felicity shuddered and wrapped her arms tightly around herself. Thinking like that wouldn't help, she told herself firmly, but it was very hard not to when you found yourself alone in a magical forest in the pitch dark in the dead of night.

She felt vulnerable and lost but she couldn't see well enough to walk anywhere and didn't want to move far in case Bob came through the cairns and couldn't find her. So she hunkered down against the trunk of a nearby tree and sat, as time ticked by, hugging her knees close to her chest for warmth and comfort.

Somewhere in the distance an owl shrieked, its cry cutting through the air like a swift, sharp sword. She shuddered again – pity the prey. Closing her eyes, Felicity tried to block out the sounds slowly emerging around her, or was it simply that her ears were becoming more attuned to the forest as she sat in silence, waiting for Bob? The rustle of the leaves overhead, the shriek of the owl, the flap of beating wings …

Felicity squeezed her eyes shut more tightly, huddled up more closely and willed morning – and Bob – to come.

## Chapter Seventeen
# Forest Fairies

She must have fallen asleep again in the night, for when Felicity awoke, the eerie darkness had been replaced by the fractured but nevertheless warm and inviting glow of morning.

She slowly stretched out her limbs – she had curled up against the solid trunk of what appeared to be a huge oak tree, surrounded by soft green moss. Bleary eyed, it took Felicity a few moments to adjust to the dewy light. It was obviously morning but the thickly spread canopy of leaves overhead hid the strong beams of the sun, so only golden streams of light and pockets of rays penetrated to the forest floor below. It gave a pretty, but mysterious, look to the forest. It was neither completely dark nor brightly lit and the air was cool and still as a result. There was no cheerful birdsong here; no signs of life – fairy, animal or otherwise. Yet.

In fact, Felicity realised, the Enchanted Forest seemed almost to be sleeping. A heavy hush blanketed the forest as she recalled how many rustlings, hoots and even shrieks she had heard far off in the night, just hours before. Indeed, even the leaves no longer stirred. Tall trees reached for the sky, their leafy canopies a natural ceiling to this magical haven.

Felicity glanced quickly around, taking in the scene in a single swoop. Trees everywhere, moss and grass underfoot and no evidence of where she had come through the cairns. The cairns that Bob was also to have come through, she suddenly remembered with horror. Where was the brownie? Surely he would have been here by now if the spell had worked? She jumped to her feet, ignoring the slight lightheadedness this caused, and began hunting through the nearby vegetation for her friend.

She searched the long grass and behind the trees, running frantically around where she had lain, until she wasn't even sure anymore which tree had been hers. In fact, they all looked the same and Felicity realised with a sinking feeling that it would be incredibly easy to get lost in this forest, enchanted or otherwise.

She sat down again, drew her knees up to her chin, rested her head on them and thought. She could wait for Bob, but a night had already passed and he wasn't here. He must have ended up somewhere else – somewhere Felicity had no way of finding. She would simply have to hope they would run into each other again somewhere on their journeys, as Bob had promised, and that perhaps he could use his magic to speed that up.

She sighed and glanced around her again. That meant only one thing. She was alone once more and she would have to solve the second riddle by herself. She gulped. Never had she needed Bob's help more than now, and now, he wasn't here.

She blinked tears back angrily – she would not allow them to fall. The Riddler – Fairyland – was *not* going to defeat her. At least she had had most of a good night's sleep – the moss had been surprisingly comfortable in its springiness and it thankfully wasn't cold. Cool, but not cold.

Still she *was* hungry and she needed to find out which direction to go and try not to walk round in circles as she did so, which she feared could be all too easily done here. There was nothing for it – she would just have to start walking.

Scrambling to her feet, Felicity scanned the forest. As she really had no idea which direction to take, she chose a route at random. The grass muffled her footsteps, which she noted would also make it more difficult for her to hear others approaching. She determined to stay on her guard as best she could. You never knew what could be lurking in an enchanted forest. She pondered the riddle while she walked, but it seemed impossible to know what it was she had to take from the witch. She shuddered. The witch would not be happy if she stole from her.

After what felt like hours of endless walking, Felicity began to tire of seeing nothing but tree trunks and grass. She had no notion of whether she was in the middle of the forest or on the outskirts, although she suspected the latter. She only hoped she would find something, anything to help her – and soon. She trudged on, each step almost the one where she would sit and rest again, but every time, Felicity pushed herself to continue onwards, keeping her eyes peeled for fruit or wild nuts. It felt like ages since she'd eaten with Bob and Drundle.

It wasn't long before she realised the forest was getting thicker. The tall trees seemed to gather closer together, whispering secrets to one another as their leaves rustled in the breeze. Felicity swept branches out of her face as she walked, finally stumbling upon a worn and dusty rabbit path.

'Something to follow at least,' she muttered. 'Run on by rabbits and maybe even fairies. I've seen neither here so far, but I'll follow it all the same.'

The path twisted and turned through the forest, but Felicity found that it cleverly avoided most of the branches, so she had a much clearer view ahead and wasn't constantly moving woody boughs this way and that. Her feet, however, grew heavier with each step and when the path brought her into a small clearing, cosy with bushes and delicate blooms, she took the opportunity to sink onto the grass for a few minutes' rest.

Thin branches swayed elegantly above her in the breeze, their green leafy fingers playing a soundless tune in the air as they moved, while full, fat bushes punctuated the circular space, some with deep-green waxy leaves. Beautiful wildflowers – some Felicity recognised from her Granny Stone's garden – were scattered all around. Shiny golden buttercups and bluebells with their frilly purple-blue petals bordered the copse with smatterings of lilac and pale pink and orange woven in amongst them.

She spied a patch of wild red roses growing alongside a clutch of white flowers, whose petals fluttered occasionally to the forest floor at the touch of the breeze, gentle as it was. There were purple petals, vivid orange, scarlet, pink, striped and spotted – the colours clashed together to form a living tapestry that Felicity just couldn't tear her eyes away from.

And the longer she looked, the more convinced she was that the flowers were multiplying under her gaze. She narrowed her eyes suspiciously. Surely those white lilies hadn't been there before? And those foxgloves – they *definitely* hadn't been there before. Something was happening here – magic was afoot: it must be.

A crop of primroses had also appeared now, not far from where Felicity sat. They were one of her favourite wildflowers and she stretched her hand out to touch one. They began to flutter like wings, then swirled upwards, a whirlwind of pale yellow that spiralled in front of her and then around her head, tickling her neck and cheeks as they passed. Felicity giggled. The primroses continued on their way skywards and she watched as they danced and twirled their way up into the trees, until they were swallowed by the green gods towering above and were lost to her.

Deciding it was time to move on, she stood up. Then she saw them.

Some were big, some small, some spotted, some plain, but, undeniably, they were *all* mushrooms. Felicity turned around, panicked. They were behind her, in front of her, beside her – they *encircled* her. She was trapped and the breeze had died.

She swallowed and took a small step forward. She took another and another until she stood at the edge of the fairy ring.

*Please*, she prayed inwardly. *Please let me step across.* She lifted her foot and leapt over the mushroom barrier.

'I did it!' she cried. 'I'm free – I'm out! The fairies haven't got me!'

But when she looked again, Felicity was still in the ring.

'That's impossible,' she said loudly. 'I jumped out. And I'll do it again – watch me!' she said, to no one she could see but someone she suspected might be watching.

She jumped again and then again and when she was tired of jumping and still found herself in the ring, she gave up and sat down in the middle of her mushroom prison. How was she ever to find the witch now?

'*Dance with us and we will help you …*' The voices floated through the air.

Something tinkled behind Felicity, but when she looked, all she saw were bluebells, standing as tall and proud as their thick stems would let them.

'*Dance, dance, we love to dance. Dance with us tonight, by moonlight, sweet moon bright, so silver it glows. Dance in the air, with your wings, on your toes.*'

Musical laughter followed the whispered words, though Felicity couldn't see anyone or anything.

'Fairies,' she said quietly. 'But good or bad? They all play tricks I suppose.'

She closed her eyes. *Trust no one*, she thought. *Play them at their own game and learn from them, but trust not a single one of them, no matter how enchanting they may seem.*

When she opened her eyes the copse was alive with butterflies, the flowers sprinkled with them too. One flew up to her – it had large red wings spotted with gold circles and tipped in black, the top and bottom ends tapering off into thin points. It took Felicity a few seconds to realise the body was no black furry caterpillar. It was dressed in red gauze, slippered with golden shoes and had a small oval face with eyes the colour of ebony. Small pointy ears peeked out from under a bob of golden hair and Felicity blinked in slow fascination as the fairy stared back.

Quick as a flash, however, it was gone, darting away before Felicity could study it more closely. It had joined the myriad others flitting to and fro across the copse and was soon lost in the flurry of fairies.

'Wait, come back,' Felicity called. 'I need to get out of here!'

'*Dance with us. Dance, dance,*' sang the fairies, their melodic voices harmonising together. '*Tonight, tonight, when the moon is bright. We dance, you dance, while away the night.*'

Felicity could only watch helplessly as the magical montage of winged creatures swirled around her, spinning faster and faster until their colours bled into one another and they were one brightly coloured mass which floated over the trees and off into the forest.

She looked round the copse in dismay. Tonight – would she have to wait in this ring all the rest of the day and then dance the night away with those fairies? What if they never let her go, making her dance every night for the rest of her life?

She remembered her grandmother telling her tales of how the fairy folk tricked humans into their fairy rings and then kept them imprisoned for all eternity, forced forever to be their dancing partners and join them in their midnight revelries. Few escaped and she couldn't even remember the most important part of the stories – how those few who *did* get away had managed it. She was being thwarted at every turn, it seemed, and she didn't know what else to do. She had no magic, no allies, nothing. She had the Riddler's words and a lost friend – stories in her head … How would those help her? Could she somehow trick the fairies into releasing her? Make a pact?

She thought and thought all the rest of the day as she sat huddled in the centre of the fairy ring. Silence swamped her but as the day wore on Felicity concentrated more intently, until she had a plan.

As the evening gloom grew around her; as the shadows lengthened and the cool night breeze began to blow; as the forest yawned and stretched from its daylight slumber, awakening to the magic of the night,

Felicity smiled to herself, for she knew now her weapon. Having racked her brain and thought upon every fairy story she'd ever read and every tale her Granny Stone and her mother had told her, she'd remembered one small but significant fact about fairies.

They were a proud race and primped and preened so they always looked their best, parading their beauty at midnight dances and feasts. They revelled in praise and flattery – sought always to be considered clever – so Felicity was confident she knew how to outwit them.

Vanity would be their downfall.

## Chapter Eighteen
# Midnight Revelry

Bathed in fresh moonlight, Felicity waited for the fairies, nervous with anticipation but also anxious to put her plan into action to see if it would work. *It must work,* she thought.

With no way of knowing what the hour was, her watch still frozen in time, Felicity could only guess when the fairy flock would come and that, she was certain, would be when the moon, hanging full and fat in the sky, was at its brightest. In the meantime the forest around her appeared to be shifting – shaking off the last scraps of day. What would happen now?

As her eyes adjusted to the growing gloom, Felicity found she had no need to become accustomed to the deeper darkness, as soft, twinkling lights began pulsing from the trees around the copse. They decorated the foliage like Christmas-tree lights, glinting and winking down at her. Silver thread – spiders' webs, perhaps – glistened with glittering drops of dew, delicate creations which encircled the copse like wire or a protective barrier.

Miniature yellow lanterns also festooned the clearing now, hung by no one Felicity had seen but bringing yet more light to the ever darkening hour. The flowers, dressed in the night's gold and silver, revealed flashes of rich colour. Bluebells gently tinkled, hushed whispers floated past Felicity's ears and the air grew heavy with expectation. It wasn't cold and yet she shivered as she bided her time in this place of bewitchment and enchantment.

Strange pipe music drifted along the breeze, its melody soothing and sweet, like a gentle lullaby meant for a restless child. Soft fluting intermingled with the notes – the perfect harmony, but created by whom? Felicity shook her head but her eyes drooped nevertheless. She mustn't be lulled. She must keep her wits, think clearly – escape – but she wanted more than anything to listen to the fairy music forever, for how could sounds so simple and pure intend any harm?

She had closed her eyes – for how long she didn't know – but at last, Felicity forced them open, battling slumber, and saw at once a scene transformed. It made her immediately more alert, for while she had dozed, magic had truly struck. She shook her head, blinked, then closed her eyes, counted to five and looked again. A queer sensation came over her, as if she had stood up too fast. Her head felt light and yet she couldn't help but drink in the scene.

Trees towered above her as they never had before – tall, terrifying trunks from which the biggest boughs and largest leaves extended. They had positively doubled – no, trebled, quadrupled in size, Felicity thought, as she pulled herself up with the help of the nearest mushroom.

Her hand froze as she realised what had happened. The trees hadn't grown, no – *she* had shrunk! Shrunk to the size of a fairy! The ring of magic mushrooms still encircled her but they were now more the size of tables and were covered as such, with pretty lace tablecloths, so delicate they looked as if they had been spun by spiders and sewn together by mice.

Laughter lilted up above her. The fairies were coming.

Felicity knew she had no escape but still tried to run from the ring, just in case. She was knocked immediately back by the invisible force-field.

*Of course*, she thought. There was no point in the fairies keeping her if she was human size. She couldn't properly join them in her dancing if she was *big*. But how, if she escaped, would she ever get back to full size again?

Her mind muddled with worry, Felicity failed to notice she now had company. She was standing before a mushroom but took a step back when she realised a rather grand elf was staring at her from the back of a pure white unicorn. The magical horse shook its flowing mane and looked at Felicity with unblinking ice-blue eyes.

The elf smiled a cold smile. There was no warmth in her jet-black stare as she said, 'Welcome, Felicity. The night's revelries are about to begin. Dance with us.'

An influx of fairy folk descended upon the mushroom ring – fairies and elves and pixies and who knew what else. Mounted on tiny unicorns with wings like silver gossamer, on candy-coloured ponies, freshly painted miniature rocking horses and even on small furry bats, the fairies flew down and around the ring or just kept circling it in the air. Their laughter filled the night yet Felicity did not feel like joining them at all. For what did *she* have to laugh about?

Her 'welcome elf' had melted into the swirling throng and Felicity almost dared hope she might be ignored but it was, of course, not to be, for very quickly the fairies tired of their frolics and greetings to one another and turned their attention to their prisoner.

Felicity felt dozens and dozens of unblinking fairy eyes upon her as she stood tentatively by her mushroom. Sapphire, emerald, black – every pair glittered against the night, a necklace of curiosity suspended above the fairy ring and no doubt ready to choke her at will. Two fairies grabbed Felicity by the hands and pulled her away from the mushroom, laughing merrily, their pink petal dresses billowing softly around their lithe bodies in the breeze.

'She shall dance with *us* first,' they called out with glee. 'Dance with us, dance with us, child!'

More fairies joined hands around her, forming a circle of dainty dancers and Felicity had no choice but to join in. Round and round they swirled, the soft fluting music playing all the while in the background.

She was out of breath when the first dance ended, but before she had quite got it back, two new fairies replaced her original dance partners and off they went again. Her feet were aching already and Felicity felt her cheeks glowing red. Surely she wasn't to dance continuously with *every* fairy in the dell? There must be hundreds. Yet every time the music stopped, she was gripped again by new hands – some with long, thin, bony fingers, some small and more delicate, but all cold to the touch. Their grip was firm and Felicity couldn't wrench herself free. The few times she tried, the fairies only clenched her more tightly, crushing her fingers and making the whole experience even more agonising.

Her legs had turned to jelly and her head was dizzy from dancing when at last the music stopped and didn't immediately start again. Felicity's hands were dropped and she rubbed them, watching as more mushrooms erupted from the ground nearby, sprouted tablecloths and were then surrounded by tinier mushrooms – seats, she assumed.

Fairies swooped down from above, while those already on the ground darted towards the mushroom tables with obvious glee. Felicity, however, hung back. Firstly, she couldn't leave the ring to go to the tables, and secondly, she wasn't sure she should eat fairy food or drink without an invitation, and even then, it still probably wasn't safe. Who knew what it could do to her?

Her hopes of being forgotten, however, were soon dashed as a pretty pixie stepped nimbly up to her. She had short messy hair of deep chestnut, which stuck out at odd angles from her head. Her ears were long, thin and more pointed than some of the others' – a clear giveaway of her race –and her eyes, chocolate brown, were flecked with purple. She was wearing a ragged lilac dress which glittered down to her bare feet. The creature extended a hand with long, thin fingers, giving Felicity a smile.

'Are you hungry?' she asked. Without waiting for an answer she added, 'Come with me and I'll take you to the best table – the one with the crumbliest cakes, the most sumptuous sandwiches and the best sparkling dewberry juice!' Felicity shook her head. 'No thanks,' she said. 'Besides, I'm your prisoner, remember? Don't you feed me prison food or something?'

'Oh, I wouldn't say you were a *prisoner* exactly,' said the pixie. 'More of a special guest who doesn't have to leave. You can stay here and dance with us every full moon and feast and sing and have fun with us all!'

'Yes, but I *want* to leave,' said Felicity. 'I *need* to leave. I only stepped into the fairy ring by accident. I'm trying to find Witch Wood to solve a riddle so I can get home and I still have to help the Pebble People find out who's stealing their pebbles and how to stop them. I can't stay here! Won't you help me?'

The pixie shook her head. 'I can't help you escape. It would be breaking one of the most sacred fairy laws,' she said. 'I don't know what they would do … Lock me up, maybe, or cut off my wings and give me to the goblins.' She shuddered. 'I just can't. But I *am* sorry. It seems that you're on a quest – not many are that we come across – but I'm afraid you'll just have to stay here.'

Felicity felt a pang of regret as she remembered Twinkle's fate in the goblin caves. She didn't want another fairy to have to endure the same, but she needed to escape and hopefully her plan wouldn't get this one in trouble.

'I'm sure you're clever enough to outwit the rest of the fairies,' she said with a smile. 'In fact, you're wearing purple – isn't that a regal shade and aren't all royals extremely educated?'

The pixie looked happy with the compliments but then she frowned. 'Of course I'm *clever*,' she said, tossing her head. 'But a clever pixie wouldn't risk helping a prisoner to escape. In fact, a clever pixie would probably report you for suggesting such a crime!'

'No! Wait!' said Felicity, as the pixie lifted her arm as if to beckon over another fairy. 'You're right. It was a silly thing to ask. But I wonder if I might request something else?'

The pixie narrowed her eyes, but waited for Felicity to speak.

'I may be fairy-sized now, but I'm not a fairy, am I?'

'Of course not.'

'So … I don't know any magic. But *you* do. Would you teach me something? Please? I can't escape from the fairy ring anyway – no one knows how *that* is done – but if I have to stay here then I would love to learn. I've always wanted to do magic.'

The pixie's face brightened. 'Well, I see no reason why I can't *show* you a simple spell,' she said. 'It will be nothing that will enable you to leave the ring, of course, though *that*,' she scoffed, 'is more easily done than you might think.' Felicity held her breath but the little creature gave nothing else away, though her eyes flicked over to a nearby unicorn as she gave a smug smile.

The movement was subtle but Felicity's spirits soared as an idea unfurled in her mind. Was it possible that she could escape the fairy ring by flying out of it on a magical unicorn? Why else would the pixie have glanced over to it at that very moment? It could be nothing, but it was certainly worth a try.

She waited as the pixie demonstrated a spell to turn grass into candy canes, her mind in overdrive. How could she get rid of her and catch a unicorn? Would it obey her and where would she go?

'If I had wanted to find Witch Wood from here,' she asked, 'before I was caught in the ring, that is, how would I have done it? I'm sure you know how to get *anywhere* in the realm, what with your superior magic ...'

The pixie sniffed. 'Well, of course,' she said. 'I would go directly to the Great Oak tree. But you needn't worry yourself about that, as you're going nowhere.' She laughed. 'Anyway, enough talking. I'm hungry, so if you're not eating, I'll see you later.'

And with that, the pixie disappeared into the fairy throng, though she left Felicity with hope in her heart. She looked around the ring, edging herself slowly towards the perimeter, away from the food-laden mushrooms and towards a solitary unicorn. When she reached it, she patted its velvety nose and whispered where she wanted to go. The unicorn immediately lowered itself to the ground and she slid onto its back. Clearly it had no allegiances to fairy rules.

The fairies were eating their fill, none paying their prisoner any attention – for the moment. As Felicity watched, a little fat fairy fell off his mushroom, he was laughing so hard, then jumped right up again and stuffed a cream cake into his mouth. The others around him laughed loudly and continued eating. Felicity wondered how they could consume so much, considering the majority of the folk were thin as rakes, with sharp, pointed faces.

Without further ado, she nudged the unicorn with her knees. It stood up and then rose into the air in a smooth motion, snowy-white wings outstretched. She gasped at the sudden rush of cold air as they soared upwards, but when she got her breath back, she dared to look down at the scene she had left behind.

The fairies, growing ever smaller, continued to feast, laughter and fluting continued to fill the air and the tiny lights still sparkled from the trees and surrounding vegetation. She could see no sign as yet that she had been missed. All was as it had been. As the scene slowly faded away and the unicorn rose higher, Felicity settled herself more comfortably upon its broad back, entwining her fingers firmly in the beautiful silvery mane for fear of falling off. It made her feel more secure but, oddly, she didn't feel scared at all. If the fairies caught her, though, who knew what they might do to her?

But in the meantime, however, she had resumed her travels and that was all that mattered. She was one step closer to home.

*\*\*\**

Hours could have passed, or was it only minutes? Felicity couldn't tell, but for the first time in quite a while she was able to relax and enjoy her journey. She could barely believe she was soaring silently through the sky on the back of a unicorn. It was as if she was in a dream, although even Felicity had never dreamed such a thing as this.

Despite the late hour, she could see quite clearly the view beneath her, thanks to the full moon drenching everything in silvery light. Most of the scenery was tree tops, but here and there Felicity glimpsed more midnight revelries taking place in the Enchanted Forest. Musical laughter would sometimes float up to her through the still night air and twinkling fairy lights decorating the trees hinted at the merriment below.

As the sky gradually lightened, Felicity could make out the odd river or lake, but only in snatched glimpses, as the thickly wooded forest floor revealed fewer and fewer opportunities to see through the foliage. As fun as it was trying to locate potential landmarks, however, her eyes eventually began to droop. She was awoken with a soft bump and, almost losing her balance, instinctively grabbed a chunk of the unicorn's silky mane. It snorted and pawed the ground.

Wondering how long she'd been asleep, Felicity realised she had been very lucky not to have tumbled from the unicorn's back during their journey. They had travelled all night and it now appeared to be early morning, which meant the Enchanted Forest was a great deal larger than she could possibly have imagined.

'I really *was* just on the outskirts before,' she murmured.

The unicorn pawed the ground again and looked at Felicity.

'OK, I get it – this is my stop,' she said, sliding a little reluctantly from its back.

Her legs ached from sitting for so long and she shook the stiffness from her joints.

The unicorn bowed its head, the glittering icicle-like horn pointing behind her to the most enormous tree she had ever laid eyes on. There could surely be no mistaking it – *this* was the Great Oak. She turned to thank her magical travelling companion. The unicorn, however, had gone.

# Chapter Nineteen
# Oak Magic

The Great Oak towered over Felicity. It would have dwarfed her even if she hadn't been the size of a fairy – that much was quite clear.

The topmost branches extended so far into the lightening sky that she couldn't see how high the Great Oak actually grew. The trunk meanwhile – gnarled and covered with tiny fissures and cracks created by birds, insects and who knew what else – was so thick at the base she couldn't see round it and Felicity wondered how long it would take her to walk a complete circuit of the tree.

She had no time for that, however – she had to figure out how the Great Oak could help her. If only Bob was here. He might have heard of this Great Oak and what it was capable of. Just where had he ended up, she wondered? It made her sad to think of him lost somewhere and worrying about her, but at least he was more familiar with the geography of the Fairy Realm and its perilous ways. Would she ever see him again? She truly hoped so.

She couldn't, however, do anything about Bob right now, no matter how much she wanted to, so all that was left was the tree. She just wasn't sure what it, or she, was supposed to do. She didn't have long to wait for inspiration.

'State your purpose.' The voice was whispery, soft and inhuman.

'Who said that?' asked Felicity hesitantly. 'Where, I mean, *who* are you?'

'My name is unnecessary. I am here, I am there, I am everywhere,' murmured the voice.

Felicity looked around. She still couldn't see anyone. There was nothing but the trees.

'You're the Great Oak!' she exclaimed, clarity dawning as she remembered about the Whispering Trees.

'My name is immaterial,' whispered the voice once more. 'State your purpose.'

Felicity thought it best not to waste time as the tree (yes, she was considering a *tree's* feelings) might get angry and refuse to help her.

'Well, you see – I was speaking with a pixie and she told me the quickest way to get to Witch Wood was to go to the Great Oak – to you,' she said. 'So … I was wondering if you could help me?'

'You want to travel to Witch Wood?' asked the Great Oak. 'Few do.'

Felicity sighed. 'It's more that I *need* to go to Witch Wood,' she said. 'I have to solve a riddle, you see.'

'Ah – so you're Felicity,' said the tree. 'Yes, I can assist. I can open the door, but then it is up to you to decide your fate.'

'How do you know my –?'

'I *know*,' replied the Great Oak. 'About you, your journey, your quest. Pebbles, potions ... *riddles*. Trees talk. To find Witch Wood you must enter within and look for the Plummeting Pool. It will take you where you need to go. Now, I bid you farewell.'

And no matter what Felicity said thereafter, the Great Oak uttered not one syllable more.

'Door, *what* door?' she muttered under her breath. The words were barely out of her mouth, however, when she spied a small red handle burrowed into the base of the tree trunk.

'*That* certainly wasn't there before.'

She picked her way over a couple of thick protruding roots and turned the doorknob. At once, a golden light gleamed, outlining an oval-shaped door in the bark. Felicity pushed and the knotted wood opened into the tree. Glancing behind her, she swallowed and then stepped over the threshold into darkness.

A glowing orb of light appeared before her and Felicity knew instinctively she had to follow it. She could feel the weight of the empty air around her – sense the vast inner space of this ancient tree – yet she reached out on either side of her and touched bark. She was clearly only on the outer edge of the Great Oak, the first layer in, and as she followed the orb, Felicity's feet soon found perfectly cut steps carved into the wood and leading upwards.

Up and up and round and round they went – she couldn't guess how many steps she'd climbed – but at last the orb stopped and promptly exploded into a sparkling mass of tiny white stars. They fluttered and fell around Felicity, melting away as soon as they touched the surrounding surfaces. A long coil of golden cord hung in front of her. She tugged it and let out a gasp as more rope firmly tangled itself around her arms and whisked her off her feet. She was pulled upwards so quickly she barely caught her breath and then, just as fast as they had caught her, the ropes fell away and Felicity was free.

The room she found herself in was round and panelled with cupboards – rows and rows of them. A tiny square table sat in the middle, with a coral carpet beneath it. Each cupboard was painted black – the only thing differentiating one from the other was silver handles moulded into different shapes for each little door. Here there was a star, there a moon, a rocking horse, a dragonfly, a leaf, a shell – too many to count, as they ran from roof to floor and filled all the space in between.

'I guess I choose a cupboard,' said Felicity and she studied her options.

She finally settled on an acorn-shaped handle, just because she thought it might be more applicable, given that she was inside an oak tree. It was only as she pulled open the door and looked inside that she realised a water-themed handle might have been better, but it was too late now.

Inky darkness greeted her. Felicity had chosen a cupboard at head height, so she had no need to hunker down or stretch to see inside. As her eyes adjusted to the gloom, she realised the door was stretching, so she stood back and watched as it slowly elongated into a gaping entrance.

'Now I go in,' she murmured.

She stepped over the threshold, then turned to look back, but the door slammed shut in her face. Felicity grappled for a handle, but found nothing but smooth, unblemished wood. Her heart beat a little faster and she turned around, her eyes drinking in the darkness and gradually becoming accustomed to it.

She started as she saw a figure before her and then realised it was her own reflection staring anxiously back from the tall mirror which filled the wall ahead. Perhaps it was a magic mirror? In fact, it was most probably exactly that, considering where she was and, given her situation, Felicity thought it was worth a try at least.

'Mirror, show me Bob!' she said with authority.

Her reflection stared back.

'I wish to see my friend Bob the Brownie,' Felicity tried again. 'Please.'

Again, nothing.

'Well, what's the point of you then!' she said in frustration. 'A room in a tree with a mirror – why?'

She stepped forward and reached her hand out to touch the smooth glassy surface. As she did, the mirror shimmered and rippled like water. Felicity snatched her hand back and watched as the mirror slowly brought an image into focus, wavering and wobbling until a figure appeared on the glass – a small brownie-like figure. It was Bob.

He was walking along a path – where, Felicity could not say – but he was obviously alive and well. She sighed with relief. If only she could find him, but she had to search for the pebbles and solve the riddles and he seemed to be safe – for now. A thought popped into her head.

'Sorry, Bob,' she whispered. 'Show me the stolen pebbles, please,' she commanded the mirror and reached out to touch it again. At once the surface shifted and shimmered and slowly revealed another scene – this time piles of glistening pebbles heaped high on top of one another, filling the glass.

'There's no way of telling where *they* are either,' Felicity grumbled. 'How on earth can I find them and solve these impossible riddles at the same time? There are no clues which are of any use to me!'

She hesitated. 'Show me Witch Wood.'

The mirror clouded over, dark ripples moving across its surface. The image it now revealed was filled with shadows and twisted tree branches, with dozens and dozens of jet-black crows perched upon them.

As Felicity peered closer, one of the witch's crows suddenly looked her in the eye and flew forward, shrieking loudly. Felicity stumbled backwards and gasped as the crow's beak smashed against the mirror, its dark wings beating strongly on the glass.

'No, that's impossible!' she exclaimed. 'Show me the witch's spire,' she said, but the crows flocked angrily en masse towards the mirror, screaming and pecking and blocking Felicity's view.

'Show me home!' she shouted, but the image stayed the same. 'Why won't you change?'

She backed as far away as she could from the mirror and closed her eyes to the crows. They definitely knew she was coming now – she had been foolish. She was trapped in a tree and had shown her enemies where she was and what she looked like. That is – if they didn't know already.

Felicity jumped up and began beating against the mirror.

'Go away! Go away!' she shouted. 'I'm *not* afraid of you – do you hear? I'm not –'

Felicity's fist slammed through thin air as the mirror vanished before her. She only just stopped herself from falling through the gap it had left behind, but something nevertheless lured her towards it and, without a moment's thought, she stepped through the entrance. A passageway, dimly lit, beckoned her deeper into the Great Oak and she followed the light gladly.

This time, however, Felicity wasn't alone in the tree tunnel.

She guessed she must now be nearer the centre of the Great Oak, as all manner of creatures began passing her by the further along she went, some going in the same direction, but most scurrying off into countless other dimly lit passageways and secret shady tunnels.

Small squirrels scuttled past her, big bushy red tails held high. Tiny tree-folk (Felicity assumed they must live here, as they wore leafy garments and had slightly gnarled nut-brown skin) moved past her in groups of two or three at a time. Some threw her curious glances but most were too preoccupied with their own business to pay her much heed. Felicity wondered what they were doing, where they were going and what was in their little baskets, which *everyone* seemed to have.

The floor of the tunnel here was also different, as it was patterned with an assortment of colourful shapes and designs. A tall fairy dressed in flowing green silk brushed past her, long silver wings tickling Felicity's arm as she passed. Her hair was buttercup yellow and Felicity thought she looked graceful and very beautiful. Perhaps *she* knew where the Plummeting Pool was.

She trailed behind the golden-haired fairy, dodging an odd assortment of oncoming folk along the way and keeping her eyes fixed firmly on those glorious silver wings. Silver wings she bumped into when the fairy abruptly stopped. She swung round and seized Felicity by the wrist, sapphire eyes flashing.

'What business do you have here?' she hissed. 'Why are you following me?'

Felicity gasped. 'Well?' the fairy demanded, gripping her wrist even tighter. 'Answer me, or I'll hand you over to the dungeon master immediately. How dare you spy on me!'

'No, please,' said Felicity. 'I wasn't *spying* on you. I was following you because I'm lost and I was going to ask you for directions.'

The fairy's eyes narrowed. 'I suppose you might be telling the truth,' she said suspiciously. 'Yes, you have an odd look about you. You're not from around here, are you?'

'No. I'm looking for the Plummeting Pool. Do you know which way it is?'

The fairy's features softened a little and she dropped Felicity's wrist. 'Just follow the painted water droplets on the floor,' she said. 'That will lead you to the pool. And please – don't make a habit of following folk.'

The fairy turned, her silk dress swirling out around her, and just like that, she was gone.

Felicity studied the floor with its colourful patterns and symbols, looking for the water droplets the fairy had mentioned. She'd only glanced at the ground before but realised now that the designs weren't meaningless shapes as she'd supposed – they were actually a series of the *same* shapes repeated over and over. Once she knew what she was looking for, she quickly spotted the string of blue water droplets painted onto the wood. The trail to the Plummeting Pool.

It wound in and around a string of painted wands, while trails of tiny puddings and a series of small mirrors also decorated the ground, along with various other symbols. The floor was a map! Hurrying, Felicity walked briskly in the direction of the droplets. On and on they went, taking her up steep slopes and along busy passages, down stairs and past places she wished she could stop at but didn't dare.

She saw a shop selling needle-thin wands which trailed glitter in the air when the fairy customers waved them, and a pudding shop which wafted delicious smells in her direction and made her mouth water.

There were large painted doors, small hidden doors, windows and tunnels and more and more creatures and tree-folk along the way as well, all hurrying about their business. Felicity wished she had the time to explore but knew she should press on, so she reluctantly left the tree-folk behind as she followed the painted droplets, finally reaching the Plummeting Pool.

The track tailed off before an entrance hung with long slivers of ribbon, each one a deep shade of blue. Felicity passed through it and entered a large, cool room. It was poorly lit, shadows shrouding hidden corners and crevices, but she saw the Plummeting Pool before her.

It was like a large, liquid eye in the centre of the room, still as ice and with a circumference far exceeding what she had expected. A stone wall rimmed the pool, low enough to trip over if you weren't paying attention. It was an invitation to go onwards – to continue with her adventure, not knowing what it would bring next.

As she neared the pool, Felicity saw steps cut roughly into the right side of the circular well-like structure, with more mirroring them on the opposite side. She would have to climb down and immerse herself in the water. Hopefully, the pool would do the rest. She would just have to trust the magic of the Great Oak.

'Right,' she muttered. 'Well, let's hope this works.'

She climbed over the side of the Plummeting Pool, onto the steps, and stared down into cold, deep and very dark water. Heart hammering in her chest, Felicity set her jaw, took a deep breath and gently lowered herself downwards.

The water immediately wrapped her in its icy grip, encasing her in cold and leaving her gasping for air. She bobbed towards the pool's centre, not quite sure what was about to happen, when she felt something tugging at her legs. Realising that it was some sort of current, Felicity felt it pull harder at her, growing more intense as she neared the middle of the Plummeting Pool.

And then, before she knew what was happening, she was truly in the water's strong grip, as she was pulled into the swirling mass of a whirlpool which had, to her horror, sprung up from within the murky depths stretching below her.

Powerless to prevent herself from being dragged under, she struggled nonetheless, desperately trying to force her head above water to gulp down snatches of air. The pool took her down deeper, however, the light of the cavern above fading to black and Felicity's hopes with it. Down and down she was dragged by the whirlpool, now spinning faster and faster around her than before. Her surroundings reduced to a watery blur, a weakened Felicity felt her eyes closing. Her legs gave a final kick and, after what seemed like only brief minutes, she succumbed to the pressure of trying to hold her breath for so long …

Her eyes shot immediately open. She was breathing! Underwater! Yet it felt strangely like air was entering her lungs, not water. She felt her neck, trembling fingers making contact with what appeared to be tiny gills. All around her was darkness and yet she found she could still see – there just wasn't anything there to look at. Except perhaps for one small thing.

Her tail.

## Chapter Twenty
# The Plummeting Pool

Felicity floated in amazement for a few moments, gazing dumbstruck at the graceful mermaid's tail which had appeared in place of her legs. She didn't even want to think about where *they* had gone to. How could they just disappear? Magic, of course. It had taken them and it would surely bring them back – at least she certainly hoped so.

Her tail was seaweed green and drifted away from her body like an alien creature. Sense told her, however, that using it was the only way she would make it through the Plummeting Pool alive, and so Felicity clumsily propelled herself round with her newly acquired appendage and swam deeper down into the water.

She was very quickly learning not to be surprised by the strange things which happened here in the Fairy Realm. It was easier than she expected to manoeuvre through the Plummeting Pool without her legs – in fact, it was much simpler having a powerful tail to push herself forward with, and Felicity soon got used to the motion.

The pool was still and silent as she made her descent. The only ripples created in the water came from Felicity's own movements and she savoured the silky feel of cool water on her skin as she went. It was actually a welcome relief, after all the walking and hurrying about she had done recently, to be able now to refresh herself in the pool.

She couldn't quite get used to the sensation of breathing underwater, though – she kept expecting the water to clog up her lungs but it simply seemed to evaporate when she inhaled, and exhaling saw only small bubbles drift out of her nose and mouth.

Further on she swam, cutting through the water with clean arm strokes and keeping momentum with the constant swishing of her tail. It grew steadily murkier the further Felicity travelled into the pool's depths, but with her mermaid's tail had come mermaid sight and she found herself more than capable of seeing her way. She did begin to wonder, however, after a long time swimming, when the Plummeting Pool would spit her out of the Great Oak. She was itching to be on her way to Witch Wood to solve the next riddle.

As she swam on, Felicity's mind began to wander and she thought again about the pebbles and about Bob and how she might find *him*. As a result, she almost didn't notice that the Plummeting Pool was narrowing and just managed to lower her arms to her sides in time. Now swimming true mermaid style, only her long emerald tail pushed her steadily onwards. She continued in her silent swimming for another short while until her head butted into a wooden trapdoor. She gasped.

More startled than hurt, Felicity swallowed back her rising panic and nudged the trapdoor gently with the top of her head. She spied a small coil of rope dangling discreetly down the side of the door and, after a couple of attempts, managed to grab it between her teeth. She pulled as hard as she could. A low groan emanated from the wood, but the door was moving away from her, so Felicity kept on with her task until there was enough space to swim through the gap she'd created.

She found herself back in open water – still within the tree, she wondered, or far beneath it? Either way, she was no longer confined to the narrow tunnel of the Plummeting Pool. Taking advantage of the chance to stretch her muscles, Felicity sped through the water, swishing and swirling around until she was quite dizzy. It was an exhilarating feeling and she had to stop for a few minutes afterwards to catch her breath.

She saw three tunnels branching away from her, but these were, for once, signposted. One read 'To the Forest'

– a possibility; the second indicated 'To the Woods'; and the third read 'To the Sea'.

'Well, I just hope the woods here are the right ones,' she murmured. She swam to the entrance, hesitated, then said: 'To Witch Wood!'

A strong current caught Felicity and dragged her through the opening, the water whooshing beneath her as she was swept along. It was definitely one of her more enjoyable experiences so far and, of course, was over altogether too soon.

The water level gradually dropped, and with each new bend Felicity found it a little lower, until her head finally emerged above the water and she was breathing air again. She was suddenly thrown into the air and found herself falling, falling, falling and then splashing rather abruptly into more water.

She spluttered and swam to the surface. It was night but she was outside – she had left the Great Oak and, by the feel of it, her tail too was gone. Any sadness she felt at this, however, quickly evaporated with the thrill of being in the open air again – even if that air was in a dangerous Enchanted Forest. She had reached her destination, which was supposed to be 'The Woods', but which woods? *Witch* Wood? She certainly hoped so.

\*\*\*

Felicity swam towards the shore, which wasn't very far away. She didn't count swimming as one of her strengths, although her mermaid experience had certainly boosted her confidence in that regard. Pulling herself up out of the water, her sodden skirt and jumper clinging cold and uncomfortable to her skin, she sank gratefully to the ground. She seemed to have returned to her own size again too. The Great Oak had obviously worked its magic on her in more ways than one.

Soft moonshine dusted an army of poker-straight evergreens ahead, on the opposite side of the lake from where she had emerged. They fringed the clearing like sharp teeth, piercing the starry sky. Felicity looked for the Great Oak's watery tunnel, but there was no sign of it.

The rest of the lake was bordered by a mixture of trees with odd, shadowy shapes dangling from their branches, which circled round behind her.

Felicity saw the hint of several possible paths leading off into the thick of them and decided to investigate. She was tired and soaking wet, but sitting there wondering about things wasn't going to help. She needed to find food and shelter and get dry … and hopefully find the witch's spire too. Standing up, she tried to wring out her wet, heavy clothes but it did little good – they weren't going to dry off anytime soon.

A flapping sound made her turn and she glimpsed a large black bird flying swiftly into the woods. One of the witches' messengers? Or a witch incognito? She shivered. Something else had caught her attention, however, and she approached the trees with caution.

A pulsing red glow seemed to be coming from the bottom of one of the trunks. Crouching down to take a closer look, Felicity saw what looked like a jewel embedded in the timber. Why would a ruby be stuck into a tree trunk? Instinctively, she reached out to touch it, her fingers brushing against the red stone. The tree shivered, and as it did, the entire trunk became studded with jewels.

Felicity's eyes widened. It was beautiful.

Most of the stones were precious gems like the large ruby which had first caught her eye, while others looked like tiny frozen raindrops iced into the wood and glittering like crystal. Dark blue sapphires, gold coins, shards of emerald and an assortment of other precious stones were wedged deep into the trunk and along its myriad branches. Felicity looked up and gasped.

Huge teardrop-shaped diamonds hung down instead of leaves. The tree was now dripping with necklaces, bracelets, rings and too many jewels to count. It was mesmerising and she suddenly yearned to see it in the daylight, when golden sun would transform the tree into a true glittering goddess. She remembered Bob's warning about taking fairy jewels, however, and knew her Granny Stone had warned of the same in her stories, so she didn't dare try to take something as a souvenir or trading piece. Regretfully, she turned away from the spectacular tree and went to inspect another, excited by her discovery.

The next tree was altogether different but no less intriguing, with leaves made entirely from burnished copper, veins of molten metal running through the trunk. The next bore wooden toys from its boughs – tiny hand-carved rocking horses, trains, bats, bricks and even dolls. It was all very strange.

Another tree had a silver face with closed eyes carved into its trunk, with nothing but long wisps of silver thread flowing from its branches. This one particularly unnerved Felicity, as it looked altogether too much like a mad old lady with long silver hair trapped in the tree, ready to wake at a moment's notice. Other trees were hung with tiny trinkets and odd objects but one tempted Felicity to stop in her tracks.

It was slender and birch-like and blooming from its branches were plump purple plums, smooth yellow pears, juicy oranges and just about every other fruit Felicity could imagine. In her hunger, the sight was even more mouth-watering and – she hesitated.

She knew the risks of picking the fruit, yet something, not just her hunger, was urging her on. The tree itself seemed almost to be calling out to her somehow. Felicity looked at the long bright bananas, soft fuzzy peaches and ripe red apples before her. She was still contemplating whether to pluck her favourite from a branch when something thudded to the ground and rolled against her foot.

She looked down and saw a fruit she didn't recognise. It was round but not obviously an apple, orange, plum or anything else. It was more golden than the vivid yellow of the bananas, yet not a peach. The surface was smooth and it was visibly bursting with fresh, sweet juices.

Without a further thought Felicity bent down and picked up the golden fruit, raising it to her lips and telling herself what had fallen from the tree was not the same as what had been picked. She sank her teeth into the soft flesh, savouring the sweet taste of the pink pulp inside. A little dribbled down her chin and she wiped it away with her sleeve.

She devoured the food and was about to throw away the stone when she realised this was no ordinary stone. What she held was a little golden ball. She shook it gently and heard something knocking against the inside. Unsure what to do with it, Felicity decided on impulse that she would hold onto it for now. After all, she'd already eaten the fruit and, who knew, it might come in useful. So she slipped the precious object into the small pouch in her pocket, along with her enchanted pebble.

The tree was now curling up its branches, folding them neatly away as a fern would roll up its fronds in winter, and Felicity backed away from it. She watched to see what would happen next but, for some reason, wasn't frightened of whatever that might be.

The tree continued winding in each of its many branches, cleverly concealing the fruit as it did so. When everything was completely curled, it looked even odder than before – just a trunk with a series of bumps up either side of it. As Felicity looked on, these too suddenly disappeared and, before she could blink, the trunk slid swiftly down into the soil. She ran over to where it had been but already the grass was growing over to conceal any evidence that a tree had ever been there.

The tree's sudden disappearance unsettled her and she decided it was time to move on. Magic was at work here, that much was clear, and who was to say what might happen next? She didn't know what any of it meant, but she thought it best not to hang around.

A rabbit path trailed off into the woods ahead, moonlight slanting down through the foliage and casting jagged shadows upon it. Of the possible routes to take, however, it looked the most inviting, so Felicity made her way towards it, leaving the silent lake behind a little wistfully. It was such a peaceful and serene place – beautiful in a haunted sort of way. Why were there trees bearing such strange gifts when there was no one around to appreciate them? Or perhaps the folk who lived here simply wished not to be seen.

As she made her way along the path, Felicity was kept suitably distracted by the wooded wonders around her, which continued on into the forest. There were bushes sprouting baubles and ribbons that glowed in the gloom and more trees with exotic and mysterious objects, with everything from spoons to jewellery, but no more tantalising food. Passing these by, a tree up ahead caught her eye and she hurried towards it.

Draped over a thick branch was a mossy-coloured hooded cloak. Beside it hung a full-length midnight-blue gown, the bodice decorated with a leafless tree of silver thread, the roots tracing a sparkling track down the middle of the skirt and trailing delicately around the hemline. Long tapered sleeves ended in cuffs of snow-white fur. Hanging from smaller branches below was an assortment of underclothes and, most wonderful of all, a pair of exquisite green shoes. They looked just as Felicity imagined a pair of fairy slippers would – fashioned from soft, supple leather, with pointed toes tipped with a sprinkling of silver dust. They had small square heels and looked exactly her size. She longed to get out of her own wet, dirty clothes and put the beautiful garments in front of her on instead, but she didn't dare.

Then she spied the note.

Attached to the cloak with a silver star-shaped brooch was a small scroll of parchment. Felicity unpinned it gently, unrolling the paper to read the message scrawled inside in unruly, spidery handwriting.

It said simply, *'For Felicity – a gift from a friend.'*

She read the note a couple more times, battling her urge to take down the clothes.

'What friend?' she muttered. 'I had only one here – Bob – and now he's gone.'

She wondered who this mysterious benefactor was and how he or she knew she would be coming this way – and would need dry clothes. Were they watching her now?

'Don't over-think things, Felicity,' she scolded herself. 'Just be grateful for the help until you find out what's going on.'

Glancing around to check no one was watching, she quickly and carefully dressed herself, making sure to move her pouch of treasures into her new cloak pocket. Feeling much better, Felicity folded her old skirt and jumper and placed them under a bush. She knew she would probably never find them again but she didn't want to carry them with her and perhaps someone else in need might come across them and put them to some use.

The dark grassy path wound on through the trees but was becoming more overgrown with every step, and Felicity feared that soon she would be making her way unguided through the wood. It seemed to be closing in around her more and more, enveloping her in its thick, leafy branches and blocking out most of the light. On and on she went, blindly tracking her way to somewhere – she hoped.

***

On Felicity went, winding in and out of trees, which were gradually becoming more ordinary, keeping an eye out for anything unusual – a landmark or a sign – anything to give her a clue as to where she might be heading.

The further she went into the wood the more alive it seemed to become, as if it had been holding its breath but was now slowly starting to wake up. Gentle rustlings of woodland animals sounded around her, leaves whispered in the breeze, and somewhere, an owl hooted. It was all actually quite peaceful.

Then a twig cracked.

Felicity stopped in her tracks. She listened, holding her breath, but whoever had made the noise seemed to have stopped too, realising their cover had been blown. Should she call out? Run? But where to and, knowing Fairyland as she did, whoever was stalking her could very probably outrun her or catch her by magic. So she waited for a few minutes and then spoke.

'Hello? I know somebody's there. I – I won't harm you.'

Silence hung heavy in the air for a few heart-stopping seconds. Then a huge black shape emerged from the shadows.

## Chapter Twenty-One
# Mezra

Out of the bushes came a large black beast with shaggy fur and coal-coloured eyes. It padded silently in front of Felicity, who didn't dare move, revealing a long and equally shaggy tail and saucer-sized paws. The beast stood almost as tall as Felicity herself. Up close, she realised it was actually an incredibly large *dog*, though from a distance it could easily have been mistaken for a bear. It moved ahead, then stopped, turning back to look at her.

'He wants me to follow,' she whispered in surprise. 'Well, he hasn't harmed me and I think I'm quite lost, so perhaps he'll lead me somewhere useful. I just hope it isn't to his lair …'

Shaking slightly, Felicity followed the big Black Dog, who never made a noise but occasionally turned back to check she was still behind him. She instinctively felt safe with the huge hound, and surely no one would dare challenge or harm her if he was by her side? He was a comforting presence on an otherwise lonely journey. She just hoped she was right to trust him.

Their trek through the woods took the pair past shadowy dells where Felicity caught glimpses of fairy folk at their night-time revelries, dancing disjointedly and eerily in and out of the trees. Soft tinkling bells and beautiful flute music occasionally floated along the breeze and she felt herself unconsciously drawn to their source. Each time she had the urge to leave, however, the Black Dog seemed to sense it and would turn, nudge her on the shoulder with its nose and awake her from the gentle trance she hadn't even known she'd been under.

Finally, as Felicity struggled to keep her eyes open and was beginning to drag her feet, the Black Dog stopped. They'd reached a dell encircled by thick leafy trees and bushes. The beast approached a gnarled tree with a stream flowing past it and waited. He pawed the ground three times, then turned tail and swiftly bounded off into the woods.

'Wait!' Felicity called.

But the Black Dog was gone. She approached the tree with curiosity and studied the trunk, looking for anything unusual.

'Aha – you've arrived!' said a voice behind her. Felicity spun round and saw an old man, slightly stooped, watching her. He had blueberry-coloured eyes that crinkled at the corners as he offered her a welcoming smile. His hair was whipped-cream white and trailed down his back, almost to his toes, from under an old-fashioned night-cap.

He wore a long, shabby blue shift, patched up here and there with odd bits of material, the points of scuffed brown shoes peeking out from under the torn and raggedy hem. In his right hand, he held a knobbly wooden staff. The old man looked at Felicity with an amused expression and she realised she'd been staring.

'Are you a – a wizard?' she asked.

'Wizard, magician – perhaps both, my child! But, first, let us go inside, for there are eyes and ears out here which had best be kept at bay. Follow me and come quickly. Questions after!'

The wizard shuffled off back the way he must have come – towards a mass of bushes – and seeing no other option, Felicity followed.

There was no path that she could see, but her new companion ploughed on through the bushes, so she trailed after him, wondering where they were going and if she could really trust this strange character.

Something shrieked in the darkness and the wizard shuffled faster. 'Quickly,' he said. 'There are things lurking here which never lurked before, so we must be on our guard. Ah, here we are.' Felicity bumped into him as he stopped abruptly in another small clearing, just big enough for the two of them.

They were surrounded by thick fir trees and shrubbery – everything seemed to grow in this wood, she mused. The wizard tapped his staff on the ground and muttered a few hurried and strange-sounding words. Something shifted in the soil.

'Down here,' he instructed. He held out his staff, muttered more words and at once a soft glow as strong as any lantern's shone from it, revealing an opening in the ground.

The little man disappeared into it, and Felicity hurriedly followed, as another shriek split the air, closer now. Leading the way, the wizard hurried down a series of steps cut roughly into the earth, then along a short tunnel, round a corner, down more steps (Felicity counted about thirty), through a longer passageway, down ten more steps and, finally, along a short tunnel to a little door with a small round window at the top, a silver knocker and a silver handle. There was, however, no keyhole.

The door swung open at the wizard's touch and he waved Felicity inside. With a glance over his shoulder, he then followed her in and the door swung closed behind them.

'Well, sit down, sit down! We have much to discuss and not much time! Make yourself comfortable and I'll fix us some tea.'

Felicity gratefully obeyed and settled herself in a low cushioned chair beside a fire which was burning merrily but, somehow, without giving off any smoke. Magic of course.

Indeed, magic was evident everywhere, as Felicity looked around the cluttered but comfortable home. The fire was the focal point, with a semicircle of chairs positioned strategically around it. Obviously Felicity wasn't the only recent visitor to the wizard's underground abode.

The fire faced the front door, with a round, faded blue mat covering the rough earthen ground in front of it. To the left of the door, from where she sat, Felicity saw what appeared to be the wizard's kitchen – a small porcelain sink was set into the far wall, where the wizard was busying himself, filling a kettle with water and then bringing it over to hang above the fire to boil.

A little washing line also hung near the sink, but instead of clothes, a series of pots, pans and other household objects dangled from it, as the wizard didn't appear to have any cupboards. All that served as such were one or two dug-out holes, in which sat a mismatched collection of cups and plates and a squat little teapot. The walls to either side of the sink were painted a strange luminescent silver, which shone oddly in the firelight and the glow from numerous small lanterns hanging overhead. The ceiling itself was a reflection of the night sky – a shimmering ebony, splashed with sparkling stars and a sliver of moon, which all looked so real, Felicity wanted to reach out and touch them.

Glancing over her shoulder, she noticed a red door and wondered what was behind it. It couldn't be a study, as books of all shapes and sizes spilled messily from a large square table wedged against the wall behind her. Clearly, the wizard did most of his business in this very room.

By the time she had had a good look around, the kettle had begun to whistle and the wizard had set a toadstool-shaped table before her with, Felicity saw with dismay – two *empty* cups, plates and bowls. An empty milk jug sat in the middle, along with dull grey cutlery. Where was the food?

The wizard settled himself in a chair opposite and filled the teapot with hot water, then sat back, steepled his fingers and smiled at Felicity.

'What will you be having to eat, my dear?' he asked, grinning mischievously. 'Why don't you just copy me, eh?' He lifted the teapot, said, 'Strong tea please pot!'

and at once steaming brown tea poured into his waiting cup.

Next, he took his knife and tapped the plate in front of him. 'Salmon-and-cucumber sandwiches, please, plate – and some sausages and a chicken pie. Oh, and I think perhaps a crunchy salad and some fresh bread rolls, with a pat of butter too!'

At once, salmon-and-cucumber sandwiches appeared on the wizard's plate, followed by fat juicy sausages and a small round pie. Next, some bright-green salad with plump red tomatoes, crisp sweetcorn, peppers and onions appeared, along with a basket full of soft bread rolls, which immediately made the wizard's home smell like a bakery. Felicity's stomach rumbled. A pat of yellow butter plopped down beside the bread.

'Milk, please, jug!' The wizard tapped the milk jug and Felicity saw creamy white milk appear out of nowhere.

'Oh, I almost forgot!' He tapped the bowl. 'Strawberries and cream, please! And how about a chocolate cake and some plums as well? Thank you! Now, my dear – what will *you* be having?' His eyes twinkled at Felicity.

Not sure they needed any more food, but excited to see what would happen, Felicity picked up her knife and tapped her own plate. 'Er, some chicken and mashed potato, please, plate!' And it appeared. Felicity was delighted. The wizard waved his hand for her to order more.

She added a small portion of vegetables and a tomato-and-egg salad to her menu, opting to share the wizard's bread rolls and butter. She also had tea, not so strong, as well as fresh lemonade, to accompany her own dessert of chocolate cake and lemon meringue pie with ice-cream. It was a lot of food, but then again, Felicity was extremely hungry after all her adventuring!

'Now,' said the wizard. 'Let's talk.'

***

Talk was exactly what the unlikely pair did next and in great detail, for Felicity soon found they had much and more to discuss.

'First of all,' he said, 'introductions. I know your name is Felicity but you don't know mine – well, it's not such a closely guarded secret as some around here. You can call me Mezra.'

He took a sip of tea. 'I discovered the Pebble People's plans to bring you here, or someone like you anyway, not long before you arrived, through undisclosed sources and magicks of my own – just in time to keep an eye on you when the big event happened. It's not often that someone, particularly a *human*, is invited into the Fairy Realm, you know. They usually come by trickery or trap, lured here under false pretences or through some fool behaviour of their own.'

'But wasn't I lured here too – by the pebble?'

The wizard shook his head vehemently. 'No, child, not at all!' he exclaimed. 'You were summoned, yes, but it was an invitation nonetheless. That particular pebble wouldn't have been left lying exposed for just anyone to pick up. It was enchanted specifically for the one who could solve the pebble mystery and that person turned out to be you. If anyone else had taken it, it would have lost its magic immediately and the Pebble People would have tried again.'

'But why me? I still don't understand. And, I hope you don't mind me saying, but if you've been watching me all along then why haven't you helped me until now? In fact – *how* have you been watching me?'

The wizard swallowed a mouthful of salmon-and-cucumber sandwich and sighed. 'To meddle in such things isn't always helpful, and anyway, I wanted to see if you could be trusted first. Then that dratted Riddler kept interfering and I do like to keep out of his way, tiresome creature that he is.

'But while you have proven yourself admirably in the riddle fiasco so far, the problem of the pebbles remains.

So, I thought that perhaps now was the time to intervene.

'As for how I've been keeping track of you, well, you'll understand there are some things a wizard just doesn't share, but suffice it to say that I have my ways, and when I saw you were headed in this direction, well – this was my chance to assist.'

'I see,' said Felicity. 'I would certainly appreciate any help you can give, starting with directions to the witch's spire in Witch Wood. I really have no idea where I'm going.'

'Precisely why I stepped in, my dear,' said Mezra. 'Witch Wood is a place to be entered with caution, so you'll need all the help you can get. And you must be extra vigilant, for, as I said, there are darker forces now lurking above ground that are no doubt a consequence of the pebbles going missing. Those shrieks we heard were harpies – or storm spirits – and you'd better hope you never meet them, for they'll tear you to shreds. Underground talk has it that they're preying on anything that moves. They haven't been seen around here for centuries!'

All Felicity remembered about harpies was from an old myth her grandmother had once told her. They were grotesque monsters with the head of a woman attached to the body of a bird of prey, their feet fitted with razor-sharp talons which they used to snatch people away. She shuddered.

'There are rumours,' the wizard continued, 'that more and more of these and other evil creatures are infiltrating the realm the longer the pebbles are missing. I thought at first the black witches and the goblins were the culprits, but now I'm not so sure. They have been meeting in secret together, though, which is why you so easily evaded the goblins when you first arrived. I only know this because I heard the trees whispering about one such meeting, but even they have become guarded and are keeping their knowledge to themselves these days. I have been unable to find out any more, as the witches have cast powerful concealment spells over themselves and are not as easily watched as you, my dear, but they seem unsettled and angry, which suggests they aren't the ones in control.

'Because of the dark forces seeping through of late, I have been using my own powers to protect my home, but I am an old man and my magic is not as strong as it once was. That's why I wanted to help *you*.

'The Black Dog who led you here, by the way, is often thought evil but is really more of a traveller's companion, and he owed me a favour, so I asked him to bring you to me and, well, here we are. In the magical masquerade that is the Fairy Realm – where nothing is quite what it appears – you have muddled your way through to me despite the odds, so it is time perhaps that you received a bit of wizardly help! Clothes included.' He smiled.

'Now, I haven't figured out why *you* specifically were chosen to solve this mystery, but I do know that so far you have proved that, somehow, you *affect* Fairyland. It's right that you're here. You must of course solve your three riddles to have any hope of returning home, but the most important part of your visit here is the pebbles. Find them and things will change.'

Something else was bothering Felicity. 'What about the lake where the strange jewelled trees were?' she asked. 'What *was* that place?'

'That, my dear, was the Lagoon of Lost Desires, where the dreams, the treasures, the joys once held dear by the fairies and all who inhabit the realm drift off to when they – the fairies – for some reason or other lose their essence.

'When hope turns to fear, happiness to despair, love to hate, the folk of the realm lose something of themselves and there it ends up, taking the form of all that you saw – a toy to represent a broken childhood dream; a jewel to signify a lost love or passion; fruit, the hope that once perhaps fuelled someone's hunger for life. It is a sad, melancholic place, yet beautiful too.

Sometimes those desires can be won back, but often they stay lost, haunting the lagoon for eternity, with new treasures added daily to the trees.'

'What about this?' asked Felicity. She fumbled for her pouch and took out the golden ball from the fruit she'd eaten. 'Do you know what it is? I thought it might be significant.'

The wizard smiled and took the ball from her.

'This is extremely significant,' he said, squeezing the ball until it cracked. Felicity gasped as the golden shell fell away to reveal a gold ring set with a large ruby.

'The Lagoon of Lost Desires has bestowed a special gift upon you, for with this you can create your own glamour and fool whoever is looking upon your face that you are someone or some*thing* else. Powerful magic indeed, but it will not last for long without fairy powers to maintain it, so must be used wisely and only when in dire need.

'When the time comes, just slip the ring on, and as it heats up you must imagine yourself into someone else. When the ruby has changed from red to green, you will be glamoured, but how long exactly this will last for, alas, there is no way of knowing, so you must be brisk about your business. When the stone is red again, your glamour will be gone and the ring will not work immediately afterwards. I don't know why it was gifted to you, but perhaps the realm is reaching out to help you restore it …'

Felicity looked at the ring. She just hoped she would know the right time to use it. Mezra handed it back to her and she pocketed it again. By this time they'd munched their way through most of the sumptuous feast and she felt rather full. She yawned.

'Right, off to bed with you!' said the wizard. 'You have a long way yet to go and you need to rest.' He rose stiffly. 'This way!'

Felicity followed Mezra to the little door behind her chair, the one she'd wondered about earlier. He led her into a passageway which ended in three more doors, all in a row. He opened the one to her right.

'You can sleep in here tonight, and come the morning, I'll send you on your way. We'll talk again before you leave.'

With that, the wizard left her alone and Felicity looked around, pleased to see a small comfy-looking bed with a quilted duvet and plump, welcoming pillows. A small fire burned at its base and a faded red mat covered the ground beside it. A couple of shelves hewn into the wall opposite held some dusty books but Felicity was too tired to look at them, and without further ado, she carefully took off her pretty emerald shoes and her cloak and crept into the bed. She was fast asleep within minutes, her last thoughts as she drifted into slumber of the wizard – of all he had said and why he was helping her.

## Chapter Twenty-Two
# Maps and More

When she awoke, Felicity couldn't tell if it was morning or night but assumed morning, as she'd arrived late at Mezra's home and felt as if she'd slept for hours.

She swung herself out of bed and found a basin of water, a facecloth and a soft furry towel set out for her use. She freshened up then looked around for a toilet. Afraid she might have to resort to a pot, she spied another door she hadn't noticed the night before, camouflaged against the earthen wall in the corner. She opened it and found, to her relief, a small hole in the ground, with 'Lavatory' written on a sign beside it.

So far, the great outdoors had served her purposes but Felicity definitely preferred the bathroom – for what it was. When she was finished, there was a flushing sound and when she looked down the hole there was nothing left but dry earth. Strange, but magic she supposed. Practical magic. Feeling more alert and rested than she had since she had first entered Fairyland, Felicity ran her fingers through her hair before joining Mezra.

She found the wizard busying himself with the breakfast dishes and accepted his invitation to sit by the freshly crackling fire. He brought over the empty crockery and utensils as he had the night before and set them out before Felicity on the mushroom table. He gestured at her to order, so Felicity picked up her fork, tapped her plate and said, 'Some scrambled eggs and bacon, please, plate!'

Immediately, a mass of fluffy bright-yellow scrambled egg appeared, along with four sizzling rashers of bacon. Felicity asked for toast and tea to accompany her meal, and at once a plate stacked with buttery bread and a steaming pot of tea appeared. The wizard was a little more restrained with *his* requests this morning, ordering just pancakes with sugar and lemon along with his tea.

'Now, my dear,' he said, when they were midway through their breakfast and Felicity had told him in detail all about her second riddle. 'Do you have any other questions you would like to ask me before you set off again?' His eyes looked enquiringly into Felicity's and, though earlier she had had millions of questions, she suddenly seemed to forget most of them. She struggled for something. 'Well, the pebbles,' she said. 'Do you have any idea who might be behind the stealing and why? You said you didn't think it was the black witches and the goblins …'

'Ah, you see, the problem is that anyone in the Fairy Realm might be suspected of having dealings in this predicament,' said Mezra. 'And, while I don't believe the witches and goblins are stealing them, I do suspect they have a vested interest in what's happening. I doubt they're meeting together to discuss rescuing the realm – more likely they want some part of the evil that's happening and are seeking to control it themselves, instead of whoever is behind all of this.'

Mezra paused and studied Felicity, who knew she must look as downhearted as she felt. It was all very well solving the riddles, but what if she couldn't help the Pebble People and had to stay here even longer, even if she *did* satisfy the Riddler? With so little to go on, she didn't know what she was to do.

'Whoever is behind this can't be working alone, though, so best to beware of everyone and suspect all you meet. Except me, of course.' He smiled. 'Hopefully time will reveal all and unravel this mystery. I will, however, be able to provide you with the directions you seek. The witch's spire is not easy to find, but I have something that will guide you close to it. From there, you will have to use your intuition to locate her precise positioning, as few know how to enter it.'

The wizard walked over to the table groaning under the weight of his heaped books, which sat in the corner behind Felicity. He reached underneath and pulled out an old chest, which wouldn't have looked out of place on a pirate ship. It had a large steel lock but was otherwise made of old darkened wood. He muttered under his breath and the lock sprang open with a soft click. Mezra scrambled about inside, finally saying 'Aha!' and lifting out an old piece of rolled up parchment. He returned to Felicity and sat down with a grin on his face.

'With this,' he said triumphantly, 'you should find your journey to the witch's spire a *lot* easier.'

'What is it?' Felicity asked curiously, too polite to say that it looked like plain blank paper from where she was sitting.

'*This* is a magic map,' whispered the wizard. 'They are few and far between and so you must guard it carefully.

'Like most magical objects, if it were to fall into the wrong hands it could be used for all sorts of mischief. However, the holder of the magic map must first know how to use it, otherwise it is quite useless – watch.' Mezra unrolled the scroll, which remained blank, and when laid flat it was about the size of a large dinner platter. Then he chanted, 'Rimmel, rommel, rimmel roo, tell me the way and tell it true. Reveal the trail to the witch's spire. Rimmel, rommel, rimmel roo, tell me the way and tell it true!'

Faint lines began to appear on the surface of the scroll and, as Felicity watched, she saw they were taking on the form of a map. A speck of gold glowed upon it and she guessed that must be near the witch's spire.

'Be sure to say the rhyme once before and once after your request for direction,' said Mezra.

'Rimmel, rommel, rimmel roo,' repeated Felicity. 'I won't forget.'

'The map is a little temperamental, I'm afraid,' added the wizard. 'That is why you must treat it with respect and not overuse it, or else it might lead you the wrong way. But don't worry,' he added hurriedly, 'I know you'll look after it. The image will last for as long as you need it, usually until you reach your destination, and then will disappear. In dangerous situations it will also go blank as a mechanism of self-defence but will reappear when you ask it again. This will only happen twice, however, so more than two misadventures and you will have to go it alone. Best to memorise as much of the map as you can now before you leave – just to be safe.

'In new hands (as the map belongs to me), it may or may not obey your requests thereafter and may even fly back to me, its owner. It's hard to tell. And remember – the map is a guide and can sometimes be vague, so follow it with caution. It shows the correct way but will not reveal any magical beings and places of enchantment you might encounter on your journey, so be wary of that.

'Now, time to get going, I think – we've talked long enough! Just keep your eyes and ears open for any signs of suspicious activity – of folk who might be involved in the pebble smuggling – but don't look *too* hard, as it is often when we seek too intensely after something that we miss it altogether. I will hold the fort here. Let's hope for all our sakes that you are successful in your quests!'

Mezra took the map and handed it to Felicity, who studied the spidery black lines marking out where she needed to go. They seemed to wind around an awful lot but she hoped it would all become clear once she was outside following them.

The wizard appeared to have packed her a bag for the trip – a beautiful, rich purple-velvet bag with a pretty pattern sewn onto it with silver thread. Inside was a small pot of fairy ointment, which he instructed would lift any fairy glamours she came across if she rubbed some on her eyelids, along with a glass bottle of water, some sandwiches and an apple. There was also a small silver platter, a goblet and a knife, fork and spoon, which Mezra told her would do just what the cutlery and crockery here had done for her, so she need never be hungry or risk consuming enchanted fairy food or drink.

Meanwhile, a small purse nestled amongst all of this, holding three gold pieces and two silver coins. Felicity placed the magic map inside and slung the bag over her shoulder, where it sat comfortably. She then fetched her cloak from the bedroom – which had mysteriously changed into a library filled wall-to-wall with books – and she was ready to go.

Although the anticipation of what lay ahead slightly scared her, she was also eager to be off again, the sooner to solve the riddles and the pebble mystery and go home. She had to admit to herself that she also had renewed excitement about exploring the realm a little more, armed as she now was with the magical back-up from Mezra.

'Right, time to be off!' said the wizard. 'I won't go up with you this time, in case we're spotted together. Better to keep a low profile – you never know whose eyes might be watching. But I wish you luck and I will try to keep up with your progress if I can.'

Felicity repeated her thanks and then watched as Mezra drew a chalk circle on the earthen floor.

'Now, my dear, step inside,' he said. Felicity obeyed.

'Close your eyes and count to ten,' instructed the wizard. 'When you open them you will be back in the wood, not far from where we are now, but far enough away not to court suspicion if you're seen. The map will show you your position and from there, well, it's up to you!'

Mezra patted her on the shoulder and then stepped back from the circle. He muttered some words under his breath and drew a battered gold wand from his left sleeve, waving it as one might a sparkler at Hallowe'en and creating similar silvery swirls in the air. As he did so, the chalk ring began to glow brightly and the soil started to stir in little brown puffs around Felicity's feet. She squeezed her eyes shut and began to count.

Before she had even reached ten, Felicity felt she was no longer underground but kept to the instructions as she had been told anyway, not opening her eyes until she had finished. When she did, she saw she was indeed back outside.

She fumbled in her new purple bag for the map and pulled it out, unfolding the wrinkled parchment with care. It was true what Mezra had said – it showed where she was with a small glowing golden dot on the page.

The morning sun shone in shafts through the trees, with glimpses of blue sky overhead. Birdsong filtered through the air and she found some small comfort in the company of the little mammals. The map indicated her route with a gold dotted line, which wound through the trees ahead and then seemed to run straight for a bit before becoming much more twisted. Felicity frowned, wondering what that particular stretch of wood might contain, but then shrugged her shoulders and decided she would deal with whatever it was when the time came.

And so, she resumed her trek into Witch Wood, anticipating another long, lonely walk with only the birds above for company and only herself to talk to.

She couldn't have been more wrong.

## Chapter Twenty-Three
# Moss Magic

'Oh, please, someone help me. Oh dear, oh dear, what am I going to *do*?'

The mournful voice stopped Felicity in her tracks and she tried to work out which direction it was coming from. Straight ahead by the sounds of it – the way she needed to go.

'Oh dear, oh dear,' the voice said again, the words followed this time by a heavy sigh. 'Why *me*, why *now*?'

Felicity knew she could either continue onwards as she had been and run into whoever it was, or skirt around them and risk straying too far off course and losing her way. She was bound to meet someone eventually, however, and this person sounded more distressed than dangerous, so she decided she'd risk it.

So far, she'd followed the map as best she could, but even with the glowing line showing her the way, it had been more difficult than she'd expected to work out its route, due to the absence of any sort of path in the wood.

As a result, she'd made a few wrong turns but had been able to get back on course when she looked at the map and saw her dot had left the golden line.

She'd kept her eyes peeled for mushroom clumps and fairy rings, determined not to unwittingly step into one again, as she knew she might not be so lucky in escaping it this time if she did. Until now, however, she hadn't come across an actual person and she was curious to see who was up ahead. Feeling a little nervous, Felicity scanned the trees and bushes for signs of whoever had spoken. She was just beginning to think she'd imagined the voice when it sounded again.

'Why me, why me, why *me*?'

It was coming from just above her. She looked up and, to her surprise, saw a tiny, raggedy creature bundled up in a net which was swinging from one of the higher branches. It was suspended so high up, she hadn't noticed it as she'd approached. As she stared, the creature spied her and immediately began wriggling about inside the netted prison, which only seemed to make him or her become even more entangled in it.

'Hi! Hi! You down there! Can you help me?'

The little figure was covered in what looked like some sort of mossy material and Felicity could see an assortment of flower heads protruding from unruly long hair. A thin face poked out from under the messy mass, two hazelnut-coloured eyes staring at her accusingly.

'What are you waiting for?' he exclaimed, for the voice was male, she now realised. 'I can't wait up here all day! I've got things to do. I'll give you a gift if you do …'

Still Felicity hesitated, until the mossy man said, 'Look, I won't hurt you or anything – I give you my word on that. Just please release me before *they* come.'

'They who?' said Felicity, stepping closer to the netting.

'The witches, of course! Who else?' exclaimed the trapped little man. 'Please – you have to hurry. I can't get out of here by myself – they've enchanted the net. Can you undo it?'

Felicity was about to say no, of course not, *she* had no magic, but then remembered the ointment the wizard had given her. She rummaged around in her bag and withdrew it triumphantly.

'I have this!' she said. 'Will that help?'

The mossy man narrowed his eyes. He sighed. 'That will lift a fairy glamour and reveal the true identity of a magical masquerade, but it won't undo a spell like this.'

He looked so glum that Felicity felt immediately sorry for him.

'Well, I could rub some on the netting anyway – just to see,' she said.

The mossy man shrugged his shoulders, so Felicity unscrewed the lid from the little jar and dabbed a small bit of ointment onto her fingers. She then reached as far as she could and rubbed it onto the net above her. At once, it seemed to come alive, writhing and wriggling in the air. The mossy man let out a yelp as the bits of netting around him turned a wispy white and then, miraculously, drifted away. He, of course, dropped to the ground like a stone, where he sat dazed for a few seconds before rubbing his head and grinning.

'Clouds,' he said to Felicity. 'They must have stolen wisps of cloud from the sky and conjured them into a net to trap me, or whichever unsuspecting soul happened to be passing by. A few minutes earlier and it could have been you! But no – it was the foolish Moss Man who got caught.

'When you rubbed that ointment onto the bindings, the clouds revealed their true form and floated off back to the atmosphere! It's a sly trick to play, though, using the likes of that to catch people, for you have no way of seeing it to avoid it! Thank you, thank you, *thank* you!'

Felicity put the pot back in her bag, suspicion creeping over her. Had the trap been laid for *her*? If so, she'd only just missed it. 'Well, I'm glad that worked,' she said, 'because I really don't have anything else I could have used.'

'All the same, you tried what you had and it did the job. Others mightn't have bothered. Now, what about a gift for your trouble?'

The Moss Man stood up and began fumbling around in his clothes, if 'clothes' was indeed the right word to describe them, for they seemed to be made entirely of a velvety green moss. Felicity could smell an earthy odour around him – not unpleasant but rather, fresh, and full of life. His hands were long and bony and his face, bronzed by the sun, was elongated and thin, with a protruding hook nose. Dark-green straggly hair completed his odd look, with scented blooms poking their heads out through the tatted mass in a higgledy-piggledy fashion, making him look quite comical.

'Aha! Here we go!' he said, picking up a tiny cloth pouch from the ground and waving it in her face. 'Must have fallen off me,' he muttered, withdrawing a necklace made of interlinked yellow flowers and green stems. He noted Felicity's confusion.

'It's a necklace for you,' he said. 'St John's Wort – a plant with special natural powers. I know the healing properties of all the plants and wild things in these woods for, as I said before, I am the Moss Man.

'This I give to you for courage, for protection and for more easily detecting magic when you come across it. If it had stayed on my person before, I wouldn't have been in such a predicament! 'As a necklace it will strengthen you and keep you healthy but you can also break the stems apart and use pieces separately to aid you in times

234

of peril – for protection against lightning, storms or evil spirits, for example.'

'Thank you,' said Felicity, accepting the pouch. 'That's very kind.'

'Yes, well, you helped me,' said the Moss Man. 'Just one thing. You must not utter a word of my sighting or tell anyone I gave you this gift. There are many who would seek my powers and secret knowledge, not least the witches of this wood, and they must never know how to find me or where I might be. Can you promise me that?'

'Yes, of course,' said Felicity.

'Then I thank you again and shall take my leave of you,' said the Moss Man. He threw her another quick grin, then vaulted into the tree from which he had only minutes before been hanging from, and disappeared.

***

Growing more used to strange people disappearing on her in even stranger ways, Felicity shook her head in bemusement when the Moss Man vanished, but she was grateful for his gift and knew there was no point hanging around. According to her map, she still had quite a distance to cover before she reached the part of the wood where the witch lived. The Moss Man had reminded her, however, that witches lurked all around here, which gave her the chills. Granted she had a little hocus-pocus at her disposal now, but would she remember how to use it all – and quickly enough – if she was confronted?

Stopping briefly along the way for lunch from her enchanted crockery, Felicity pushed on with her journey, staying on the alert. As the afternoon drew in and nothing unusual happened, she pushed the thoughts of hidden magic and traps to the back of her mind. She didn't directly encounter any more fairy folk, but she suspected her presence had been noted. In fact, she was fairly certain concealed eyes were watching her every move, but as no one confronted her, Felicity felt confident anyone tracking her was merely curious and meant no harm. Not yet anyway.

She stopped every so often to check her progress on the magic map and was dismayed each time to see that it looked as though she'd hardly moved. Yet to her, it felt as if she'd already walked for miles. Just how long was it going to take her to reach the witch's spire?

She was so preoccupied that it took her longer than it should have to notice the silence that had dropped down around her. This part of the wood was even more closely knitted with trees than the way she'd just come. The birdsong had gone, while the scuttling and scurrying sounds from the undergrc

and comforting backgro·

simply with the sound of

Only leaves whispe

breeze, their branches

blocking out the sun v

was saturated with su

make out shapes – solid, jaggeᵣ

ominously before her – yet still she walkeᾱ, aᴗ

were reeling her in with an invisible rope.

As she drew nearer, the shapes sharpened and Felicity saw they were in fact huge standing stones, not black and bumpy like rocks, but smooth and sculpted. There were five altogether, each a different colour and roughly oval in shape. A dull yellow stone, the farthest away from her, stood straight ahead, while just below it, to the left, was a grey stone mottled with white. Opposite was a reddish brown stone and behind Felicity was a white and a purple-blue stone, spaced apart from one another.

In the centre of the stones, where she now stood, lay a pile of broken twigs and branches – a fire, waiting to be lit. A creeping suspicion came upon her that someone or some*thing* was coming, as she realised that was probably why the woodland creatures had fled. They had felt it and she had not. They'd gone somewhere safe but she e middle of whatever was about to

omething told her it wasn't going to be

to hide and fast. Bushes were everywhere

rovide good cover but Felicity wanted a tree

ould be able to see what was going on. If she

just hide inside a hollow or perhaps climb one to

a safe view.

Spying a medium-sized tree with a branch just low enough for her to reach, she ran towards it. Without thinking, for she could feel a subtle change in the wind and noticed that even the trees had stopped their whisperings now, Felicity swung herself up and scrambled as high as she safely could, settling down comfortably and parting the leaves just enough to give a view of the stones. From her vantage point she could see they formed the five points of a star. She only hoped she was well enough hidden from anyone on the ground.

She didn't have to wait long. Within a few minutes, everything changed.

First, came the smell of wood smoke laced with strange fragrances. The air was perfumed with mystery and suspense, with fear and unease; longing mingled with doubt and distress, mixed up with wishful thinking and desire. Felicity didn't know how she knew these things – she just did.

Then came the flames.

Five curling plumes of smoke snaked their way in from five different parts of the wood, entering the centre of the star-shaped space and then plunging into the assembled kindling. It burst into flames of gold and orange, electric blue and deep blood red, of emerald green and buttercup yellow and, finally, of black. Felicity had never seen *black* flames on a fire before and she felt shivers tip-toe up and down her spine.

Then came the crows.

Gripping the branch to stop herself from tumbling off, Felicity tried to work out where the cacophony of cries was coming from but could see nothing. The calls collided with the silence, shattering it to pieces with ugly shrieks and scoldings, and then she saw the black birds themselves enter the clearing. They flapped noisily towards the black-flamed fire – five crows to match the five standing stones and the five smoke plumes. Each bird flew anticlockwise around the fire three times before settling on the ground, each in front of one of the stones. Then silence once more.

Felicity watched, breath bated, her knuckles white from clenching the branch so hard, eyes focused on the scene below. The crows arched their sleek black necks, wings spread wide to either side, and then the most extraordinary thing happened. The stretching didn't stop.

As the crows' necks arched, they elongated, giving the birds the appearance of stunted flamingos. Their wings also extended slowly, writhing in the firelight like black feathered snakes trying to escape their very skins.

The crows' flamingo-like necks were joined by flamingo-type legs next – stick-thin appendages which grew until the creatures reached almost the height of the standing stones. The legs were no longer those of a bird's, however, as each pair now seemed to be wearing differently coloured striped stockings, all ending in black buckled shoes.

Their torsos were now encased in ebony fabric embossed with sparkling silver stars, hats and eyes, while the remaining feathers grew downwards to become flowing black skirts.

Wings had become arms ending in long bony fingers – fingers tipped with gnarled, pointed fingernails, all painted black. Necks were no longer feathered and crow-like but had smooth skin and the foundations of five heads.

Five heads of five witches – with hats on top.

## Chapter Twenty-Four
# Witches

Felicity's heart was pounding but she remained rooted to the spot, drinking in the scene. The witches stretched again, flexing their arms and necks and legs to ease out the stiffness that had resulted from being crows.

They wore black pointed hats, decorated to match their embroidered bodices, with long red hair, black hair and locks of mahogany, silver and gold flowing out from under the brims. Far from looking like the haggard, warty witches Felicity had expected, they were in fact quite youthful and each striking, if not beautiful, in their own way.

Each now also wore a cloak of black silk, which flowed like water down their backs and seemed to be constantly in motion. Huddling around the gothic flames, the witches began speaking in low voices, too low for Felicity to hear what was being said. She didn't dare move any closer, but it was clear something was wrong.

The gesticulations went on for a while, the mutterings ebbing and flowing in volume so that, once or twice, Felicity picked up a few words – enough to know that she really wished she could listen clearly to the discussion. The snatches of conversation gave her enough information to know that they were discussing the goblins, the stones and something which was happening tomorrow. Just what were they up to, she wondered?

She leaned forward just a fraction and her branch gave a quiet but distinct creak. Felicity froze, but it was too late. The witches had looked up, eyes piercing the leafy canopy above them for the source of the sound.

Barely breathing, Felicity was sure she'd blown her cover and so was immensely relieved when at that moment a flock of crows emerged from the trees opposite. They circled the witches before perching on the standing stones, the rest fluttering to the ground. She waited to see if they too would transform into witches but they remained crows. She remembered how Bob had told her that some witches could take the form of crows but that not all crows were witches, although many were willing messengers and accomplices of covens throughout the realm and therefore not to be trusted. For now, though, Felicity was grateful for their appearance, and what was more, it sparked an idea.

She could use her ring from the Lagoon of Lost Desires to glamour herself into a crow and fly down to hear what the witches were plotting. Even better, she realised with a smile, she could also fly *with* the witches back to wherever they'd come from and, hopefully, find the witch she needed to solve her second riddle. It was the perfect plan, and surely much quicker than following the map. She just needed to remove the ring from her bag without drawing any attention to herself …

It was as if the trees were against her. Felicity groaned inwardly when her branch creaked loudly just as she located the ring. Once again, the witches scoured the treetops but then turned back to the fire. This time, however, they didn't continue with their discussions but instead began chanting, low at first, then faster and more furiously, their arms stretched towards the black-flamed blaze and their voices raised. As Felicity looked on, mouth agape, the ebony flames seemed to reach out and touch the witches' beckoning arms. She could hear their repetitive chant now.

'*Rise – Black Shadow Fingers, Black Shadow Fingers, Black Shadow Fingers …*'

Coldness cloaked Felicity as she saw the Black Shadow Fingers, long, black fingers of flame, rise from the fire and begin to search – for her. She gulped and fumbled with the ring, slipping it onto her finger with haste.

The Black Shadow Fingers stretched closer towards the trees and she squeezed her eyes shut, desperately imagining herself as a crow perched on the branch and not a girl. She felt the ring slowly begin to heat up, which spurred her on to focus more deeply on what she would look like as a bird. Black feathers, a beak, beady eyes, wings, stick-thin legs, talons ...

She wondered briefly if it would hurt – the transformation – but a shudder simply ran through her as the ring reached its hottest temperature. She opened her eyes. The stone had turned green and she was swaddled in glossy black feathers, the ring somewhere amongst those on her left wing. The magic had worked and she'd barely felt a thing! Felicity's purple bag had also shrunk but was thankfully still there – treasures intact – although her clothes had disappeared. She just had to trust they would materialise again when the time came to change back. In the meantime, she hoped she would be able to get lost well enough among the other crows so no one would notice the tiny bag slung over her back.

Meanwhile, the Black Shadow Fingers – those writhing, pointed tentacles of unnatural length and substance – searched on. Their hot black flames flickered upwards into the trees and through the bushes, yet failed to ignite the foliage through which they passed. More trailed across the ground as Felicity realised the fire had produced not just one but *five* pairs of creepy fingers – all stretching out with one purpose.

She fluttered her wings self-consciously, waiting. The Black Shadow Fingers whipping through the treetops around her were growing rapidly closer, and suddenly they were there, hot flames breathing upon her. Felicity knew what she had to do, so she hoped for the best, spread her wings and jumped. She glided on the thermals created by the Black Shadow Fingers, hovering mid-air for a few seconds before she flapped, forgetting for a moment the peril she was in, so wonderful was the feeling of floating.

The eerie appendages hesitated but then continued with their sweep of the area. As Felicity joined the assembled crowd of crows below, the witch with silver cobwebs on her bodice pointed at her in disgust. As the other witches realised what had happened, the spell was broken and all five pairs of Black Shadow Fingers were dragged back into the fire, shrieking as they went. It became momentarily engorged as it reabsorbed them, then settled down again into a steady burn. The crows stared at Felicity with distaste but thankfully paid no more attention to her, instead pecking and jostling each other noisily.

Evening was now rapidly approaching and the witches appeared to be getting ready to leave the copse. Felicity still couldn't make out their muted mutterings but was grateful that they too had paid her no more heed. Obviously, whatever it was they were discussing was much more important than a crow interrupting their meeting.

The red-headed witch suddenly clapped her hands together and the fire, as if drenched with water, sputtered out.

'I'm *not* flying back as a crow,' the silver-haired witch declared adamantly. 'There's no need on the return flight anyway and I'm fed up having to hide all the time.'

'Yes, well, we none of us like it much but sometimes glamour is necessary, as you very well know,' said the red-headed witch. 'But I agree. On the way back there is little need for it. Dusk is fast approaching and with it we shall fly properly!'

Felicity saw that each witch now held a broomstick, each unique to its owner, of course – be it smooth and polished, gnarled and knobbly, etched with intricate carvings or splashed with spots of coloured paint. She couldn't believe she was about to witness five witches fly away – and what was more, *she* was going to fly with them! The witches perched elegantly on their broomsticks, muttered a few words and then rose effortlessly into the darkening sky, cloaks billowing out behind them.

Felicity couldn't help thinking they were an impressive sight, despite the fear fluttering in her tiny crow stomach at having to follow them. She hoped that doing so, however, would help with both her riddle and the pebble mystery.

The crows rose as one huge flock and she lost herself easily in their collective mass of black feathers as they tailed the witches away from the copse. Below her, the ground fell away, though this was a truly different experience from her ride on the fairy unicorn. Soon they were soaring above even the tallest treetops – a blanket of green which betrayed no hint of the magical life sheltering below it.

Oddly enough, Felicity felt the same, yet also very different. She was still Felicity but her eyes were sharper, picking out details she knew she would never have seen as a girl, and her wings, outstretched, felt lovely and light. She was actually beginning to enjoy herself when she realised the crows were thinning out, birds from the side falling away from the flock.

Wondering what her next move should be, she noticed the mahogany-haired witch break away from the coven and disappear down into the wood. A little further on, the golden-haired witch did the same, soon followed by the red-haired witch and then the silver-haired witch. With each one, a small assembly of crows also left, so now Felicity remained with just the black-haired witch and only a handful of birds. She had no idea which witch she should follow, so she simply opted for the final witch, hoping it was the right thing to do.

Without warning, the black-haired witch veered her broomstick – a twisted and varnished piece of dark wood – off to the left. Felicity followed.

***

Down they went, the wind whipping through Felicity's feathers and clearing her mind of all thoughts as she focused on the flight. Although the evening was darkening, the wood here was already black, trees thickly blotting out the sky. Her new and improved eyesight, however, helped her navigate, as she dodged branches and boughs and ducked under other obstacles. The wood was quiet and still and the witch pressed on. She finally landed, however, and the crows, including Felicity, perched in the trees to watch her.

The witch had disembarked among a group of tall, spiky pine trees, the grass below littered with brown rocks and stones which seemed to form a scattered sort of path which she now followed. She was soon swallowed up by the pines and Felicity followed discreetly from branch to branch above her. Intent as she was on her journey, the witch appeared not to notice her – and besides, other crows mirrored Felicity's moves as lookouts, so she wasn't alone.

The scattered path led the witch to a small mound with a hawthorn on either side and Felicity watched as the witch knelt, bowed her head and muttered something. Before she knew what had happened, the hillside had opened up, the witch had entered it and Felicity – well, Felicity had followed her in.

## Chapter Twenty-Five
# The Witch's Spire

As soon as they passed through the entrance in the hillside, it was sewn seamlessly together again behind them. Although darkness was now cloaking the wood outside, inside the mound black candles as tall as pokers burned brightly in antique silver candelabras, casting misshapen shadows on the walls.

Felicity had been underground a few times since entering the realm, but this was different. The air hung heavy around her, an occasional spark crackling in the charged atmosphere. She had barely taken the time to glance around her but it was seconds too long, as when she looked for the witch, she had disappeared.

Alone, Felicity flapped her wings nervously, hovering at the mouth of a tunnel which dipped into shadow a little way ahead.

The witch could only have taken the same route, as Felicity saw no other entrances. She had no idea how long her glamour would last, so she flew into the murky blackness, hoping for the best.

The hillside had led straight into what Felicity soon regarded as the longest underground passage in the world, or at least the realm. Shadows clung to every surface around her as she flew, making her sticky with nerves.

Now and again, she passed candles weeping wax down slim stems but releasing enough light to allow her to move onwards without fear of flying into the walls. Further along, the candles were replaced by ornate lanterns, which creaked as they swung above Felicity's head, although just what was making them move, she had no idea. Some were stained glass, so the light thrown into the tunnel became a mysterious fractured rainbow which danced along beside her.

As she flew onwards, drawings appeared on the walls of the passageway, which had slowly changed from packed earth to stone. Silver stars and moons shimmered here – strange symbols and colourful birds glimmered there.

Flying faster and faster now, Felicity's wings beat furiously, propelling her onwards to somewhere she wasn't sure she wanted to reach but knew she had to go. And then, just as she felt sure she was never going to find her witch, the tunnel fell away.

Felicity had been moving so quickly she was taken completely by surprise at the space now yawning beneath and around her, as she realised she'd just flown over a huge staircase cut steeply into the earth below. Not just one but three, she soon discovered, stopping mid-flight and backtracking for a closer look, as two smaller staircases shouldered the grand central one in the middle, all of them draining down to what looked like a very deep well. Worn paths pointed away from this well to the entrances of several shadowy tunnels scattered around it.

If she'd been walking rather than flying, Felicity would have had to brave climbing down one, and she shuddered, as none had banisters and all were precarious and practically vertical.

Looking up, she saw the ceiling swept high above her in a huge dome. Carvings dug deep into the stone showed a tangle of swirled symbols and mythical beasts stretching across the entire canopy. Hovering in the vast cavern, she wondered what it could be for.

Below her, the black-haired witch had just completed her descent and she disappeared into one of the tunnels. Felicity hesitated. Straight ahead, at her bird's-eye level, was a higher passageway that appeared to be accessible only to those with wings, which, at the moment, included her. What had the riddle said? *'Through whispering woods – go low, then high ...'* Well, she'd gone underground to reach this point, so that was the low. Maybe this was her opportunity to 'go high' and find the witch's spire.

Torn about what to do, Felicity made a split-second decision. She would only be able to access the higher passage with wings and she had them now as a crow, so she shouldn't waste this chance. There was bound to be another opportunity to find out what the witches were up to. Besides, her mother used to say that sometimes things happened for a reason. Felicity fleetingly wondered if her mum still thought that, but snipped the thread of the idea before it had a chance to be spun.

So, leaving the staircases and tunnels in her wake, she flew onwards – and upwards, as the route ahead followed a steep incline. This time, the walls no longer showed painted pictures but instead revealed gnarled roots and pieces of sharp wood sticking out from packed earth. She had to dodge around them, trying not to damage her wings as the tunnel rose ever higher.

Everything had been so silent up until now that when the first sounds wafted through the stagnant, soil-soaked air, Felicity picked them up immediately. Chanting.

Feeling incredibly tired, but spurred on by the sound, she continued on, the chanting growing louder with every charged flap of her wings. The roots around her, however, were now thicker and she slowed to dodge around them. At last, she was forced to fly to the ground and hop along over twisted roots and branches, bits of dead wood and other rotting vegetation, until she was brought to an abrupt halt by a thicket of thorns.

*** 

Before she could work out the best way to creep into what she hoped was the witch's spire, Felicity's cover was blown. She felt a bony hand close around her body and wrench her through the thorns, tearing out a few of her feathers in the process.

'You're late!' a croaky voice proclaimed. 'Can't wait all night as well as all day for you! Well, where is it?'

Felicity stared fearfully into cruel emerald eyes which looked as if they had been plucked from a beautiful, younger witch and pressed into the wizened face of the old hag before her.

The witch had sharp, angular features, with a jagged chin and a lightning bolt of a nose. She had no warts, but wrinkles aplenty, and skin that appeared paper thin and almost luminescent. Arched eyebrows – silver – matched bedraggled silver-grey hair, which hung lank round the witch's bony face, making it seem even smaller and shrewder.

Felicity struggled, trying to escape the steely stare of this frankly terrifying old woman. The hand only gripped her more tightly.

'Where is what?' she forced out, assuming the witch understood 'crow'.

'Don't play games with me!' screeched the witch in frustration. She shook Felicity hard. 'My ingredient, my ingredient,' she muttered. 'I must have it. I must be ready for tomorrow.' Her fingers suddenly released their grip and Felicity flapped her wings just in time to stop herself falling to the ground. The witch was still mumbling to herself, pulling at her hair and seemingly forgetting all about Felicity as she hobbled away from her.

Felicity followed her into a large circular room with stone walls, which had been cleverly concealed by the thorns from the tunnel side. Was this the witch's spire? If so, the stony half must face outwards to Witch Wood, she thought, while the other half hugged the hillside – growing out of it like a parasite.

'The Hunter is getting closer,' muttered the witch. 'I must be ready.' Then, '*I must be ready!*' she screamed, seizing a glass jar and throwing it against the wall. It smashed to smithereens, shards of glass glittering in the gloom of her home. She grabbed more potion bottles from a nearby table, hurling them wildly at the walls and forcing Felicity to seek shelter behind a chair. When the witch had calmed down, she ambled over to a large cauldron bubbling by a crackling fire. She held her hands over the smoking surface, mumbling as she did so, and Felicity watched in astonishment as the spilled liquids from the broken jars and bottles evaporated from the walls and from the floor and drifted over to the cauldron – a huge, squat iron-clad beast with four black clawed feet.

They mingled with the smoke, turning it into a rainbow of colour. The shattered glass then gathered in the air to form a jagged ball-like shape and flew into the witch's pot. When the witch plunged her bony fingers inside, Felicity gasped, but her shock turned quickly to disbelief and wonderment when she saw the witch lift out a glittering glass – no, *crystal* – ball, which momentarily threw pure white light around the cave before settling down to a soft pulsing glow. The witch smiled a crooked smile to herself and Felicity felt sure she was quite, *quite* mad.

She watched as the old crone lowered herself into a creaking rocking chair by the fire, cradling the crystal. Her room was modest, with the fire and accompanying cauldron, a bed, a small table and chair, and a chunk of wall filled with potions – a circular window in its centre. Through it, Felicity spied the moon, so she knew without a doubt that she was at the top of the spire. This was definitely her witch!

Crystal ball before her, the witch moved her hands over its smooth surface, which at once shimmered and changed, shapes forming inside. Felicity flew a little closer to get a better look. The ball showed a mass of white pebbles.

'It is time,' whispered the witch. 'It is time and I must soon go, but first I must sleep, for there is much to be done and I am not yet at my full strength. Rat–*chet!*' she shrieked.

A little knock-kneed creature darted out from behind a red velvet curtain which hung by the side of the witch's bed, one end attached to the wall.

'Ratchet, I am almost ready to leave,' said the witch sharply. 'Gather up my belongings while I sleep and wake me at moonrise tomorrow, for I must rest all the day to be at full strength for tomorrow night's meeting. My sleeping draught will ensure I'm not woken by any of your noise.' She pulled a bottle from her pocket and gulped down its contents. 'And don't let this out of your sight. I'll need it for my divining.' She handed him the crystal ball.

Ratchet took the magical object and then scurried around the room as the witch stumbled into her bed, drawing the heavy red curtain to hide her from view.

'Oh, and kill that wretched crow,' she rasped. 'It's the wrong one and it's seen too much. Bird for breakfast, I think!'

## Chapter Twenty-Six
# Carpet Tricks

Felicity froze at the witch's words. Her eyes met the bulging grey stare of the old crone's servant, who licked his lips and offered her a quivering smile. Arms outstretched, he came towards her and Felicity's only thought was that she couldn't be a crow anymore.

She pulled at the ring in desperation, hoping against hope that she would change back into her old self if she could only get it off. Gripping it with some difficulty in her beak, she gave a final sharp tug as she flew away from Ratchet and perched on the mantel above the fire.

The ring popped off and before she knew it she was staring at an extremely startled servant, her legs dangling over the ledge. She jumped down and grabbed the skinny creature before he could alert the witch, clamping her hand over his mouth. He struggled feebly but the surprise had obviously taken him aback and Felicity worked quickly, stuffing a nearby rag into his mouth and tying his hands together with a piece of ribbon she snatched up from the floor. It was a good thing the witch was messy, she thought with relief.

Felicity was quite impressed with her work, as she'd never tied anyone up before, but she did feel a little guilty. She could either do this or get caught, however, and she didn't fancy being the witch's new slave – or breakfast. She grabbed the ring from the floor and put it back in her bag.

'I don't know if this is right, but it just *must* be,' she muttered, running over to where Ratchet had placed the crystal ball among the potions on the wall. 'If she needs it for her divining, then it must be something she'll miss, and it came from the cauldron, which is heated by fire …'

She placed the magic object carefully in her bag, Ratchet's eyes bulging in his tiny head, which he shook furiously. He was lying on the floor and Felicity knew he would get into a lot of trouble for this but it couldn't be helped. Then a thought struck her. She was no longer a crow – how would she get away? She ran to the window and saw that she'd been right – they were at the top of a tower and below was nothing but treetops. The only entrance seemed to be the one she'd entered as a crow, but there was no way she could backtrack without wings. Mezra had told her the ring wouldn't work again immediately after being used – how could she have forgotten?

There was only one thing for it – she would have to ask the servant for help.

Ratchet was struggling quietly with his bonds and jumped when Felicity tapped him on the shoulder.

'If I release you will you show me the way out?' she whispered.

He took a few seconds to mull this over, then glanced at the red curtain concealing his mistress and nodded glumly.

'Do *not* shout when I take this off,' she warned, as she untied his gag. 'You'll be in as much trouble as me – if not more – for allowing this to happen: remember that.'

Again Ratchet nodded so Felicity freed him. He was as silent as he had promised and stared sullenly at her – but with a bit of fear. She felt ashamed and patted the little creature on the shoulder.

'How do I get out?' she asked him gently.

He pointed to the wall of potions.

'Can you show me?' she said, approaching the shelves of bottles and jars.

Ratchet followed and climbed up onto the lowest protruding shelf. He reached high for a squat, square jar containing a dark liquid. He lifted this away and pressed part of the rock wall, then jumped down again. Felicity waited for the wall to swing away and reveal an escape passage. It didn't.

Instead, a small drawer at the very bottom, underneath the lowest shelf, quietly slid open. Ratchet rubbed his hands in glee and crouched down to pull something out, a goofy grin on his face. Felicity couldn't work out what it was – a cloth of some kind? It was red and patterned – pretty, with golden tassels – but how would *that* help?

Ratchet stood up triumphantly, the roll of fabric clutched tightly to his small, bony frame. His eyes were pleading and Felicity knew what was coming. He wanted to escape with her and, in all honesty, she couldn't really blame him. Who wanted to be a witch's servant, especially when you'd just helped her potential prisoner/breakfast escape and lost her a crystal ball into the bargain?

'OK,' she whispered, nodding. 'You can come. But how do we get out of here and what *is* that?'

Ratchet looked fit to burst with pride and excitement. 'First of all, my name is *Hat*chet, not *Rat*chet,' he said, in the lowest of voices. 'As for this – it's a magic carpet! All we do is get onto it and tell it where we want to go.'

He looked at her enquiringly. 'Where do you want to go?'

Felicity looked at it in amazement. She had heard tales of such things, of course, but had never dreamed she would actually *see* one for herself.

'I … I have no idea, actually,' she confessed, realising for the first time on her journey that she really didn't know what the next step was. 'As long as we can get out of here and go somewhere safe, that's all I care about for now,' she said. 'Why don't you decide?'

Hatchet grinned and hopped onto the rug. Felicity stepped on beside him. The carpet could have comfortably accommodated perhaps two other bodies, so there was plenty of room for them to sit with space around them.

Hatchet grasped two pieces of thickly coiled and cleverly camouflaged bits of material, winding them around one ankle and then the other and binding two more around his wrists. Felicity felt around for her own pieces and secured herself firmly. She felt safer now and nodded at the odd little creature beside her.

Hatchet squeezed his eyes shut, took a breath and then uttered a low chant:

*'Oh, magic carpet, this song is for you,*
*Oh, magic carpet, your power please ring true.*
*Take us away, oh, with speed and with haste,*
*Take us away to a far distant place.*
*Oh, magic carpet, I ask of you now –*

*Fly us to "anywhere" – we don't mind how!'*

Felicity stared at Hatchet in astonishment.

'What do you mean, *anywhere*?' she hissed. 'Anywhere in Fairyland could be, well, *anywhere*! Who knows the things that might live there or what dangers there will be. Tell it somewhere else, quick!'

But the carpet had already begun to twitch, its corners curling up around them ready for take-off. Hatchet shook his head in reply.

'Once told where to go, the magic carpet won't stop until it takes you there,' he mumbled. 'You can't get off until we reach our destination,' he added mournfully. 'The magic can't be broken.'

'I wish you'd told me about all these rules *before* you told it where to go,' hissed Felicity. 'If only –'

But her sentence hung in the air, as indeed then did Felicity and Hatchet, as the magic carpet lurched forwards and upwards and then shot through the thorns, which parted to let them pass. It whooshed along so fast Felicity's hair was torn back from her face – like a russet scarf flying behind her – and she struggled to sit up.

The carpet sped along the tunnels she had already flapped through as a crow – or so she thought anyway: she couldn't possibly tell *which* way they were going, as everything was a blur. She saw that Hatchet had lain back – whether on purpose or thrown by the force of the carpet's flight she didn't know – but Felicity soon followed suit, immediately feeling more comfortable and secure. She was also less frightened in this position – closing her eyes, she felt a pleasant and peaceful rocking sensation as the carpet hurried onwards, twisting and turning through the witches' lair.

She hoped she'd solved the second riddle. What if she hadn't and had to start again? Would she even be *able* to start again? Felicity couldn't bear to think of that so instead she turned her attention to 'anywhere'.

Where *was* 'anywhere'? Would it be a good place or an evil place? Would the Rhyming Riddler find her there? Surely he would – he had always seemed able to track her down before. She longed to see him in his colourful robe, mysterious pouches with untold secrets and treasures swinging from his waist. To hear her final riddle and get one step closer to home. Her grandmother … she just wanted to go home and be with her Granny Stone.

Fresh thoughts of home tumbled into Felicity's mind, mixing with her muddled thoughts of the realm like clothes in a washing machine – clashing and clambering against one another and ending up a tangled ball of everything.

She'd drifted off into a deep sleep, her dreams showing Bob still by her side, helping her, then taking her home to her grandmother. She was nowhere and everywhere, maybe even anywhere – somewhere she ought not to be.

## Chapter Twenty-Seven
# Exchanges

It turned out that 'anywhere' didn't take all that long to get to. Or so it seemed to Felicity.

She felt as if she'd just closed her eyes and she was there, although, in reality, it had taken much longer than she could have imagined, despite the speed of the magic carpet. She didn't know it, but she was now a long way from the witch's spire, having crossed the realm swiftly during the night.

She woke with a start as the carpet bumped its passengers rather ungraciously onto the ground. Above them, the mid-morning sun shone golden as honey from a turquoise sky dressed in marshmallow clouds.

Felicity unravelled the carpet bonds from her wrists and ankles, rubbing them gently as they had become stiff during the flight. She looked around to see where they were. The carpet had deposited them on a small hill which sloped gently down to a magnificent pair of bronze gates, the metal twisted at the top, like the antlers of a wild stag, so that it almost looked alive. Between the huge gates, which were wide open and shouldered on each side by pine trees bristling with thick, impenetrable green needles, more metal coiled around to spell out a word – 'Any-Ware'.

Felicity stared at the name, stunned that the carpet had actually taken them to a physical place called 'Anywhere' – well, 'Any-*Ware*'. She was glad they'd landed where they had, however, because what lay below them was a sprawling mass of mayhem. Hundreds, maybe thousands of voices – high and sharp, low and deep, loud, shrieking and all sorts besides – ripened the air, as fairy folk chattered and shouted at one another. At any rate, it woke Hatchet up and he stared along with Felicity, mouth agape.

There were wooden stalls and small stalls, painted stalls and tall stalls – stalls of all shapes, sizes and colours sprinkled like petals over the floor of the valley below. Flags flew from some, bright banners from others. Some stalls had striped bunting, some none at all. Everywhere Felicity looked there were traders and all were shouting their wares. Then it clicked.

'Wares' were items for sale, so Any-Ware must be a place where you could buy anything you wanted. Studying the busy scene, Felicity also realised it wasn't just stalls filling the space. Huge, sturdy shire horses plodded through the melee, trailing cumbersome carts behind them; pedlars proudly proclaimed the treasures they had stuffed into big, bulky sacks slung over their shoulders; caravans – wooden, with brightly coloured cloth canopies – trundled slowly by; and here and there Felicity thought she could make out little grey stone structures amongst the sea of colour painting the valley.

Then there were the people – the fairy folk – and Felicity found them the most fascinating of all. Again, grateful for their perfect vantage point, she could see pointed witches' hats poking up through the crowd, like panicked periscopes in an ocean swimming with strange and exotic creatures. Accompanying cloaks swirled ominously behind these witchy folk, pouring over any small creature which found itself in the way. Fairies flew overhead – obviously escaping to the sky so they could see better and thus freeing themselves from the jostling crowd below.

Brownies the colour of autumn leaves could also be seen here and there in splodges of earthy neutrals, breaking up the glitterati of sparkling white elves and fairies. Was Bob one of them, she wondered? Felicity could have kept watching the folk all day but was aware of the carpet moving restlessly beneath her and Hatchet.

'It wants to be off,' said Hatchet wistfully. 'Pity.'

Felicity looked at him in alarm. 'Can't we keep it? I mean, so we can go somewhere else if this place turns out to be dangerous?'

Hatchet shook his head. ''Fraid not. Only one trip at a time, and anyway it's borrowed magic – from my mistress. I mean, *her*, the witch.' His voice dropped slightly. '*She* owns the carpet and so it *has* to go back. She'll likely beat it for helping us escape, even though it didn't really have a say in the matter. It has to do what it's told – bound by magic, you see.'

It was the longest speech Felicity had heard Hatchet make so far and she was shocked by his words. 'Poor carpet!' she said sympathetically. 'Especially when it's not its fault. Are you sure we can't keep it?'

But even as she spoke she knew it was impossible. The magic was evidently more powerful and to go back to the witch was what the carpet wanted to do. It was now wriggling frantically underneath them and Felicity and Hatchet quickly rolled onto the grass. At once, the carpet sprang into the air, shook itself and then sped off into the distance. They stared after it a little wistfully before Felicity perked up.

'Look, we can't stand here moping all day,' she said, feigning cheerfulness. 'Let's go and investigate this Any-Ware. You never know what we might find.' Hatchet looked nervous but nodded his head anyway. Felicity supposed he was used to taking orders from the witch, so she elbowed him gently and said, 'Only if you want to, though. But one thing's for sure – I don't think we should stay on this hill. At least down there we can lose ourselves in the crowd.'

This seemed to brighten the little creature up and he gave Felicity a half-smile.

'I'm Felicity, by the way,' she added, suddenly realising she hadn't even introduced herself properly to him. 'And thanks for helping me. You didn't have to – you could have called the witch. Also, I'm sorry for tying you up before.'

Hatchet flashed a full smile at her this time. 'That's OK,' he said shyly. 'I always wanted to escape from her but didn't know how, or have the courage to do so.'

'But the magic carpet – you knew where that was. Why didn't you use it before?' asked Felicity.

'I, I didn't know where to go and I've been there so long I didn't think I would be able to survive out here on my own,' he said.

'She took me when I was only little. At a – a place like this, actually. She swept me up in her cloak and the next thing I knew I was her slave.'

Felicity looked at Hatchet in horror. 'That's awful!' she said. 'No wonder you aren't keen on going down there. What about your family?'

'Gone,' said Hatchet mournfully. 'Gone before I was taken. I was an orphan and I think the witch knew that. She knew I wouldn't be missed and that nobody would come looking for me.' He sniffed. 'No one ever did.'

'I'm so sorry,' said Felicity again.

She didn't know what else to say but smiled encouragingly at her new friend, as she knew that sometimes it was better not to say anything when there was nothing helpful to be added. She also knew herself, however, that distractions were a great way of taking your mind off unpleasantness, so she decided to change the subject.

'If you don't mind me asking, what type of fairy are you?' she asked.

'I'm no fairy,' said Hatchet dolefully. 'Fairies are pretty and I'm not pretty. *I* am a hobgoblin.'

'Oh!' Felicity couldn't help herself. 'A goblin? But I thought all goblins were, I mean, well …' She flushed.

'Evil?' said Hatchet. 'Yes, most are. But I'm a *hob*goblin – a distant cousin of the goblin race and not quite as violent. We're sort of like brownies, really. We do household chores, which is why the witch took me, you see – although we do often play more tricks around the house.

'Also,' he said proudly, '*I* don't eat human flesh. You *are* human, aren't you?'

'Yes,' said Felicity. She shuddered as she remembered Bob also telling her how goblins enjoyed eating people. She thought again then of poor Twinkle – she was very glad indeed to hear that Hatchet was nothing like his cousins.

'What about you?' asked the hobgoblin. 'How did you get into the realm?'

'By mistake,' said Felicity. 'Well, I mean, I accidentally picked up an enchanted pebble and it brought me here, though it was apparently all planned by the Pebble People.'

'Pebble People? I've heard of them,' said Hatchet, looking incredibly pleased with himself. 'They look after all the enchanted pebbles, don't they? They can spirit folk away to all sorts of places – some good, some not so good. I've heard mistress – I mean, the witch – talk of them.'

'Yes, well, I think she may be mixed up in some sort of plot linked to the magic pebbles,' said Felicity grimly. 'That's why the Pebble People brought me here – someone has been stealing the pebbles and draining them of their powers, and they want me to stop them. A wizard told me the witches are plotting with the goblins, perhaps to gain control of the dark forces unleashed by what's been happening. The problem is I'm still not completely sure what *is* happening.

'I think fairy folk are stealing the pebbles for someone who is tampering with them for whatever reason, and this is allowing evil creatures and their black magic into the realm. I just need to find out who this is and where they are, so I can somehow stop them!'

Hatchet's eyes had widened. 'You're certainly on a marvellous adventure,' he said. 'And wait – you were a *crow* when I first saw you! How did that happen?'

Felicity smiled. 'I've got a lot to tell,' she said. 'And I suppose now is as good a time as any to tell it!'

So, she took a deep breath and as they made their way downhill to the bustling Any-Ware, Felicity told the hobgoblin of her adventures in the Fairy Realm so far – of everyone she had met, the perils she had faced and the challenges which still lay ahead.

## Chapter Twenty-Eight

# Any-Ware

'Stay close,' said Felicity, as they walked through the towering gates to Any-Ware, which made the two travellers look like ants. Hatchet gripped her cloak tightly.

To their left, wooden stalls groaning under the weight of their wares were manned by extraordinary creatures Felicity couldn't put a name to. They seemed to be selling a type of lotion and one was busy rubbing the cream onto a nervous-looking brownie. She watched to see what would happen and was quite surprised when the brownie's arm turned a startling shade of green. He yelled in surprise.

'What kind of muck is this you're selling?' he shouted angrily. 'I wanted *tanned* skin so I wouldn't stick out like a sore thumb amongst all the other brownies and now you've turned it *green*! Fix it!' The creature selling the lotion, which resembled a dwarf but had a long nose almost like an elephant's trunk, motioned to one of its fellow traders. Without speaking, he was silently handed another jar and he rubbed some of its contents onto the brownie. This time the arm changed to bright pink, and Felicity and Hatchet hurriedly moved on as the brownie launched into another verbal rant at the poor mute traders.

More stalls lined the right side, selling scarves and cloaks, hats and various other items of clothing, but up ahead, Felicity could see the traders became much more spread out and higgledy-piggledy, hence the overall chaos of the place, as streams of folk browsed from all directions.

A host of delicious smells perfumed the air, along with some particularly strange aromas, which Felicity guessed must come from the brewing of potions. It made her excited and wary at the same time. Despite all that had happened, here she was in the Fairy Realm, positively *surrounded* by fairies and all sorts of magical folk, something she'd never dared dream might happen when dream of Fairyland was all she had once done.

They passed witches hunched over bubbling black pots – some young and beautiful, some old and haggard – and watched laughing pixies try on gossamer dresses. They also saw a well-dressed fairy purchase a diamond dewdrop necklace, handing over five gold pieces to a gleeful dwarf, who had a choice array of sparkling gems displayed on a mini Ferris wheel by his cart.

Hatchet's eyes nearly popped out of his head at the sight of the gold, the jewels and the beautiful fairy combined, but he walked on by with Felicity who, in turn, envied the fairy her gorgeous piece of jewellery.

'What about finding some food?' she asked the hobgoblin. 'Aren't you hungry? I can smell something wonderful. In fact, lots of lovely smells seem to be coming from over there. Let's go and see if we can get something.'

They were just approaching what appeared to be a bakery, where a plump, red-faced dame was busily piling pancakes onto a large plate, when Felicity stopped in her tracks and slapped her forehead.

'I almost forgot!' she exclaimed. 'I have the magic plate and goblet for food. We certainly don't need to waste our money *buying* anything. I can just ask the crockery for it!'

Hatchet looked confused and Felicity grinned. 'Come on,' she said. 'I'll show you.'

They ate a little distance away from the traders, under a shady tree which gave them a good view of Any-Ware. Felicity, inspired by the old dame they had passed, asked for hot pancakes with lemon and sugar and bacon, along with fresh, creamy milk to drink, and she and Hatchet tucked in hungrily. The hobgoblin looked as if he hadn't eaten a square meal in months. Afterwards, they shared a huge slice of rhubarb pie and then sat back against the rough tree trunk, savouring the moment.

'Do you think the witch will come after us?' Felicity asked, watching an elf try on some incredibly long pointed shoes.

'No, I don't think so – not immediately anyway,' said Hatchet. 'She'll sleep all the day and then do whatever it is she was talking about tonight – I don't know what or where that is – so she certainly won't waste her time tracking *me* down.'

'Well, that's something at least,' said Felicity. 'I mean, that she won't be coming after us at once. It gives us a head start and is one less problem for us to worry about. Now all I have to do is find the Riddler and give him this crystal ball (that's hoping I have what he asked for), get my third and final riddle, solve it, find Bob and the pebbles and save the day for the Pebble People, and then go home.' She frowned, her brow furrowing. 'Nothing much then!'

Hatchet, however, looked distinctly cheerful. 'I'm just happy to be free!' he said. 'And I'll help you.'

There it was – all that fretting and Felicity realised she should also be feeling happy for being free as well. Not only free, but *safe* now too. She should be grateful. She *was* grateful! Something which had been nipping at the edge of her thoughts, however, now crept back into her mind.

'Hatchet – do you know anything about those staircases near the witch's spire?' she asked. 'Do you know where they lead to?'

'I think the witches sometimes meet there to work magic, but I have no idea where they go,' said her friend. 'Sorry.'

'What about the witch?' said Felicity. 'When I turned up it sounded as if she'd been expecting another crow to bring her something. Do you know what that was?'

'I certainly do!' said Hatchet. 'And I'm glad she didn't get it, although the crow may still have found its way back to her. My mistress – former mistress – is aeons old and to travel beyond her spire for any length of time now she needs a special elixir to give her the strength to do it. The spell which makes this requires certain powerful ingredients and, because she never wanted to let me out of her sight, she sent crows to fetch her the things she needed. The potion itself usually makes her look a little younger as well, so she won't be happy if she can't brew it up. She won't last long on the ground without it!'

Felicity grimaced. 'It all sounds a bit ghoulish to me,' she said, shuddering. 'Almost like bringing a corpse back to life! Anyway, whether she's coming after us or not, we'd better get moving,' she said, brushing some stray crumbs from her clothes and standing up.

Once the enchanted crockery had worked its magic and cleaned itself up, Felicity popped it all back in her bag. Then they slipped back into the busy crowd once more, glancing curiously at the various new stalls and traders they passed. They saw a skinny witch girl selling equally skinny pink rats' tails from one stall, while an elf had a little table filled with fairy buns dipped in snow-white icing and decorated with sparkling pink sprinkles on another.

At one point, they noticed a strange crooked man peddling long, hooked walking sticks and Felicity watched in surprise as an old woman picked one up only for it to turn into a snake and slither away. The old woman shrieked and threw the man an angry look, but he simply handed her another stick with a sly grin and this one behaved itself.

On they walked, gentle pipe music now drifting in and around the other sounds of Any-Ware. Everything was so colourful, the folk so, well, *magical*, that Felicity couldn't help but stare. However, she knew they didn't have time to hang around and so she made a beeline for what looked like the exit, leaving the eclectic traders and their interesting customers behind.

They left Any-Ware under the shadow of two more huge gates, this time made of dark ebony, then stopped in a small, secluded clearing sheltered on either side by thick, waxy bushes. What now?

Perhaps the crystal ball could give her some answers before the Riddler arrived. Pulling it out of her bag, Felicity was going to ask it about the pebbles when Bob popped into her head again. She really wanted to know where her friend had disappeared to, so she cleared her throat.

'Where is my friend Bob the Brownie? Please – show him to me clearly. Thank you.'

At once, the crystal clouded over so that it was almost white, before this gradually faded away to reveal trees – lots of trees – and walking through them was Bob.

'He looks like he's in the forest!' Felicity exclaimed. 'He must have found his way there after all. Thanks for showing me, crystal ball. I wish he'd find us, but he's back there – and we've travelled far to Any-Ware.' She frowned and glanced around as the ball began to clear.

Just then a pair of long, knobbly hands snatched it from her grasp. Felicity gasped and looked up to see the Rhyming Riddler's smug face staring back at her from the middle of the bushes.

'Not so fast, my dear,' he said. 'Don't need you using up all the magic here. Well done, though, I say – well done! You solved your second rhyme … and in the nick of time.' He waggled a finger at her. 'But the ball is for *me*. For you, my dear – let's see. A riddle, I think, to bring you back from the brink.'

'Do you have to rhyme *all* the time?' said Felicity crossly. 'And I wasn't using up all the magic – I just wanted to find out about the pebbles. It's tragic –'

'Pebbles, pebbles, *pebbles*. Taken by the rebels,' said the Rhyming Riddler. '*You're* helping the Pebble People, not I. So don't you use my crystal ball to scry!' He looked gleefully at her.

'OK, OK – if that's what you say,' said Felicity, growing more and more annoyed by the second. 'You won't help with the pebbles, so tell me quick. What's the next riddle? What's the next trick?'

The Riddler somersaulted out of the hedge and into the clearing. Felicity was surprised at how spry he was but then remembered he was magic.

'For this endeavour, you must be clever,' said the Riddler.

'I *can* be clever,' Felicity said firmly.

'Fast of speed and slow to greed,' he went on.

Felicity looked at him impatiently, willing him to get on with it but biting her tongue. Not annoying the fairy folk was her new thing. 'OK,' sighed the Riddler. 'You have no pen – so listen up then!

*'When rocks seem wrong, when perspective is gone,*

*When a cliff isn't always a cliff.*

*There you will find a secret untold and a legend, they say,*
*of a tiff.*

*Beware when you're there of who you might meet and*
*always look out for the feet …*

*Be they friend or foe, well, nobody knows,*

*And therein lies a win or defeat!*

'OK,' the Rhyming Riddler clapped his hands, 'that's all, folks!'

And he was gone.

## Chapter Twenty-Nine
# Galloping Gallitraps

After yet another hasty exit from the Riddler, Felicity felt more than a little fed up. He'd taken the crystal ball before she could use it to find out more about the pebbles. Perhaps she should have asked the magical object about them first, but she'd been so anxious about Bob. What now, though? They had the map to direct them – they just still didn't know where they needed to be directed *to*.

'OK, we both have no idea what the riddle refers to, am I right?' she said.

Hatchet nodded.

'So … we can either go back to Any-Ware and find someone to help us, or we can press on and hope we bump into someone along the way. *Or* we can wait here and work out what it means ourselves.' She sighed. The idea of going back the way they'd come didn't particularly appeal.

'I think moving forward is better,' she said, decided upon the matter. 'We might not know exactly where we're headed but we won't get any closer to our destination by backtracking.'

Feeling more in control having made the decision, Felicity gathered her things together and looked to the sky. It was already darkening and it gave her the chills. Another day almost past. How many was that now since she'd been here and how much time did it mean she'd lost back home?

If only they knew where the witches' meeting was taking place – and what they were planning. In the meantime, they would just have to keep moving and see where that took them. And so, Felicity and Hatchet left the clearing and made their way into the woods which stretched just beyond.

'Fairyland certainly seems to have a lot of trees and woodland,' said Felicity, as they picked their way over fallen bits of branches and onto a winding rabbit path.

'All the better for folk to mix together in secret and make magic,' said Hatchet knowingly. 'And of course, most fairies live underground – beneath and inside the trees, hidden from sight – and where better than in a dark, secluded forest or wood? Such areas also grow a lot of food and provide valuable natural ingredients for spells and potions, and they supply countless flowers for fairy dresses, so they're incredibly important to all of the folk.'

'When you put it like that it makes perfect sense,' said Felicity, wondering what sort of flower *she* would pick for her own fairy dress if she was an elf or pixie. A satiny yellow tulip, perhaps – or a scarlet foxglove …

'Will *you* live in a wood then? When this is all over?' she asked.

'I think perhaps a cool little cave somewhere by the sea would suit me better,' said Hatchet. 'But we'll see.'

They walked on in comfortable silence, deep in their own thoughts – Felicity running over the riddle again and again in her head so she wouldn't forget it. The afternoon wore on and they stopped briefly for food before travelling onwards, each apprehensive about what might be around the corner. Soon dusk crept in around them and when they finally stopped the stars were piercing the sky overhead. They'd left the wood behind and were now in open moorland – dark, deserted and more than a little dreary. The air was laced with the smell of damp moss and rich, wormy mud.

Although night was steadily deepening, they decided to walk a little further to see if they could find shelter. They were thinking of settling down anyway, shelter or not, when the sound of tiny hoof-beats came trip-trapping over the still air.

'Pixies,' whispered Hatchet.

***

Felicity scoured the open landscape, but she couldn't see any of the little folk around them. Yet she could quite clearly hear the gentle pounding of hoof-beats in the distance.

'Why can't I see them?' she asked in a hushed voice. 'Can you? They sound so close.'

'I can't see them yet,' said Hatchet. 'But they're here all right, galloping on their horses, and I think it would be best to avoid them if we can. Tricksy pixies – they like to lead travellers astray and if you step inside the pixie ring you'll be taken prisoner. You can't trust them.'

'Oh, well, let's avoid them then,' said Felicity. 'Much as I'd like to catch a glimpse of them on their tiny horses, I'd really rather not be held prisoner again!'

Unable to see where exactly the pixies were, Felicity and Hatchet edged carefully away from where they imagined the hoof-beats were coming from. The only problem was, each time they thought they'd successfully evaded the riders, the pounding of hooves would start up again nearby.

'It's no use,' groaned Hatchet. 'They must have spotted us long ago and have been playing with us all the time we've been trying to slip past. We aren't inside the pixie circle yet or we'd be able to see them. The pixies call them 'gallitraps' and use them for racing their horses and ponies, so they're a bit bigger than ordinary fairy rings, which makes it more difficult to know if you're in one!'

Felicity didn't like the sound of that. 'I assume you become their prisoner only if you step fully inside the circle?' she asked.

Hatchet nodded. 'One foot inside allows you to see them, though, with or without their glamour up,' he said. 'If you're outside the ring they decide how and when you see them. Put both feet in, however, and you'll be trapped and at their mercy.'

Felicity sighed. She didn't want to be a prisoner again. Why on earth were the folk here so obsessed with capturing people anyway?

'How can we find them?' she said. 'If we know where exactly they are, then we can avoid them better. Wait a minute.' She'd just had a thought. 'I have some St John's Wort. We can each wear some of it and it will protect us from the pixie magic.'

'It's worth a try,' said Hatchet. 'But first we need to find the gallitrap. Do you have anything else that might help?' Felicity fumbled in her bag and then spotted the jar of ointment Mezra had given her.

'This!' she said triumphantly. 'If we rub it in our eyes it will reveal any glamours, so surely it will let us see the pixies if they're under a glamour?'

'I should think it will!' said Hatchet. 'Let's try it. The sooner we see them the better, as I dislike all of this masquerading and disguise.'

Felicity took some ointment from the jar and rubbed a little on each eyelid. Hatchet did likewise. And when they opened their eyes, there were the pixies.

***

Closer than Felicity had expected, the pixies raced around the gallitrap – which was huge – in steady streams just beyond them, swarming over what had appeared to be bare, scrubby moorland encased in nothing but murky darkness just seconds before. It was now alive with pixie riders and their assorted mass of ponies and horses – lanterns swinging from tall, thin sticks held by some of the riders to guide them. They flowed past Felicity like a vast rushing river – an unstoppable force.

The pixies themselves looked as wild as anything. They had flame-red hair and were dressed in browns and blacks and greens, blending in with both their surroundings and their mounts. Whooping and calling to one another, they urged their animals on faster and faster, taking no notice, or so it seemed, of Felicity and Hatchet. Some carried tiny whips, which sliced through the air, whistling as they went, such was the speed at which the pixies flung them to and fro. Meanwhile, the ponies pounded on, whinnying and kicking up their heels.

Felicity carefully pulled apart the St John's Wort necklace and formed two small bracelets, which she and Hatchet each put on.

'They're impatient are pixies,' said Hatchet. 'So perhaps we'd better just wait until they move on – they're bound to tire soon, especially once they sense the St John's Wort and know we're protected. Oh, and I just remembered, you should turn your cloak inside-out – just in case – as it will help to protect you from any of their mischief if they try to make you lose your bearings.'

'Well, I'm lost anyway, but I'll do it all the same,' said Felicity, turning her cloak the other way around. 'Actually – as we *are* lost, I have a bit of an idea. Couldn't we enter the gallitrap and borrow two of their ponies for a while? It would help us travel faster and if the pixies are moving on soon, then they might lead us somewhere useful. We really could do with some help – any help. Also, the gallitrap would camouflage us better if there are witches flying overhead. What do you think?'

Felicity looked at Hatchet with excited eyes. The hobgoblin looked nervous, but then gave a shaky grin. 'OK – I'm in,' he said.

'Take my hand,' said Felicity, who was both nervous and excited. It was a risk, but one she felt sure was right to take.

Hatchet gripped her hand tight in his bony fingers. They looked at one another encouragingly and then jumped into the pixie ring.

***

Inside the gallitrap Felicity and Hatchet were surrounded by high-pitched shouts and whoops, along with the swirl of activity made by charging horses and ponies. Now the size of the pixies themselves, they stayed close to the edge of the ring, but a grinning pixie had spotted them and came riding over with two ponies.

'Here you go!' he said. 'Come and race with us – we're just about to head off.' He frowned as he noticed Felicity's cloak and their bracelets, then gave them a sly grin. 'Come!' He turned tail and disappeared back into the pixie throng.

Felicity glanced at Hatchet as she patted a chestnut pony with a white blaze on its forehead. Hatchet approached the other, a dappled grey which head-butted his shoulder playfully before the hobgoblin leapt up onto its bare back. Felicity struggled to do the same, but with a little considerate kneeling from her pony, she too was soon safely astride.

She gripped the sides of her mount tightly with her legs and threaded her fingers firmly through its soft mane. She was ready. She had no idea where the ponies would take them but their energy was infectious and she felt excitement grip her. The pixie riders, she now noticed, were indeed beginning to move off, breaking away from their circular gallop and charging straight ahead. Before Felicity had time to urge her pony onwards, it had trotted off to join them.

Once they were in amongst the pixies, there was no hope of Felicity and Hatchet talking to one another, so they each tried to steer their ponies closer together to avoid being separated. They continued like this for quite a while, the scenery a dark blur around them, so Felicity couldn't be sure where they were – the moor, a forest, field or wood. All she knew was that the ponies were galloping faster than she could have imagined and she had to hold on for dear life. Her hair was ripped back from her face – her inside-out cloak billowing like a ship's sail – and she felt almost delirious with the speed and the whooping of the pixies and the sheer magic of it all.

Despite this, however, she was glad when the ponies started to slow to a canter, then a trot and, finally, to a brisk walk. Her cheeks were flushed from the journey, her hair tangled and her heart racing. What now?

She didn't have to wait long to find out, as she saw the pixies were now herding their ponies into pairs, in preparation for crossing a bridge up ahead. Hatchet and Felicity positioned themselves just in time to make sure they were side by side when their turn came.

They were at the edge of a high, rocky cliff and would have to make their way carefully across a narrow bridge of rock. Felicity was worried the ponies might slip on the smooth stone but they seemed to manage all right, so she just gripped her pony's mane tighter and tried not to feel queasy about the breathtaking but terrifying views, as there was a sheer vertical drop on either side of them.

Below, foamy waves smashed against glassy rocks, flecks of foam drifting up from time to time to settle on the riders as they made the perilous crossing. Felicity could just make out the open sea at one end of the ravine and gave up trying to think how travelling worked in the Fairy Realm. She was glad, however, to be back at the seaside, as it reminded her of home and made her even more determined to get back there.

The ponies trip-trapped over the bridge, all making it safely across to the other side, where the pixies had gathered in one huge mass. They seemed to be waiting for someone or for something to happen. This side of the cliff was grassy, with gentle green hills sloping away from them. Beyond that, Felicity couldn't begin to guess what lay ahead.

Thick darkness draped itself over the gathered assembly and Felicity and Hatchet made a point of keeping to the very edge of the throng, away from the lanterns and the main thrust of the crowd. They too waited expectantly, wondering what was about to happen.

Without warning, the pixies hushed and Felicity smelt a sharp earthiness – of freshly turned soil and moss – which seemed to seep into her every pore. A voice spoke up. It had an air of authority and was shrill yet firm at the same time.

'Listen up pixies!' it said loudly.

Felicity looked to see who was speaking but couldn't make out which direction the voice was coming from. It seemed to be everywhere at once.

'The situation is now more perilous than ever,' the mysterious voice continued. 'Pebbles are still going missing and I'm very sad to say that there are pixies here tonight who have had a hand in this wicked, deceptive behaviour.' Not a pixie moved or spoke. The atmosphere was strained, expectation suspended in the air, taut as a tightrope. 'We will find those pixies who betrayed the laws of the realm and endangered the folk within it and we will try them accordingly,' continued the voice. 'They will be imprisoned and, if all evidence is approved, their fate will then be decided.

'Anyone found here this night with pebbles in their possession will be sorely and justly punished. Let the searching begin!'

## Chapter Thirty
# Pixies and Pebbles

Felicity looked at Hatchet with horror, suddenly very conscious of the pebble in her bag. If the pixies discovered it, then what – imprisonment? Something worse? It didn't bear thinking about. They couldn't be caught.

'At least they aren't *all* in on it,' whispered Hatchet helpfully. 'Then we really *could* have been in trouble.'

'But we *are* in trouble, don't you see?' hissed Felicity. 'I still have my pebble from the Pebble People. It may have already worked its magic, but it certainly won't look very good.'

Hatchet's face fell and, despite the darkness, visibly paled just a little. Their ponies were standing side by side and Felicity leaned in again to whisper to the hobgoblin. 'What if we explain about what we're trying to do?' she said. 'Surely they'd have to believe us?'

'They don't *have* to believe or *do* anything,' said Hatchet. 'And by the tone of that voice, I don't think they're going to be in the mood to hear excuses from two people who are very obviously not pixies and who have tricked them with St John's Wort.'

'Who was that anyway?' said Felicity.

'It must be the pixie king,' whispered Hatchet. 'There's only one king of the Fairy Realm, but the pixies also have their own, though he still has to answer to the main one.'

'Well, I don't fancy meeting him,' Felicity whispered back. 'We'll just have to try to slip away while they're doing their search. We're close enough to the edge of the crowd, so we could sneak off if we're careful. It's dark enough that we might just manage it without being seen.'

That much was true, as the sky was a nightmarish black, with a fat, silver teardrop of a moon trickling only a faint glow onto the ground below.

'We'll have to leave the ponies, though,' said Hatchet. 'We don't want to anger the pixies even more by stealing from them!'

'OK,' said Felicity, although she would be sorry to say goodbye to her pony. It was a sweet, amiable animal and it had been nice to have a rest from walking all the time.

'Let's go then,' said Hatchet. 'Better make it quick!'

The pixies up ahead were moving aside to let what Felicity assumed was the pixie king pass, murmuring nervously as they did so. It wouldn't be long until they were discovered. They slid silently from their ponies and began to edge away from the throng. If they could just make their way over the hill lying a little way ahead then they would be concealed from view and could run without being seen. Getting to that point, however, would be a challenge. Indeed, as the pair tried to push past the few pixies in their way they soon found more than a little retaliation, as suspicious eyes turned on them. The pixies stood firmly against them and Felicity realised with a sinking feeling that they wouldn't be allowed past.

The pixies' eyes glinted darkly. At that moment, however, there was a shriek from another part of the crowd. A pixie must have been seized. It was a small disturbance but enough of a distraction for Felicity and Hatchet to break away from the little folk.

Felicity's heart raced as her legs pumped furiously to take her from the panicked pixies. She knew the St John's Wort had worked and that they'd crossed the gallitrap boundary when she realised she was back to her normal size again. Sensing Hatchet just behind her, she kept on running – over the hill and down the other side – arms flailing, her skirt and cloak streaming behind her as she went. The terrain here was sandy underfoot, yet grass also grew – tall, sharp grass which sliced at Felicity's fingers and stung her skin as she sped through it. The blades were almost waist-high and she thought they could fling themselves onto the ground and hide among it if needs be. It might buy them some time at least.

They ran through the grass for what felt like longer than it probably was, stumbling onto a narrow moonlit rabbit – or perhaps pixie – path that wound on and on. Felicity could still hear the sea, the aroma of salt suspended in the air and flooding her nostrils with the comforting smell of home. The dunes dipped and rolled ahead of them until, at last, they fanned out into open space. It was exposed but it was also dark and Felicity and Hatchet stopped to catch their breath, both tired from the exertions of their escape.

'Look,' said Hatchet, pointing. 'Two moons now.'

Felicity looked and, sure enough, a second moon had joined the silver teardrop one from before. The new moon was pale blue and hung right beside the other – like an eerie mismatched sibling.

'Once in a blue moon,' she murmured.

'What?' said Hatchet.

'Once in a blue moon,' Felicity repeated. 'It's a saying I've heard but I didn't think there actually *was* such a thing as a blue moon. I mean, no one's ever really seen one. It's just something people say – an expression – like, when something unusual happens or, I don't know, to refer to something that very rarely or never happens, you say "once in a blue moon".'

'Well, one thing's for sure,' said Hatchet. 'Even in this realm a blue moon isn't natural. We'd best not be out in the open if something's about to happen.'

'It must be to do with the dark forces being unleashed because of the pebbles,' said Felicity. 'A second moon from another place …'

She shivered, goosebumps pricking her arms and the nape of her neck despite her warm cloak, which she now turned back the way it was supposed to be worn. 'Right, let's go,' she said.

Walking briskly, the pair scoured the gloomy landscape as best they could for signs of shelter, but could see none. Felicity was worried. She really didn't want to have to sleep outdoors tonight, where anyone or anything could find them. At this moment she wanted more than anything to be back in her Granny Stone's cosy cottage, *hearing* about fairy stories instead of being *in* one.

'There!' said Hatchet, after they'd walked further on.

He pointed ahead of them, to the left. 'There's something over there – a building. Let's see what it is.'

As they got closer to the shadowy structure, Felicity thought it was a stone cottage, but then realised it was little more than a ramshackle out-house, long deserted.

A hawthorn tree grew to one side and Hatchet paled at the sight of it.

'What's wrong?' she said.

'The tree of the witch!' groaned the hobgoblin. 'That's what it is! We can't stay here if witches are about. Hawthorns are like signposts to them, and if they're going to stop anywhere, it's sure to be where these grow.'

He grabbed Felicity's arm and pulled her away. 'We must move on. Quickly!'

Disappointed they couldn't stay and sleep, but now worried about witches again, Felicity gladly followed her friend. They would just have to keep on running. And run they did, leaving the grassy fields behind and entering yet more wooded territory. Not long afterwards, Hatchet gave a sigh of relief.

'Look!' he said, grabbing Felicity's cloak to stop her. He pointed a little way off to their left. 'It's an oak tree – a safe haven for fairies. We've found our shelter for the night!'

'An oak?' said Felicity. 'How can that help us? Unless it's like the Great Oak I was in …'

'Not the same, no, but helpful nevertheless,' said Hatchet. 'All oak trees afford natural protection to the fairy folk from witches and the like – their magic can't work against the ancient powers of this hallowed protector. If we seek shelter here we'll certainly be safe overnight.'

They ran to the oak tree, which was fairly large but nothing compared to the Great Oak. Felicity guessed that *that* magnificent tree, however, was one of a kind.

'I hope I remember how to do this,' muttered Hatchet. 'I only saw a friend do it once, before I was taken by the witch, but that was a long time ago.'

He rapped the trunk three times with his knuckles, then three times more, followed by a single knock and a whispered word. Nothing happened, so he did the same again, this time using a different word. After a few seconds the roots at the base parted, the earth fell away and an opening was revealed.

He grinned. 'After you!'

***

Despite the fact she was now underground yet again, Felicity was extremely glad to be safe, for a time at least, from the sneaking night outside and whoever happened to be lurking in it.

The tree trunk led them down into a dim tunnel, where roots brushed against Felicity's hair and a rich, earthy aroma once more flavoured the air. She seemed to have shrunk enough to fit the space and assumed it was all part of the oak's protective magic. After all, it couldn't protect folk if it couldn't accommodate them.

'Where will this lead us?' she asked Hatchet. She didn't really want a run-in with fairies of any kind right now – she just wanted to rest and refuel and try to work out what her third and final riddle meant.

'I can't be certain,' said the hobgoblin. 'But I sense that somebody has been along this way fairly recently. There's something else … I can't quite put my finger on it.'

'A paw would be better,' said a soft, muffled voice.

Felicity and Hatchet stopped in their tracks.

'Who said that?' said Felicity. 'Is someone there? We don't mean any harm. We just want shelter.'

'You're on a quest – two, in fact,' said the voice, which seemed to be coming from somewhere to their left, though Felicity could see no one.

'How do you know that?' she asked in surprise, her fear momentarily forgotten.

'You hear things down here,' said the voice. 'All sorts of things – Hunter.'

'Hunter? I'm no hunter!' said Felicity.

'You hunt for the pebbles. You hunt for those who stole them.

'You hunt for answers to your riddles. You *are* the Hunter and you'd better be quick, because they know you're coming and they aren't going to give up without a fight!'

'Who knows I'm coming? The witches? Please, come forward so I can at least see who I'm speaking to.'

Something in the darkness moved and two eyes appeared startlingly close to Felicity and Hatchet, who leapt back in surprise. As the figure shuffled forward from the shadows, Felicity could make out two long, upright ears and were those – *whiskers*?

'A rabbit!' announced Hatchet with relief. 'It's just a rabbit – thank goodness!'

'*Just* a rabbit! *Just* a rabbit!' exclaimed the furry mammal. 'Now hold on just a minute – who are *you* calling *just* a rabbit, *hob*goblin?'

'Wait, please. We don't want to fight with you, sir,' said Felicity, glaring at Hatchet as best she could in the gloom. 'I'd really like to find out more about what you've heard. Is there somewhere we could go to talk – away from the open tunnel, perhaps?'

'There might be,' sniffed the rabbit. 'My burrow – or one of them at least – isn't far from here. I heard you through the tunnels and came to see who it was. Apart from me, there haven't been many folk through here recently.'

'You heard us? How?' said Felicity, who thought they'd been moving quietly.

'Vibrations,' said the rabbit proudly. 'I could feel the vibrations you made as you walked. Now, follow me!'

Felicity caught a flash of bobtail and made after it as the rabbit disappeared down a tunnel off to the side. She hadn't even noticed there *were* any side tunnels, which made her wonder just who else might be watching and listening to them in secret.

They followed the rabbit quickly as he bounded along, their eyes well-adjusted now to the darkness. It wasn't long before they reached a burrow and were shepherded inside by their host. The interior was modest – a circular room neatly dug out of the soil and lightly strewn with fresh, clean straw, which carpeted the furthest section of the rabbit's home. An oil lamp cast soft shadows around them from an alcove in the wall. Other than that, the burrow was empty.

'So,' said the rabbit, once they'd gathered safely inside. 'What do you want to know?'

'As much as you can tell us, I suppose,' said Felicity, not quite sure where to start. There were so many questions she could and indeed probably *should* ask but, as often happened in these situations, her mind now failed to settle on any one of them.

'What did you mean about being quick?' she asked eventually. 'Is this to do with the witches' meeting we've heard about? Do they know where we are?'

The rabbit twitched his nose from side to side, long ears quivering.

'They don't know everything but they know enough,' he said finally. 'This oak – for we are still shielded by its roots – will help in fudging that knowledge, so they won't be able to detect where *exactly* you are. But rest assured, they *are* on the look-out for you and won't want you to stop them in their sorcery. And I don't just mean the witches.'

'Who else do you mean?' asked Felicity, a slight tremor creeping into her voice.

'Everyone and no one – some folk and no folk,' answered the rabbit cryptically.

'Now you sound like that wretched Riddler,' said Felicity in exasperation. 'Everyone but no one?'

'Well, I mean – it could be everyone, anyone, fairy folk or "no" folk. That is, well, animals. But not me, of course,' he added hastily.

'And how did *you* come to know of all this then?' said Hatchet. 'Of Felicity's quests and those seeking her out? The pebbles?'

'Everything travels underground,' said the rabbit knowingly. 'You should know that, hobgoblin. Fairies, elves, pixies, even goblins – *all* of them gossip. The birds, the breeze, the whispering trees … You would be surprised, human girl, who watches, listens and passes on messages. Forces seen and unseen, beings big and small – they see things and tell all.

'As for the pebbles, well, *everyone* knows about those by now, and a fair few more than you realise know the Pebble People summoned a human hunter to the realm. When you entered Fairyland and crossed the boundary between our worlds, it was sensed, my dear – not by all, but by enough. The most powerful and the tuned-in – the good and the bad.'

'I see,' said Felicity. She remembered Silvertoes and Mezra saying something similar. 'Well, what do you know about the missing pebbles and who might be behind all of this?'

'My cousins from the cliff have spoken of rebel rabbits joining forces with pixies and the like; of secret rendezvous taking place at various locations across the realm; of pebbles carefully gathered by the Collectors, otherwise known as the Smuggles, who serve the one behind it all. Whoever *that* might be …' said the rabbit.

'Of course, pebbles have been dropped during these exchanges and travels, with dire consequences for innocent fairy folk of the realm, while some of the thieves themselves have seemingly been spirited away through their carelessness.'

'The Collectors,' said Felicity. The name made them sound even more ominous.

'Do you know *why* they're stealing for this unknown person?'

'Perhaps for promises of power in exchange for the pebbles; perhaps in the hope that the one seeking the pebbles can help them find their missing relatives,' said the rabbit.

'It would explain why they are willing to risk their own safety. They are working separately from the witches and goblins, so it seems, though who is to know whom one can really trust? I know not if I should even trust you two, but I must. I must trust.'

'I should think so!' said Felicity. 'After all we've been through and still have to do. Of course you can trust us! But how do we know *you're* to be trusted rabbit?'

'It's Rufus, actually. And I wouldn't be telling you all this if I didn't know you were bona fide anyway,' he continued huffily. 'I was just saying – it's generally hard to identify the true of heart. Anyway, I *may* have some information on a recent pebble heist – if you're interested, of course.'

Felicity and Hatchet glanced at each other excitedly. 'We're interested!' they said in unison.

'Good,' said Rufus. 'Well, this recent incident involved pixies.'

Felicity nodded. She'd been expecting that, after what they'd just witnessed.

'It would appear,' said Rufus, 'that a small group of pixies was spotted with bags of pebbles just the other evening. The one who saw this wishes to remain anonymous, but I know him personally so you have no reason to doubt his word.

'The group will have moved on by now, of course, but I have news that one pixie has been spotted travelling alone with what appears to be a bag of pebbles. A risky move, as they require strong spells to be cast over them for safe transportation and a single pixie would find it hard to maintain these. Anyway, if the witches are having a meeting tonight, then all the better, for if they are distracted with that, then it will be easier for you to find this pixie, as he may well still be able to lead you to the one behind all of this.

'What I'm saying is this – you should follow him to the source of this mayhem, find the pebbles and defeat the perpetrator of these crimes!'

## Chapter Thirty-One
# Thistle Glen

Felicity wasn't sure what to make of Rufus' speech. For so long she'd been baffled about the pebbles and now here was a *rabbit* suddenly informing her he knew of a rogue pixie attempting to approach the source of all this mayhem – and they were to follow him!

'How do we know this isn't a trap and that you don't actually work for whoever's behind all of this?' she asked.

Rufus sighed. 'As I said before, you can trust me and it seems that you will just have to take my word on that. But you should know that most folk of the realm are outraged at what's been happening with the pebbles. Many have lost friends and family members to faraway lands and unknown magicks.

'They're constantly on the look-out for those stealing and moving the pebbles and most of this information travels, in some shape or form, down here – from the wind, the trees, the birds, the rabbits, fairies, elves and nymphs. A wizard here, an old crone there – whisperings have wings and so I have heard not only of the pixie, but also of you – as have the stealers of the stones. Only in such sacred, protected places as this oak are conversations ever truly concealed, but who knows what folk are lurking nearby even here?'

'To be honest, we don't have the time *not* to believe what you're saying,' said Felicity. 'With the witches' meeting tonight and with my third riddle still to solve, we need to do *some*thing.' She hesitated. 'Of course, Hatchet, you don't have to come with me. I don't want to put you in danger or make you feel obligated to help me.'

'I don't feel obligated,' said the little hobgoblin crossly. 'I want to help and I want to come with you. End of story.'

Felicity nodded. It was going to be another eventful night.

'So what now?' she asked Rufus. 'Where's this pixie and how do we find him to follow him?'

'By magic, of course,' said Rufus with a relieved smile and a twitch of his soft, snuffly nose. 'Time is of the essence. You must intercept the pixie at Thistle Glen and follow him to the source. Then it will be up to you to find a way to put an end to this pebble business. Sit close and sit still and I'll try to get you there.'

Felicity and Hatchet sat side by side on the straw-covered soil floor, wondering what magic the rabbit was about to perform.

'Now, don't move a muscle,' Rufus instructed them rather sternly. 'And close your eyes tight. You mustn't open them until you reach your destination. This is an old, old travelling spell known only to us animals and will feel very strange, but it only works if you let *it* move *you*.'

Felicity and Hatchet closed their eyes tight. Felicity had already experienced various forms of travel in the realm – what could possibly be next?

Rufus was silent, then began to chant in a low voice – words Felicity couldn't understand but which the rabbit uttered faster and faster, his voice becoming more and more frenzied as he continued rattling out the magic. She felt her body becoming lighter, weightless even, as if she was floating. It was quite a relaxing sensation. Her legs, arms and body seemed to sift and swirl through the air of their own accord and soon the coolness of the night kissed her skin. They were outside.

Delightfully dizzy, Felicity happily succumbed to the forces carrying her along, twisting and turning her in the breeze as she floated in the star-studded sky. If she had been on the ground below, her reaction may have been a little less relaxed, however, as to the watchful eyes of a prowling fox, she appeared only as a sparkling stream of particles spinning above and out of sight. But Felicity and Hatchet had no idea of the forces at hand and so enjoyed the spell until it was done and they swirled back down to earth, settling softly onto the ground. To any observers, it was as though two gusts of stardust had spiralled down to the earth. Felicity stretched and let out a yawn. She felt comfortable enough to sleep but Hatchet poked her in the ribs, jolting her back to alertness.

'We're here,' he whispered.

She sat up. They'd landed in the middle of a thistle patch. So this was Thistle Glen. Now to find the pixie. It seemed like the longest of long nights and she just wanted to get on with it: follow the pixie and find the pebbles – and whoever was behind all of this mayhem. What she would do then, well, she didn't quite know but she *did* know one thing – situations had a habit of working themselves out and, somehow, this must be resolved.

The thistles were bathed in silver moonshine and grew thickly around them. Felicity and Hatchet were, however, conveniently placed at what appeared to be the entrance, or at least *an* entrance, to the glen. Hopefully they would catch sight of the pixie as he passed by. Felicity was sure Rufus' magic would have taken them as close as possible to whoever they were meant to follow. She just hoped they were on time. In the end, they didn't have long to wait.

Hatchet had barely scrambled onto his hunkers to peep through the thistles when a tiny figure appeared a little way off on a stony path which entered the glen not far from where they were hidden. It descended into a wilderness of thick, tall thistles – and who knew what else.

Felicity and Hatchet had no idea where the little creature had come *from* – they simply became aware of a pointed pixie silhouette standing at the top of the sloping path, as if contemplating whether to go on with his journey or to retreat. A small, bulky sack was slung over his back.

And then the decision seemed to have been made. The pixie gave a last lingering look behind him, then turned back towards the glen and strode confidently, if just a *little* warily, forward.

'OK, this is it – be quiet and be careful,' warned Felicity. 'It's time to find the source!'

***

The pixie was intent on getting through the glen as quickly as possible, that much was obvious and ultimately in their favour, as he hurried along without taking much notice of his surroundings after that initial hesitation. Felicity was glad, as when the time came to slip out from their hiding place and follow him, they were able to do so without being detected. They made sure to stay as far as possible behind him, just keeping the little figure in their sight as they moved parallel through the thistles, suffering a few scratches along the way.

The glen was aptly named, as tall thistles grew thick and strong right the way through it, with small openings and the indentations of trampled plants suggesting others had recently passed this way.

The night had just enough background noise to mask any rustlings Felicity and Hatchet might have been making. A growing breeze breathed life into the thistles, their stalks swaying and waltzing in the moonlight. Occasionally a hunting owl could be heard far off, its shrieks slicing through the air like poison-tipped arrows. A barn owl, perhaps – with the screech of a banshee and the face of a ghost. It reminded Felicity of her earlier encounter with the actual banshee and she shuddered, skin prickling.

As they approached the outer edge of the glen, the thistles began to thin out and so too did their cover. The glen ended at what appeared to be a wall of impenetrable rock, but as they drew closer, a dark archway loomed in the middle. The pixie strode on determinedly, never once glancing behind him, so Felicity and Hatchet were easily able to slip in after him.

It was instantly colder here and somewhere nearby Felicity could hear water trickling. The old night-time noises from before had been replaced by the squeaks of bats as they flitted to and fro amid the inky gloom. The pixie splashed on up ahead of them, and soon Felicity and Hatchet were also treading in the icy-cold water of a stream, which flowed across their path.

Once through the archway, the landscape was even more rugged and wild than before, and it was peppered with differently sized slopes and hills, lots of winding rabbit paths and thick bushes with needle-sharp thorns. It was somewhere designed to get lost in, Felicity thought.

They followed the pixie at a respectable distance, trailing him up slopes and along stony paths as he weaved in and out of the bushes. The route became more and more twisted, however, and Felicity and Hatchet briefly lost sight of him as he rounded a sharp bend. By the time they had done the same, the pixie had vanished. A tall, dense hedge towered menacingly before them, dark and green and foreboding.

'Where did he go?' said Felicity in exasperation. 'He can't just have disappeared!'

'He must have gone in through here,' said Hatchet, pointing at the hedge.

Felicity couldn't see an opening, but it did seem to be the only place he could have gone.

'Well then,' she said. 'It looks as if we'll just have to go in after him!'

### Chapter Thirty-Two
# Through the Labyrinth

A s soon as Felicity touched the seemingly impenetrable, waxy leaves of the hedge, they parted easily, allowing both her and Hatchet to slip through.

All was quiet around them, as if the night-time noises had been commanded to hush here – their sounds muffled by the thick, bushy walls. Felicity had a sneaking suspicion they were in some sort of labyrinth, as straight silvery paths lay to the left and the right of them, with hedges running as far as she could see in both directions tapering off into darkness.

She looked at Hatchet. 'Er, which way do you think we should go?' The little hobgoblin stared back at her blankly.

'Well, I think we're in a labyrinth and you normally have to find the centre of those, right? So what if the pixie is on his way there? What happens at the centre of a labyrinth?'

'I don't know,' said Hatchet. 'I wish I could be of more help, but I don't know.'

'I guess there's only one way to find out!' said Felicity, sounding more confident than she felt. 'Let's go right, then. Both ways look the same so it's as good a choice as any.'

They walked briskly down the path for a bit, neither speaking – both intent on their task. Felicity was impatient, though, and worried they might miss the pixie.

'Why is it just straight?' she asked finally. 'Shouldn't a labyrinth twist and turn – try to confuse us? This is just leading us in a straight line to nowhere. We can't find the centre without turning in somewhere, surely.'

'How about there?' said a voice.

'Or over there?' said another.

'Or anywhere?' said a third – or was it the first voice again? Felicity couldn't tell.

She looked to see who had spoken but there was no one.

'There!' said Hatchet, pointing to the bottom of the labyrinth hedge on their left.

Hidden under the leaves were two tiny imps, both staring solemnly up at Felicity and Hatchet. They were no taller than a very tall toadstool and were dressed all in black, with eyes like chips of charcoal, sharp features and little black pointed hats and shoes. One held a tiny lantern.

'Do you know the way through the labyrinth?' Felicity asked them, both amused and curious about the little creatures. They were twig-like and had a look of mischief about them, so she knew at once she would have to take anything they said with a pinch of salt.

'We don't know *the* way,' said one imp.

'But we do know *a* way,' said the other immediately.

'Which way do *you* want?' asked the first imp, wriggling his little eyebrows at Felicity.

'Well, you only appear to know one way – *a* way,' said Felicity, suppressing a smile. 'So I guess that would be the one I'd like to know, please.'

'As you say then,' said the imps together, jumping in glee. They pointed at Felicity.

'Look hard enough, human girl and you'll soon see – the labyrinth ain't always what it appears to be! Just walk on through but be careful when you do … for the labyrinth is full of hullabaloo!'

They scurried back under the hedge again before Felicity could ask them exactly what they meant, but then she had an idea. 'They must mean there are concealed gaps and entrances through the hedges,' she said. 'We just haven't been able to spot them because they're so cleverly camouflaged!'

'I think you might be right,' said Hatchet. 'I'll have a look over here and you check your side and let's see if we can find an opening. There must be one somewhere around here.'

It was Hatchet who found the hidden entryway and much more quickly than they expected. He gave a shout of glee just moments after they began searching and Felicity ran over to where he was standing proudly.

She didn't see anything, but she knew by now that in the Fairy Realm that didn't necessarily mean something wasn't there. Sure enough, Hatchet crouched down and crept through a round hole cut carefully into the hedge. It was so well done that it was no wonder they hadn't seen it or any others so far. Not wasting any time, Felicity crawled through after the hobgoblin and was surprised to see that, instead of hedge, red-bricked walls now mapped out the labyrinth, the walls seeming to emit a ghostly glow to light the way. The ground too was paved, but with a mosaic of different coloured and oddly sized bricks.

This time, there was no doubt they were inside a labyrinth, as three possible routes lay ahead. They settled upon the one directly in front of them, Felicity figuring that it looked as if it was pointed towards the centre, or where she thought that might be anyway. They didn't want to stop for food, but she asked her crockery for some water and chocolate-chip cookies to keep them going as they walked.

The path twisted and turned quite a bit, colourful flowers and plants poking out from various parts of the crumbling labyrinth walls. A large red flower unfurled its petals as they passed and Felicity hesitated when she saw a bright blue butterfly rise up from within it. It flapped its wings when it spotted the girl staring, rearing up to show off an underbelly of orange crescents and black spots. It tutted at Felicity.

'Never a moment's peace around here,' said the butterfly huffily. 'Too many folk disturbing the peace in this labyrinth for my liking. And who might *you* be?'

'I'm Felicity,' she said in surprise. 'And this is –'

The butterfly interrupted her with another wing flap. 'Never mind who you are. Just please stop thundering about in my home and move along. You're the second to disturb me tonight.'

The butterfly's words gave Felicity hope that they were going in the right direction. Indeed, as she turned away from the flower it appeared that *was* the case, as she found herself staring straight into the inquisitive eyes of the pixie.

\*\*\*

Felicity looked at Hatchet. Now what? Before she or the hobgoblin could say anything, however, the pixie spoke.

'Come closer – I don't want anyone to hear us,' he said. 'Walls have ears, you know – and more besides.'

For want of any other option, Felicity and Hatchet huddled in close.

'OK,' said the pixie quietly, looking from one to the other. 'You were following me, correct?'

Felicity and Hatchet exchanged a glance. That much was fairly obvious, so they both nodded reluctantly.

'Well, I *knew* that anyway,' said the pixie. 'Did you honestly think I wouldn't notice you, especially considering where I'm headed?' He shook his head in bewilderment. 'Next question. You want to get to the Mystical Mansion?'

Again, Felicity and Hatchet nodded. So *that* was their destination.

'Well, it looks like we're going the same way then.' The pixie grinned, startling Felicity. Perhaps he thought they were thieves as well.

He had warm brown eyes, which reminded her of someone, but Felicity knew she certainly hadn't met him before and she most definitely remembered *everyone* she had met in the realm so far.

'To get there we must find the centre of the labyrinth, so let's do that and then we can talk further,' said the pixie. 'It's safer there.' Unsure of what magic the pixie had at his disposal, Felicity decided the best thing would be to do as he said. After all, they *did* need to get to this Mystical Mansion, if that's where the pebble thieves took their pebbles.

'OK,' she said. 'If we're all going the same way ...' She gave Hatchet a reassuring smile, hoping he would play along.

'Just don't try anything,' said the hobgoblin. 'We have magic and we *will* use it on you if you do anything funny.'

The pixie didn't look very convinced by that, but he nodded. 'Let's go then,' he said. 'This way, I think.'

With no option but to trust the pixie traitor-turned-ally, Felicity and Hatchet trooped silently after him as he led the pair through the enchanted labyrinth. He was silent from thereon in, intent upon navigating them through the many twists and turns they encountered. Felicity saw a lot of strange things along the way and sensed many more, so she was glad they had a guide, even if she wasn't quite sure whether to trust him or not.

Strange shadows scuttled around corners, while mutterings and whisperings could be heard now and again, though their messages were indecipherable. She could have sworn the paving was also rearranging itself as they walked, for when she glanced back on one or two occasions, the path looked very different from before. It could quite easily trick someone into going the wrong way and getting hopelessly lost.

At one point, a gnarled gnome scurried past them in the opposite direction, muttering distractedly and looking none of them in the eye. Another time, they turned a sharp corner and almost walked right off the edge of the path.

'How can a maze have a vertical drop in the middle of it?' muttered Felicity angrily, even though she knew the answer, of course – magic.

As they moved deeper within the living labyrinth – which gradually became a mass of leaves and bushes once more – parts of it reached for the three travellers as they passed, thin and twisted branches tangling themselves in Felicity's hair and snagging on her cloak.

'Don't let them get a grip,' their guide warned without looking back. 'Or you'll disappear off into the walls of the labyrinth and never return!'

Felicity hurriedly disentangled herself and kept well away from the sides of the path. Finally, after walking in a tight spiral which became gradually narrower and narrower, the trio arrived at what she assumed – and hoped – was the centre.

It was. 'Here we are,' said the pixie triumphantly and with obvious relief.

'Now for the hard part – tackling the Mystical Mansion.'

The labyrinth's core was star-shaped rather than circular, with what appeared to be a carousel in the middle.

'Right, now we choose a carousel character, hop on board and hope they take us where we want to go,' said the pixie, more cheerful now.

'But first …' He looked at Felicity, eyes crinkling kindly. 'Now that we are briefly protected here at the heart of the labyrinth – where the magic is strongest and acts as a barrier to outside ears – I can reveal that I am, in fact, travelling incognito and have a story to tell once our work is done. For now, though, suffice it to say …' He leaned close to Felicity. 'I'm Bob!'

Felicity stared incredulously at the pixie as he stepped away from her. How could *this* be Bob? But then, maybe the question she should be asking was why *couldn't* it be Bob? This *was* the Fairy Realm after all – a land where magical masquerades were rife. She knew she'd recognised those brown eyes. If it *was* him, then they had much to talk about. She looked at Hatchet, who shrugged.

'I know it's hard to believe, but it's true,' said the pixie, or Bob. 'We don't have time to talk much now – let's get to the Mystical Mansion first, for it is on the move and might disappear again before we get to it. If *that* happens, then we really *are* in trouble!'

Felicity nodded, her mind swimming with questions for her friend, if it truly was him. They would have to wait, however. Her instincts told her he was telling the truth, though, and that would have to be enough for now. She would have to trust *herself* on that one.

'Magical masquerade.' Bob grinned.

Felicity smiled. It did *sound* like her friend. Suppressing her burning curiosity, she asked him where the mansion was now, as they boarded the carousel.

Bob chose a green spotted horse with a blue mane, which whickered as he settled himself on its back. Felicity made her selection more carefully when she realised the animals were animated, if not quite fully alive. She picked a friendly looking white-winged pony, while Hatchet jumped onto a pink flamingo. All avoided the beautiful but intimidating Bengal tiger, the fluffy ostrich, an ill-tempered hump-backed camel and a miniature dragon – purple and green and puffing out tiny plumes of smoke from its nostrils.

As the carousel began to pick up speed and fairy pipes softly fluted, Bob answered Felicity's question.

'At the minute,' he said, 'the Mystical Mansion is on the Scary Islands, so – to the Scarys!' The carousel lurched forward with a jolt and Felicity, Hatchet and Bob only just had time to fling their arms around the necks of their animals to stay on.

The music grew wilder as it picked up, the carousel spun round at a dizzying speed and Felicity wondered just what would they find in a Mystical Mansion on the Scary Islands?

## Chapter Thirty-Three
# The Mystical Mansion

Their ride on the carousel didn't last very long, something Felicity was glad of, as the spinning was making her feel a bit nauseous. It gradually dropped its heady pace, becoming slower and slower until, at last, it shuddered to a halt. Bob scrambled off first.

'Quick,' he hissed. 'Before it takes off again!'

Already, Felicity could hear the music starting up once more and she quickly hopped off her pony, Hatchet following close behind. She watched as the carousel picked up speed, a white cloud gathering around it as it spun, until the ride was completely hidden from sight. Then the music stopped, the cloud cleared and the carousel was gone.

It had brought them, Felicity assumed, to the Scary Islands and it looked much bleaker than any part of the realm she'd visited so far. The ground was rocky, with a thin layer of scrubby grass, and the general terrain seemed full of barren hills and slopes and not much else. Did anyone live here, she wondered, and where was the Mystical Mansion in this desolate place?

Bob beckoned them over. It was still strange for Felicity to think of this pixie as her brownie friend and she was keen to have him change back to his original, familiar form.

'We must hurry. The Mystical Mansion will be at the very centre of the islands – we're on the main one. No one lives here except for a few rabbits and no one really visits much except for the seabirds, on account of the, ah, the ghosts and what not.' He glanced at Felicity, who grimaced as he continued.

'The Scary Islands are so called because they harbour all sorts of undesirables from the supernatural world – lost souls who would rather haunt a clutch of deserted islands and lament over their lives than be of any use to the rest of the realm or lie in peace.

'They'll entice any wayward traveller with their tales of woe, and once they have you in their icy death grip, they won't let you go.

'They cross over once a year, on All Hallows' Eve, to the human world – no one can catch *them*, you see, as they would fairies – and from midnight till dawn they search for souls to take. They send people mad and make them so full of fear that they lose themselves to the ghouls of the Scary Islands.'

Felicity shivered. The island was silent as a tomb, the stars stitched into the inky sky shedding little light on the small party. The moon still glowed but threw only a cold, grey glimmer down at them, while the blue moon seemed to shed none.

'In the very middle of this part of the Scarys is a huge hollow,' said Bob. 'It isn't visible until you're standing at the top looking down on it, and that's where the Mystical Mansion will be, cleverly hidden from view on an island no one ever dares visit, in a spot even fewer know about. Or so I'm led to believe, anyhow. Word has it the Mystical Mansion never stays anywhere for too long these days, so we must hurry.'

They followed Bob in single file as he led them across the island, Felicity fearful that at any minute they would encounter one of the spirits or ghosts he had spoken of. They didn't, but she was sure she could hear distant moans and wails drifting through the night air as she hurried on after her friend.

She realised that she still didn't know where Bob had gone when they separated at the cairns, so she asked him about that now, moving up beside him. 'I saw you once or twice,' she said. 'In the Great Oak and through a crystal ball. I wasn't sure where you were exactly, but at least I knew you were safe.' So Bob told his tale as they trudged onwards, and Felicity and Hatchet listened, rapt, as he spoke of how the portal had taken him, not to the Enchanted Forest, but to the Enchanted *Wood*, known for its Moonlight Markets and Starlight Dances. Where the Enchanted Forest was black and shadowy and home to dark elves and wicked fairies, the Enchanted Wood housed more pleasant creatures – though they were still prone to trickery, of course. This wood was always bright and welcoming, and at night fairy lights decorated pathways and trees to guide folk as they went about their business.

'So you see, I found it rather pleasant and extremely helpful,' said Bob, a little guiltily.

'You weren't to know we'd be separated,' said Felicity. 'I'm glad you went somewhere nice.'

As it turned out, Bob spoke to a rabbit, who sent him to an owl, who directed him to a wizard, who told him about pixies shifting enchanted pebbles to the mansion.

'That was when I had an idea,' explained the brownie. 'I asked a white witch to glamour me as a pixie and off I went with a map in my pocket and a plan in my head – to meet these pixies and, er, "borrow" a bag of pebbles from them. I'd hoped I would bump into you at some point, but thought perhaps I could solve the mystery myself. I got a *little* lost along the way, but it all actually worked in my – *our* – favour in the end. The rest … well, you know!'

Story told, they moved on in silence, heads down, following a stony dirt track across exposed and uneven ground which crept slowly upwards. From the summit they should be able to see the Mystical Mansion, Felicity hoped, and find a way in. Her heart gave a flutter of excitement at the thought that soon the pebble mystery would be solved, and then she could focus on her last riddle and on getting home. When they finally reached the top, all three stopped and gazed down at what awaited them below.

'The Mystical Mansion,' breathed Bob. He caught Felicity's eye. 'And you once thought you might never solve the pebble mystery. Well, between us, we seem to have got to where we need to be! Hopefully this will be an end to it.'

Felicity hoped so too, but it didn't look promising all of a sudden. The Mystical Mansion towered in the centre of the hollow, shining silver in the moonlight, which highlighted every angular surface and hid in shadow other unseen parts of the building. The effect was eerie and unwelcoming, as it looked jagged and dangerous, like a monster smouldering in its lair.

Lights glowed behind some of its many tall windows, like mismatched eyes in the face of this stony giant, watching and waiting. As she looked at it, however, Felicity realised that she recognised the sprawling house, except she was more used to seeing it perched at the edge of a cliff, and in much better condition. There stood the turreted tower, in darkness – the one she had always admired in her world. There was the wrought-iron balcony clutching the front of the building. Puffs of white smoke came from tall chimney pots that prodded the sky, snakes of green writhing from a smaller stack off to the left. The oddly shaped brickwork that framed the roof looked like sharp teeth in the darkness.

Then she saw the shadows.

They flitted past the windows as she watched, some slowly, others darting rather than drifting, but all strange, contorted shapes with outlines she couldn't even begin to identify. Felicity swallowed nervously.

'Who knew, eh?' said Bob. 'It was in front of us from the very start, but we just didn't know it! Anyway, the word is that the Collectors are depositing their pebbles somewhere inside and, I assume, are getting some sort of reward for doing so. We need to find this spot, drop off the pebbles I have here with me and somehow, er, save the day. Oh, and we don't have much time because, aside from anything else, the spell on this sack won't last much longer and I really don't want to be whisked away by these pebbles.'

Hatchet spoke up. '*That's* your plan?' he said. 'Just walk in and hope for the best?'

Bob bristled. 'It's all we've got. Do *you* have a better idea?'

Felicity stepped in quickly. This was no time to be arguing among themselves. 'We have no magic to speak of, but I've been brought here for a reason, so we have to try something,' she said. 'It's the only thing we *can* do. The Pebble People seem to think I can stop this, so I have to try. I promised them. Are you still in, Hatchet?'

'Of course I'm still in,' the hobgoblin muttered. 'I just think it sounds dangerous, that's all. But I'm not turning back now.'

'OK, good – and thank you both,' said Felicity. 'Let's get down there and find out what's happening once and for all.'

Bob nodded his agreement and the trio began to make their way down into the hollow at as brisk a pace as they could manage. They all felt the urgency of the situation and they all heard the increasingly loud wails at their backs. It seemed the ghosts were on the prowl and drawing ever closer.

The way down was full of obstacles – bushes and tiny gnarled trees and shrubs slowing them down and snagging on their clothes, like scraggly fingers trying to pull them back. Scratches or not, however, all were determined to reach the bottom and so they scrambled over stones and rocks, pushed through prickly bushes and kept on going until … they were there.

They halted as one at the edge of the clearing, where the Mystical Mansion stood stern and silent. Up close it looked even more grim and foreboding. Sparks crackled and fizzed from a chimney pot overhead, spraying into the night sky for mere moments before dissolving into nothing, eaten up by the hungry black atmosphere.

'Wait,' said Felicity. 'If I'm expected as "the Hunter", shouldn't I disguise myself before going inside? I still have my ring from the lagoon.' She fumbled in her bag. 'I can glamour myself into a white witch or something. Then I'll be more or less my usual size. What do you think?'

'Good idea,' said Bob. 'Better do it now, before we go any further.'

Felicity slipped on the ring and imagined herself transforming into a white witch. A shiver ran through her as the ring warmed up, and when she opened her eyes, it was green and she was indeed a witch, dressed in silver and with flowing white hair.

'Right, let's go,' she said.

They crept out from the foliage and followed a faintly trodden path towards the front door of the mansion. Many others had obviously been before them. In silence, they approached the majestic and haughty-looking building which held the answers, Felicity hoped, to a lot of her questions. When they stood before the huge oak door, studded round the edges with nuggets of cold, polished steel, Bob raised his hand to lift the knocker, shaped into the frowning face of a wizard. Before he could take hold of it, however, the door swung open.

Felicity followed her friends inside to the candlelit entrance hall, footsteps echoing their arrival. Behind them, the heavy door slammed shut, making Hatchet jump in alarm. His eyes darted anxiously from side to side, searching for someone or something, but there was no one and nothing to see.

'Now – which way to go?' said Felicity in a low voice, fighting off the fear that threatened to overwhelm her. Anticipation of the unknown was a terrifying thing.

'*Somewhere* in here is a room where the pebbles must be delivered to, but I'm afraid I never found out exactly where,' said Bob. 'The Collectors who returned never spoke specifically of where they had been, but they said that, once inside, they seemed to be guided by the stones themselves.'

A candle to Felicity's left flickered violently, as if someone had just swept past it, and she glanced round uneasily. There was no one in the murky gloom that she could see. The ceiling of the entrance hall rose high above them, while closed doors circled the empty space like tight little lips stubbornly pressed together. Heavy velvet curtains also hung here and there, no doubt concealing other entrances and doorways.

The windows, meanwhile, were curtain-less, which gave them a rather startled look, and the floor was a puzzle of bare, dusty flagstones. Here and there stood ancient candelabras with puddles of wax beneath them that looked like tiny ice-rinks. A tall staircase twisted upwards into the darkness in front of the three visitors and Felicity knew instinctively this was where they were meant to go.

'Up there,' she whispered, with steely determination. 'Does that feel right to you, Bob? You have the pebbles after all.'

'Well, I don't feel any resistance,' said the pixie–brownie, 'so I think it's worth a try.'

Felicity nodded and turned to the staircase, the others following behind.

When she reached its base she hesitated, then set her foot on the bottom step. Immediately, the staircase disappeared, yet Felicity's foot remained where it was – as if on solid wood.

'What on earth?' she exclaimed. 'Where did it go?'

She lifted her foot off the step and the stair wobbled back into view. Bob groaned. 'An invisible staircase – brilliant. It disappears from view as you climb it, to confuse you and prevent you from reaching the top.'

'Well, it's the only way we can go,' said a breathless Hatchet. 'I ran round and tried the doors down here and none would open.'

Felicity hadn't even noticed he'd been gone, but she smiled her thanks. 'We'll just have to memorise the amount of steps we can see right now and also the shape of the staircase and just take it from there,' she said, her eyes gleaming at the challenge.

She certainly wasn't going to let a staircase thwart her efforts now – not after all she'd been through. She studied the stairs, the twists and the turns, and decided she was ready. This time, when the staircase turned to empty air – or gave the impression that it had, anyway – Felicity kept going, Bob and Hatchet bringing up the rear.

It was a very odd feeling to be climbing something you couldn't see and she was thankful the banister was still there to grip onto.

She had counted about twenty steps up before the first twist to the right and then it was about five steps in that direction before the staircase had seemed to veer left sharply. After that, it would all be guesswork, as Felicity had been unable to see any further. She only hoped it didn't rise too much higher.

They navigated the turns fairly easily, considering, but Felicity began to feel more and more lightheaded as they climbed. It was too strange to be walking in empty space, despite feeling the solid staircase beneath, and the blackness pressed in close and stale around them. She had to sit down and close her eyes a couple of times, head tucked between her knees, gulping breaths of the stagnant, dusty air. But it helped enough to let her complete the ascent and she refused to look down at the dimly lit entrance hall now far below.

After climbing more than two hundred steps (Hatchet was counting softly to himself), Felicity was shuffling along yet another landing when her foot caught on something. She stopped and bent down to feel what it was.

Here, there were no candles to light their way, only murky darkness. Her heart skipped a beat as she felt a smooth surface like stone and feared she had just touched an enchanted pebble, but this was much larger, with jagged parts to it, so, hesitantly, she lifted it.

At once, everything changed. It was as if a curtain had been dropped from the front of a stage as torches with green flames licked light into the gloom and the staircase reappeared beneath them. Felicity realised they had reached the top – the staircase now opened out onto the fire-lit first floor, which had corridors stretching off to the left and right. She breathed a sigh of relief and looked to see what was in her hand.

It was a head.

## Chapter Thirty-Four
# Mansion Magic

Felicity swallowed a scream as she dropped the head. It rolled left away from her and kept on rolling long after it should have stopped, black painted eyes ogling her as it turned, until it sped through an open door and disappeared.

'What in the realm was that?' said Hatchet.

'A head. A *wooden* head,' said Felicity. 'But it was alive – I'm sure I saw it blink! How –?'

'How indeed!' Bob butted in. 'By clever and powerful enchantment – courtesy of the master or mistress of the mansion, I don't doubt! And where there's one, there'll be more. So, come on – no time to dally!'

Indeed, as he spoke, a full-bodied puppet filled the frame of the doorway. It was grotesquely disjointed, with long pointed arms extended crookedly towards them and legs splayed at awkward and painful-looking angles. The head had rejoined the puppet's body and the effect was deeply disturbing. Jagged, soulless eyes were cut roughly into the face, painted black around the edges and coloured red within, while long lashes made it look as if the puppet was shedding shards of sharp tears.

A long Pinocchio nose protruded into a very sharp point, like a harpoon poised to skewer some unsuspecting soul, and from the pinched-in torso hung rags so dirty, so laden down with the grime of untold years, they looked as though they would disintegrate upon touch. The puppet was bald and bony and smiled a pointed smile, baring black, empty space where teeth should have been. Then it sprinted towards them.

The movement was so unexpected and so quick that it took Felicity, Bob and Hatchet a crucial split second to realise they were being charged at by the creature. Bob was the first to snap to attention.

'*Run!*' he bellowed, and run they most certainly did, manic puppet in pursuit.

Not caring where they went, as long as it was far from the puppet, the three dashed away from it, down the right-hand corridor, the green torch flames flickering wildly as they passed. Felicity risked a glance back, stumbling as she did so but still managing to keep moving. The puppet had disappeared.

She stopped sharply. 'Wait!' she hissed at Bob and Hatchet. 'Where did he go?'

The others stopped just a little way ahead, panting and looking around in a panic. It was true – the puppet seemed to have vanished.

Felicity turned to Bob. 'Where now? *What* now?'

'Out of this hallway and fast!' said the pixie–brownie breathlessly. 'Before that fiend comes back. Quick, over there!'

He rushed towards a door and went to pull it open, but as soon as he touched the handle, it promptly disappeared. Bob jumped back in surprise.

'Try the next one,' urged Felicity and they ran to the next door along.

It too, however, disappeared as soon as the handle was touched. The same thing happened with two more doors, but when Felicity gripped the third after that, it swung inwards.

'This one then,' she muttered.

They all piled through, Hatchet shutting the door quietly behind them. It was dark but a light flickered on as soon as the door closed. Felicity swung round, but where the door had been there was now only bare wall. They were sealed in.

With puppets.

Petrified, the friends could only look on in horror at the population of creatures before them. All waited with bated breath – for what, they had no idea. Felicity relaxed a fraction, however, as she studied their wooden foes. These puppets were much less gruesome than the one that had chased them – more detached and eerie than wild and scary – and she felt her breathing calm a little. She stood transfixed with Bob and Hatchet, watching the tall, lanky puppets and being watched back.

The room itself was long and narrow, which meant the puppets filling it seemed to be more in number than they actually were, although Felicity still counted around twenty-three – more than enough to overwhelm the three of them anyway. They lined the sides of the room solemnly, wide eyes staring straight at the visitors.

There was nothing, or no one, else present that Felicity could see – just the puppets and a long patterned carpet stretching away from them towards a blank, lonely wall. Something dark stretched horizontally across the middle of the floor but, other than that, the space was unadorned except for an ornate chandelier dangling above them – and the chilly silence.

The mansion had vacuumed them up and Felicity's head was buzzing as she tried to think of an escape plan. The puppets were as scrawny as the angry one which had chased them, but this group was clothed in chipped paint rather than wearing tattered rags. Their skulls had painted-on black and brown hair and their sunken black-ringed eyes lured Felicity's gaze to them, much as a hypnotist might entrance an innocent spectator at his show. She knew she should look away and yet she ... just ... couldn't ...

Hatchet jumped as one of the wooden figures broke away from its companions and began taking slow steps towards them.

The approaching puppet was clearly the queen and the others her drones. Blood-red paint, faded and scratched, covered her lower half, while a pale primrose colour adorned her torso. It was her hair, however, which really marked her out as different. It hung down straight to her ankles and then curled and trailed along the floor for metres behind. It was black and shiny and alive – more alive, in fact, than any of the puppets appeared to be – a thing of beauty amongst ugliness, wriggling like a crawling baby impatient to walk.

The puppet stopped and reached forward, then curled a long, thin finger, inviting them towards her. Transfixed by her gaze, Felicity followed, not knowing why but realising she was powerless to stop her feet from moving, and her friends fell trustingly into step behind her. Even Hatchet made no protest or objection, for all were enthralled.

As the three ventured onwards, the puppet took steady steps backwards, until they had reached the midway point of the room and the darker-coloured part of the carpet. Felicity saw now, however, that it wasn't a carpet at all but an opaque pool, just about wide enough to jump across at a run.

The heads of the puppet army cracked sharply as their wooden necks swivelled round to watch them. The puppet queen glided effortlessly over the pool, Felicity and her friends waiting on the other side.

'*The pebbles,*' hissed the puppet in a wet, wooden voice.

Felicity gulped as Bob handed her the sack he had been carrying. Her hands untied the mouth of the bag, trembling just a fraction, and she lifted it towards the painted queen, showing her the contents. The puppet pointed at the pool.

Hoping it was the right thing to do, Felicity poured the pebbles into the dark, murky depths, the sack gradually lightening its load as the last of the tiny coloured stones slipped out of sight. As the final pebble hit the water, it began to glow, ribbons of dark crimson unfurling in the blackness. Felicity, Bob and Hatchet were by now all standing at the pool's edge and they watched, mesmerised, as the swirls revealed the enchanted pebbles, glowing now like bright jewels in the water. They spiralled downwards in a fantastic flurry of colour – like tiny stars whizzing around their own private galaxy, trailing sparkles of stardust. The friends watched as the pebbles one by one disappeared, the pool gradually darkening again as it swallowed them up.

The glorious red swirls which had swept the pebbles away became an impenetrable black once more, and when Felicity looked to the puppet woman for the next instruction, she had disappeared. Felicity spun round. The rest of the puppets had similarly vanished, leaving them alone in the chamber.

'Well, I'm glad *they're* gone,' said Hatchet. 'Creepy creatures.'

'Look,' interrupted Bob. 'The pool's gone too.'

'But how are we supposed to …' Felicity's words tailed off at the sight of a door set solidly into the wall ahead of them.

'*That* wasn't there before – was it?' she said, not sure anymore what was real and what wasn't.

'No, it most certainly wasn't!' said Bob. 'It must only reveal itself once the pebble price has been paid. Beyond that door, I *expect*,' he hesitated, 'is the reward – whatever it is – afforded to the bringers of the stones.'

'And it's where we must go, or at least where *I* must go,' said Felicity, 'to find this person once and for all and solve the pebble mystery.'

'Right, let's get going then,' said Hatchet and Felicity knew there was no point asking them to remain behind for their safety. Her friends were coming with her and she knew nothing would dissuade them.

The three approached the door and this time there was no resistance – it creaked open as soon as Felicity turned the enormous iron handle. It opened into a corridor carpeted in dark purple, light blinking at them from tall candelabras.

A faint smell of must mingled with the waxy smoke from the creamy coloured candles, which reminded Felicity of her mother. Her mum had liked lighting thick scented candles – usually vanilla – when she had a headache, as she had said it soothed her. Felicity couldn't say these particular candles had the same effect on her now, but they brought her a small shred of comfort nonetheless.

The corridor ran straight for a bit and then swerved off to the left. The trio said little as they approached the bend. At its turn was a set of steps leading upwards and another snaking down. Felicity, Bob and Hatchet looked at each other in dismay.

'Does any one way draw you to it?' asked Bob, his hazel eyes searching Felicity's anxiously.

She studied both stairwells. The upper one rose welcomingly into a well-lit space, yet there was something about the slightly murkier downward-facing stairs which seemed to capture her attention. When her eyes ran over the steps and explored the shadowy entry, she felt something urging her on.

'Yes – down,' she said firmly. So down they went.

Just twenty-seven steps took them to a chamber stuffed with books – on shelves, stacked high in precarious higgledy-piggledy piles all over the floor and strewn across a large oak table in the centre of the room. Bob's eyes lit up at the sight of them. A threadbare rug covered the middle section of the chamber, and to the left the glowing embers of a forgotten fire still burned. Beyond the table, just off to the right, was a curtained doorway and Hatchet headed towards it.

'Wait!' said Felicity. She stared at the messy books. 'I want to have a quick look at some of these. One or other of them might give a hint about the purpose of all this – tell us something useful. It's worth a try.'

'We really shouldn't linger,' said Bob, though he looked tempted.

'I won't be long, but I have to check,' said Felicity and she strode over to the table, pulling an opened volume towards her.

It appeared to be a sort of geography book on Fairyland, with intricate maps finely sketched across the thin parchment. The pages where the book had been left open looked strangely familiar to Felicity and she studied it more closely. The writing was scrawled in a different language, so she scrutinised the map itself. For a moment, it stirred something in her but then it seemed to shift slightly and the feeling was gone. She couldn't recognise it.

Turning her attention to another book, she saw pages filled with recipes, or more likely, she mused, spells. Another few books showed much the same but when she opened the cover of a smaller volume bound in soft green leather, with a border of light silvery wood. Felicity felt a frisson of energy run through her. She paused.

It looked like a diary, the rich creamy parchment covered in the neat handwriting of its owner. Again, Felicity couldn't read what it said but her stomach somersaulted as she realised the handwriting was very like her own. She'd loved learning how to join up her letters at school and had quickly perfected her penmanship, creating letters which looped and swirled elegantly like writing from the olden days. She didn't have time to study it properly now, but she lifted the book and slipped it in her bag before rejoining Bob and Hatchet.

Beyond the heavy curtain was another room, rectangular and filled with paintings of assorted shapes and sizes. Their oils and watercolours looked wet and slick, as if just freshly painted. They were a little creepy, so the trio moved quickly to the door at the far end, leaving the strange exhibition in their wake. They passed into yet another corridor and Felicity stopped in frustration.

'We don't seem to be getting *anywhere!*' she exclaimed. 'It's just room after room. Maybe I chose the wrong way after all.'

She looked down the corridor, which was noticeably darker than the others had been.

'Which way now?' she asked, for it ran from left to right before them, offering two more choices.

'This mansion is just like another maze,' she grumbled. Then a thought struck her. 'My map!' She rummaged in her bag. 'Maybe it will lead us!'

The map, however, was nowhere to be found, despite a very thorough search.

'It must have gone back to the wizard,' she said in dismay. 'He warned me it might do that.'

She shivered as a cold draught tickled her skin. Bob shivered too and then Hatchet. The hobgoblin looked at them in horror. 'Ghosts!' he squeaked.

Felicity felt goosebumps rise on her arms, her skin clammy. It was true that the corridor had taken on a distinctly chilly quality. 'Are you sure?' she said.

Bob shivered again. 'Yes, I think he's right,' he said grimly. 'We'd best not linger.'

Felicity's eyes widened. Her hair swirled around her shoulders as an unseen force swept past and knocked Bob clean off his feet. He slammed into the wall behind and looked dazedly back at her. The ghostly gusts seemed to be coming at them from the right, so Felicity turned left again. She helped Bob up.

'Quick, this way,' she said.

They ran down the corridor, its twists and turns slowing them down a little, the ghosts blustering behind them and nipping at their heels. Breathless, they rounded another corner and, before she could stop herself, Felicity ran smack into a tall, thin column of stone. Or so she thought until it seized her by the wrist in an iron grip.

Two enormous eyes glared at her, magnified behind thick black-rimmed glasses.

## Chapter Thirty-Five
# The Enchanter

The figure muttered a string of words dripping with magic, without removing his intense gaze from Felicity's, and she heard Bob and Hatchet yell and make struggling sounds behind her. She twisted round only to see her friends wrestling, to no avail, with thick cords of enchanted rope. The figure turned sharply and dragged Felicity after him, forcing her to follow with his unyielding grip on her wrist.

He led her through a door and Felicity's protestations were cut short as she saw piles of snowy-white pebbles, bled dry of colour and arranged methodically around the edges of the huge, echoing chamber.

The figure dragged her on and all she could do was let herself be pulled helplessly into a further chamber – this one even bigger and even more intriguing. Marble tables zigzagged across the room, covered with tubes spewing coloured smoke and exotic smells through the air, mixtures fizzling and popping. Sweet flowery scents mixed with those of freshly cut grass and damp earth, while strange spicy aromas mingled with tangy lemons and oranges. They were delicious, if not strange, combinations – neither unpleasant nor indeed perfect fragrances – the aromas of nature all thrown together in some sort of odd experiment.

The stone floor was covered with scraps of mismatched carpet and upon them sat squat sacks of pebbles, waiting for whatever it was they were there for.

Felicity was dragged to the far side of the room and pushed into a surprisingly comfy armchair. She struggled immediately to get up but every time she tried to stand, something forced her back down. She quickly realised it was impossible, and indeed foolish, to waste her energy in fighting back, so she sat and waited, wondering what was going to happen now. She hoped Bob and Hatchet were safe.

The mysterious figure was busying himself at one of the nearby marble worktops, pouring a cheery yellow liquid into a bowl and frowning when nothing happened. He then turned to a clear, curly tube bubbling with a dark-green potion and busied himself collecting a variety of ingredients. In fact, he seemed to have forgotten all about Felicity, which gave her time to catch her breath, calm down a little and observe her captor.

He was very tall and very thin and wore a high-collared black cloak with holes scattered along the bottom. There was no hat, just steel-grey hair streaked with black and messily pushed back from his face. He had a slightly pointed nose, eyes like pieces of coal and a thin mouth.

Felicity decided it was now or never. She had to do something.

'Can I ask who you are and … and what you're doing?' she said, her voice trembling slightly. 'What have you done with my friends?'

Her captor swung round, his eyes narrowing into slits. 'The Hunter speaks,' he rasped, then laughed humourlessly. He was at her side in a flash, eyes peering into hers intensely, making Felicity take a sharp breath.

'What. A. Ridiculous. Name,' he enunciated slowly. 'If anyone is "the Hunter", it is I, for *I* have suffered long and hard and will never give up until every last wretched pebble in this wretched kingdom is uncovered, bled and forced to reveal its secrets, for I *will* not rest until I find them!'

He swung away from her again and Felicity watched as he swept the contents of the table onto the floor with a crash, shattering the glass, the potion bleeding onto the floor. 'You seek me out to stop me?' he hissed. 'Well, seek me out you have, but no one – *no one* – can stop me! As for who I am – I am the most powerful enchanter in the realm and I intend to keep going for as long as I have to. Forever, if that's what it takes!'

Felicity had no doubt she had finally found the mastermind behind the pebble thefts. There was a ferocious look in the Enchanter's eyes, however, which made her feel like a gazelle locked in the hungry glare of a tiger. She needed a plan – and fast.

The Enchanter now appeared to be searching for something and when he turned round, he held a silver hand mirror, tarnished with age. He waved it at her, a sinister smile creeping across his face and sending shivers tingling up and down Felicity's spine. Goosebumps rose on her arms and even her scalp prickled as he approached. Magic was about to happen – she could feel it in the air – and it wasn't going to be the good kind, she was sure.

The Enchanter stopped in front of her and held out the mirror, plated side facing him and Felicity's pale reflection staring back at her. She jumped, then remembered she had changed herself into a white witch earlier, though as she watched the glamour fell away and her own features returned. She stared defiantly up at the Enchanter.

'Look again,' he said. The glass had clouded over, the faint smell of night – of dew-coated grass and slightly salty air – perfuming the space around them now as the mirror cleared to reveal a starry sky flecked with flying witches.

Their cloaks billowed out behind them as they cut silently through the darkness – a whole host of witches and, Felicity thought worriedly, with Hatchet's ex-mistress surely amongst them.

The Enchanter shook the mirror gently and the image fell away to reveal a swarm of goblins scrambling over messy undergrowth. Felicity gasped.

'The witches and goblins come to overthrow me,' said her captor. 'They want to harness the dark forces which have been unleashed through my experiments and put an end to my work. *You* are the least of my worries, little girl ...'

Felicity's mind worked furiously. The witches mustn't gain control or the realm might never recover, but the Enchanter did need to be stopped. Meanwhile, here she was trapped in an armchair, with her friends imprisoned somewhere in the mansion.

On impulse, she called after the Enchanter, who had turned away again. 'Wait! Who does the mirror belong to?'

The Enchanter stopped and glanced back at her, suspicion heavy in his eyes. 'What makes you think it isn't mine?'

'Well, you've stolen all of these pebbles,' said Felicity, 'so why not this magic mirror as well? Besides, it's obviously meant for a woman or a girl.'

The Enchanter pressed his lips together so tightly his mouth became nothing more than a grim line. He clutched the closest table with white-knuckled hands and breathed deeply.

'It was *hers*,' he said through gritted teeth. 'And now they're coming to ruin it all and I still haven't found her.'

Wisps of white smoke puffed out from the Enchanter's clothes and circled around his feet as his agitation increased. Scared he was about to combust before her eyes, Felicity kept going nevertheless.

'Who are you talking about?' she said. 'I'm not here to cause trouble – I promise. I just want to help the Pebble People, solve my riddles and go home. But if you tell me what happened to her – whoever she is – maybe I could help?'

The Enchanter turned towards her, eyes for a second tinged with remorse, then quickly clouding over with anger. 'It belonged to Aurelia,' he said. 'My wife.'

He seemed, then, to forget Felicity altogether as he stood entangled in his thoughts. Sadness flickered across his face, then rage, then resignation. Finally, he spoke again, but in a voice thin as a whisper. 'She's gone. Aurelia and Seraphina are gone. *Pebbles*,' he spat out.

Felicity didn't know who Seraphina was, but guessed maybe a daughter. One thing was now clear, however – it seemed the Enchanter's family had been lost and that the enchanted pebbles were the cause of it. So what, then, was the Enchanter doing collecting them all?

'Surely, surely, you aren't trying to find out where they were sent to?' she asked, half-incredulously and half-admiringly, as realisation pinched her.

A crash on the roof made her jump. It also awoke the Enchanter from his stupor and he snapped back into action.

'Yes, and find them I most certainly will!' he declared, throwing a scrawny arm up to the ceiling in defiance. 'Those cretins won't stop me either!'

A voice cut through the chamber.

'And just *who*, may I ask, would these *cretins* be that are you referring to?'

## Chapter Thirty-Six

# Witchery

T he voice was polite but jagged as broken glass. It came from the chamber but Felicity hadn't noticed anyone entering the room. She caught the faint scent of mixed spice mingled with the sweet, heady scent of hawthorn blossom.

A cloaked figure slowly materialised not far from where the Enchanter stood – a witch. Not one Felicity recognised from her adventuring, and certainly not one she wanted to be in the room with.

Her eyes swam in shadows and her gaze was dark as a graveyard. Her features were waspish but not those of a young witch, time trickling through the cracks and fissures in her skin.

Hair the colour of a filthy mop bunched around bony shoulders, covered with the token black cloak, flowing skirts of sooty black billowing underneath it and rustling now as the witch took a calculated step forward.

'Stop!' said the Enchanter, holding his palm out towards her. 'I demand that you come no closer.'

The witch arched a shapely brow.

'You've been making quite a lot of demands recently,' she said icily. 'I'm here to put an end to that – with my sisters.' She clicked her fingers and Felicity counted twelve more witches as they materialised around her.

'You've actually done us a favour, loosening the boundaries between here and the underworld – and more besides. But now it's time we took over.' She laughed.

The witches closed in on the Enchanter until they had formed a circle around him. Felicity saw sparks crackling from their fingertips as they started chanting. The Enchanter was whispering – and staring hard at Felicity. Intuitively, she lifted herself from the chair and found the resistance had gone. The Enchanter – for whatever reason – had freed her.

With the witches focused on their prisoner, Felicity slid quietly off the chair and hid behind it. How could she help? She was confused as to why the Enchanter had freed her, but perhaps all that talk of his family had softened him enough to feel sorry for her when the witches arrived. There was no time to dwell on that now, though – she could hear footsteps on the roof. She rummaged in her bag for something that might be of use, hesitating when her fingers closed around the soft leather-bound diary. Again, she felt a tingle of energy running from the book into her hand when she touched it.

The witches were chanting much louder now, along with the Enchanter, as he tried to hold back the combined force of their power. Felicity saw what looked like lightning bolts zigzagging from the witches' fingertips, the Enchanter smouldering profusely from the effort of trying to shield himself from whatever spell they were casting. An ethereal mist rose up around him, enshrouding the Enchanter within a magical cloud as his attempts to break through the circle of witches failed. He appeared to be keeping them at bay for now, thought Felicity, but he was clearly outnumbered, so it couldn't last for long.

She flicked through the creamy pages of the diary, scouring them for anything that looked remotely like a spell. She stopped in the middle of the book, where the pages were oddly much smaller than the rest, with writing so tiny it was hardly legible. The words were arranged in what looked like verses, and Felicity's heart skipped a beat. A spell? It was certainly worth a try. The light emanating from the witches was growing brighter and brighter and she could no longer see the Enchanter as they kept up their high-pitched chant. She only hoped he was still protected by his magical mist – and that what she was about to do would have some effect.

Trembling, she began to read from the book, her tongue tripping over the unusual sounds of the words. What if she wasn't saying them properly? What if it wasn't a spell – or one that would be of any use?

It was all she had, however, so Felicity read on, her voice becoming steadier and louder as she spoke, the language becoming somehow easier for her to speak, if not understand. Indeed, without any real control over herself, Felicity felt compelled to stand up and recite the spell directly at the witches in a strong, clear voice. It was written over a number of those tiny pages at the book's core, and she kept reading and turning the parchment until at last the witches realised what was happening.

What was happening was that their spell no longer appeared to be having its desired effect. As Felicity spoke, the bright light surrounding the Enchanter dimmed, until she could see him through his protective cloud. Indeed, by the time she had finished the spell, the only visible magic still in the room was the mist around him. The witches stared at her, fury in their eyes. Yet none stirred against her.

'A spell wrapped in willow wood,' spat the witch who had entered the chamber first. 'Though why it worked for a mortal is – interesting.' She looked at Felicity, eyes burning with curiosity. 'Such protection spells only work for so long against us, my dear, so we'll be back with our goblin friends – soon – to finish what we started. And next time, it won't be just *him* that we're after.'

She shot the Enchanter and then Felicity a steely stare before she and the other witches melted soundlessly from sight, the smell of spiced hawthorn lingering behind them.

\*\*\*

The Enchanter stared at Felicity as his misty cloud evaporated. He frowned. 'Let me see that,' he said, gesturing towards the book. 'Where did you get it?'

'From here,' said Felicity. 'In a room in the mansion. I thought … well, I thought the writing looked a bit like mine so I took it with me so I could look at it later, and then when the witches came I thought it might have spells inside which could help.'

'It has,' said the Enchanter, 'a protection spell at its core – one which will offer up the defence you need according to the foe you face at that time – strengthened by the border of willow wood around the edge of the book. In this case, the willow worked against the witches perfectly, for a willow tree – also known as the Tree of Enchantment or Tree of Witcheries – is full of powerful magic. Witches often bind their brooms with willow wood, but it can work against them, just like any other wood. The spell combined with the willow magic was enough to stop them in their tracks tonight but,' his eyes narrowed, 'a human should not have been able to perform it. So, the question is – who exactly are you, Hunter? And what drew you so keenly to my *wife's* book?'

Felicity didn't quite know how to respond to that and, before she knew it, she was telling the Enchanter her story, recounting her journey to the realm and all her adventures to date. She seemed to have no control over her tongue any more at all and she suspected the Enchanter had loosened it with magic. When she had finished, he asked to see the pebble which had brought her to Fairyland.

'I wonder …' he muttered. 'This was enchanted specifically for you, so it should hold the key to who you are – even though the Pebble People were unable to discern why it chose you. The magic of the stones sensed you were the one who was to come here, and my own magic might just be able to distil why exactly that was. May I?' Felicity nodded. It couldn't hurt, surely, and she didn't really want to say 'no' to the Enchanter in case he started smouldering again – or switched back to angry-captor mode.

Using curved metal tongs, he picked up the pebble, dropping it with a soft plop into a beaker of clear liquid. After a few seconds, it began to shake as the pebble vibrated, the liquid slowly turning a buttery colour, which then darkened to purple, green, red, blue and orange, before settling into a bright gold, small bubbles popping on the surface. The golden sparkle of the pebble had detached itself from the stone, which in turn was now snow white. The Enchanter poured the fizzing gold liquid into a clear, twisted tube, which wound round and round to another circular jar and then on to a complex system of smaller tubes, which ended with one very thin, straight tube extended over a small hand-carved walnut bowl.

The elixir whizzed through the tubes, singing shrilly as it went, until, finally, all that was left was a single drop of molten liquid, which wobbled and then slowly plopped into the waiting dish below. The Enchanter grabbed it and ran to another table, where Felicity could see nothing but a large square of polished silver. He turned the bowl over and the drop spattered onto the surface.

The silver tray began shimmering and shifting on the table, and as she drew closer to it, Felicity saw it was showing different scenes – of the sea, cliffs and a cottage. It then cleared to reveal a face that detached itself from the silver and drifted above the table, becoming more and more life-like by the second. It was an old woman, and as the features became more defined, Felicity froze.

It couldn't be.

'No …' said the Enchanter. 'How –?' He looked at Felicity, surprise and shock on his face. 'I know that face. It's older than it should be, but I *know* that face.'

Felicity couldn't help it. 'That's my grandmother!' she blurted out, astonished.

The Enchanter gaped at her. 'Aurelia?' he said. 'That is Aurelia – my *wife*.'

Now it was Felicity's turn to gape. Her Granny Stone's first name was Audrey.

'*You* must hold the key to everything,' said the Enchanter, hope dawning on his face. 'You were brought here to put an end to all of this and so, as it finally turns out, you have. You have ended my search – you have found her!'

His eyes became glassy with tears. 'Now I understand. The Human Realm – where time moves so much quicker than here. Of course – it was the *Human Realm* all along and I could not see it until someone from that realm showed me the truth. My mind was clogged and fogged with so many other places and times and dimensions, and yet they were taken to the one place without any real magic left! She is safe – and alive – but what of my daughter? She must be safe too, surely, when you are here – my *granddaughter* – Felicitina!

'And, if you're here and were able to work magic, then that means only one thing. You are a child of both realms, which is rare indeed – one who is able to cross safely between the two at any time, pebble or no pebble. Who knows what powers you might have and what you might be able to do with them!'

## Chapter Thirty-Seven
# Answers and Expectations

Silence stretched in the chamber as both Felicity and the Enchanter contemplated what he had just said.

Felicity was full of questions, her mind whirring from one thought to the next. Was this true? Was she *magic*? Was her grandmother – her *mother* – magic? It would certainly explain what she had seen her mother doing in the attic that time, yet she just couldn't quite believe it. How could her Granny Stone be a ... what – enchantress? Witch?

'I don't understand,' she said.

'It's simple,' said the Enchanter. 'When a magical being enters the Human Realm by their own desire, they can work their magic as normal, but when an *enchanted pebble* whisks them there by its magic, then they are trapped, no matter how much magic they know or do. That's the thing about the pebbles – they whisk you

369

away, but they don't bring you back or let you *get* back easily. Which is why they're so dangerous.

'There are endless possibilities as to where a pebble might take you. I've been experimenting on them since I lost my family, to try and locate them. By distilling the pebbles' essences, I could conjure up images of the places they would take folk to, if lifted by an unsuspecting soul, and use my powers to sense whether Aurelia and Seraphina were there. And now, thanks to you, I have found them. We must make haste and journey to the Human Realm!'

'Wait,' said Felicity, not quite knowing what to make of all this. 'I'm not magic and my granny certainly isn't magic. And besides, I can't go anywhere until I solve my final riddle and until I know the pebbles won't be stolen anymore. I promised the Pebble People.'

'Why would I want to steal pebbles now when I know where my family is?' said the Enchanter. 'Quest completed, my dear! As for your riddle, well, that is a slight problem, I'll admit, but we'll solve it quickly and get rid of that ridiculous Riddler in no time.'

'What about the folk who are still bringing you pebbles?' said Felicity. 'You have to make sure they stop stealing them. And what about all those who have disappeared off into strange lands while they were collecting pebbles for you? What are you going to do about them? Oh, and don't forget my friends, who you took prisoner!'

The Enchanter clicked his fingers and pixie Bob appeared with Hatchet in the chamber, looking bewildered by the sudden change of scene.

'I will tell the fairy folk I need no more pebbles,' he said. 'And once I get my family home perhaps I will look into finding those others lost to the pebbles, but in the meantime there is much to be done!

'Of course, had you known of your true nature before, then the Riddler could have been avoided,' he added. 'For *you* can leave Fairyland any time you wish, being a child of both realms. However, once you start solving his riddles, solve them you must, otherwise you will be bound to him forever and trapped in the Fairy Realm, no matter *who* you are. So, we will solve this riddle, then go to Aurelia and then … maybe we will track down those other lost folk.'

Felicity wasn't sure she liked the Enchanter's use of the word 'we', but help with the final riddle would be good, and she did want to get back home.

'If this is all true,' she said, frowning, 'then how did you lose your family? I've told you my story, so I think you owe me yours.'

The Enchanter sighed. 'It was a foolish error on my part,' he said. 'I should have been watching them more

371

closely. We were out on a picnic one day when my dear little daughter wandered under a willow as Aurelia and I talked. Aurelia ran after her as soon as she realised, and I followed behind, but I was too late. I saw Aurelia grab Seraphina by the arm to stop her, but she'd already reached for a pebble – she loved collecting sparkly things, you know – and they were whisked away together before my very eyes.

'From that moment, I have been searching for them day and night. I made it my mission to track down every enchanted pebble I could find, in the hope it would lead me to my family. The Pebble People only watch over the stones and, while they have their stony magic and can *read* the pebbles, they can't work out where someone has gone without seeing the pebble which took them. So I began experimenting, to see if I could find a pebble which led to wherever they were taken – more than one pebble can lead to the same place, you know – but I made errors and ended up being spirited away myself for far too long. I know that my magic has been causing problems in the realm but I just had to find them.'

'Yes,' said Felicity. 'Dangerous creatures and dark forces have come through because of what you've done, and the Pebble People have been losing their powers. You've put many people in danger and that will have to be put right.'

She didn't want to anger him, but she felt someone had to say it. Bob and Hatchet stood beside her, and she felt safe with her friends there.

The Enchanter's brow furrowed. 'Yes, well, for that I am sorry. Perhaps when we return with my family we can begin to make amends. Also, Felicitina, you must awaken your magic and be taught how to use it. That is why you must come back here with us – to *learn*!'

All Felicity wanted was to get home and speak with her Granny Stone. Who knew what she would make of these developments? Felicity couldn't imagine her living anywhere except her cottage. Also she hadn't told the Enchanter her mother had gone away, and he hadn't asked about her father … Felicity's head was swimming but she still had a riddle to solve.

'For now, at least, we must focus on the final riddle, yes?' said Bob, giving her a reassuring look. 'The rest can wait. One thing at a time – before making any sort of decision.'

Felicity nodded.

'OK, so what was the riddle?' asked her friend.

Felicity knew it from memory by now, so she recited:

*'For this endeavour you must be clever,*

*Fast of speed and slow to greed.*

*When rocks seem wrong, when perspective is gone,*

*When a cliff isn't always a cliff.*

*There you will find a secret untold and a legend they say, of a tiff.*

*Beware when you're there, of who you might meet and always look out for the feet.*

*Be they friend or foe, well, nobody knows …*

*And therein lies a win or defeat!'*

The Enchanter gave a guffaw. 'Well, *that's* ridiculously simple,' he said at once. 'It's giants and I *suspect* that the Causeway of the Giants is where you must go!'

Bob frowned and then looked admiringly at the Enchanter. 'I do believe you're right!' he exclaimed.

Hatchet, who had been silently observing them until now, spoke up. 'The Causeway of the Giants? It *does* make sense – why didn't *we* think of that?'

'I'm not an enchanter for nothing,' said the Enchanter huffily. 'Riddles pose little problem to a mind such as mine, muddled though it may be from long times spent alone in dark, troublesome places. So, you must go to the causeway and uncover this secret.

'The rocks will seem "wrong" because they're hexagonal in shape, as far as I can recall, and perspective will most certainly appear skewed, as the cliffs tower high above – higher than anywhere else – and will dwarf you most certainly. A cliff isn't always a cliff because at least one of them holds the stony form of a giant's relative – a hunchback old woman, I think – and watching out for enormous feet speaks for itself! There *are* tales of a secret surrounding these giants, and it's said two once had a ferocious fight – the "tiff", perhaps, that you speak of?

'As for being "friend or foe", well, who knows if this giant is good, that giant bad? They keep to themselves but there are tales of all sorts about them from those who have encountered the race. I myself have the ghosts of some cousins of the giant family in this very mansion and such temperamental apparitions you never did see. I'm hanged if even *I* can figure out what they're about!

'In short – nobody knows their true nature. Even the king and queen of the realm do not know, for the Causeway of the Giants is beyond the boundaries of the Fairy Realm and so is not governed by them –' The Enchanter stopped.

'Hmm, perhaps the Riddler suspects that you are different,' he murmured. 'This would appear to be a test of more than one skill then,' he mused. 'In solving the riddle, yes, but more importantly, in travelling to and *entering* the causeway, which will prove your ability to cross between multiple realms. Or – he simply wants you to fail.

'You will have to be "fast of speed" to dodge the giants and "slow to greed" to abstain from their huge wealth, because if you pocket any of their treasure, you will void the riddle. There – I think that's everything now. I can help you get to the causeway but only *you* can solve the secret and remove the bindings of the Riddler. Then you must return here and decide what to do next.'

The Enchanter had become steadily calmer and more serious as he spoke, and Felicity realised this was probably a truer reflection of his former self, before he lost his family and was almost driven to madness in trying to find them. What he said made sense, though, and she had to trust now in his powers as an enchanter – and as a seemingly new member of her family – that he was right.

'OK, well, I'd rather do it sooner than later, so – what next?' she asked. 'How do I find the Causeway of the Giants?'

The thought of another long journey didn't appeal to her in the slightest but, if it had to be, it had to be.

'Simple,' said the Enchanter. 'I can spirit you there with very little effort. But only you.' He eyed Bob and Hatchet warily.

'Now, hang on a minute,' said Bob. 'She can't go off alone to seek giants!'

'Yes, you can't hold us here,' said Hatchet. 'We're going too! I told you I'd help,' he said to Felicity. She smiled at the hobgoblin.

'I know you did and I'm grateful to both of you for offering to come along, but I think perhaps this last riddle must be completed alone and I'd feel better knowing you're both safe here at the Mystical Mansion.

'Please,' she said, as Bob and Hatchet opened their mouths to protest again. 'I think it has to be this way – for now.'

'I don't like it!' said Bob. 'Safe indeed!'

'Nor I!' said Hatchet quickly, although Felicity thought he seemed a *little* relieved at not having to face giants.

She looked imploringly and a little anxiously at Bob.

'Well, I suppose you came a long way on your own before, so you can surely do it again,' he said gruffly.

'Indeed she can!' boomed the Enchanter, startling them all. 'In the meantime, I will strengthen the willow enchantment used on the witches tonight with my own magic, though it will only protect us while inside this mansion – and, even then, for just a few days. But first, food, rest and *then* the spell.'

## Chapter Thirty-Eight
# The Causeway of the Giants

Rain lashed down the next morning as Felicity prepared for her departure to the land of the giants.

They'd rested and eaten since the excitement of the night before, dining in the Enchanter's elaborate banquet room and sleeping in cosy four-poster beds, so Felicity felt refreshed and ready for her final adventure, though she looked at the weather in dismay. The sky was overcast with dark, angry clouds which showed no sign of leaving and the sun was nowhere to be seen.

The Enchanter led them across the hallway of the mansion which, in daylight, seemed a fraction less scary. He'd explained over their late supper that he had worked various spells over his home to protect himself while he experimented, hence the puppet which had pursued them and the ghosts which had spooked them. The jagged puppets still gave Felicity the chills, though, no matter why they were there.

'This way – hurry now,' said the Enchanter and the three friends followed him underneath the staircase and down a flight of stairs hidden behind it. They entered a small circular room without windows and fitted only with a few scattered wooden shelves holding dusty bottles of who knew what.

'Felicitina,' said the Enchanter. 'You must stand here in the centre while I say the magic around you. Close your eyes and focus on the causeway and I will do my best to get you there.'

Felicity was growing to like how her name translated in the Fairy Realm – better even than the human version. She did as the Enchanter asked and nodded at Bob and Hatchet. They had already said their goodbyes and she only hoped she would soon see them again.

She closed her eyes and thought of the causeway and what she might find there, waiting for the Enchanter's words and the strange wind she had felt when Mezra had magicked her from his underground home to the wood.

She was startled, however, at the sudden sound of seagulls and a sharp breeze in her face and she opened her eyes, gasping at the coldness. She was no longer in the Mystical Mansion but on a silver path sandwiched between Fairyland and what she assumed was Giant Land. The Enchanter had promised to take her to the border between the two realms so she would have a chance to get the lay of the land and catch her breath before entering the causeway. He'd been as good as his word and Felicity marvelled at the preciseness and power of his magic. Going backwards would take her onto grass leading towards the spiky fir trees of a Fairyland forest, while stepping forward would see her walk into a thick fog to somewhere she couldn't yet actually see. Behind her was clarity – ahead of her, the unknown.

She stepped forward and felt gravel under her feet, but it took a few seconds for Felicity to make her way through the fog.

Then she saw a swirling mist hovering above the sea to her left, while to her right huge towering cliffs overshadowed the landscape and swept down to a crumbling path which disappeared around a bend. Black crows mingled with the gulls, riding the air currents around her, and she wondered if any were witches or watchers – or, indeed, just honest-to-goodness birds.

The descent was creepily quiet – if there were giants about Felicity certainly couldn't see or hear them. It filled her with a little confidence and a little fear, as the path took her onwards. Loose stones crunched under her feet. To giants, the walk was probably no more than a few short steps, but to Felicity, it was a much more time-consuming exercise. Once or twice she thought she caught the distant sound of pipes playing – not sweet fairy pipes, but mournful church piping – then the wind whispered in her ear and it was gone.

When the path finally ended, Felicity stood before a stony entranceway. The air shimmered within it, as if a bubble was stretched between the stones. 'Here goes,' she muttered, as she stepped through. The sky disappeared.

Or at least – that's what it seemed like, as something or *someone* had blotted out the view above her.

*'Oho – what do we have here then?'*

Felicity looked around for the speaker, knowing full well it must be a giant but wondering why the voice wasn't louder.

*'Mind-speak,'* murmured the voice. *'If I spoke with my full, true voice it would explode your eardrums. So I speak through my mind into yours, and I ask – who are you and what are you doing here?'*

Felicity hesitated.

*'You can speak freely or use mind-speak – as you prefer.'*

'Can – can I *see* you? Please?' she asked.

All she could make out was a fuzzy mass of – what was that? Cloud? Vapour? Dust?

*'Not at this time,'* said the voice. *'I am but the essence of myself here, but follow me and we will speak further, away*

*from here, for things watch and things spy and one who adventures to this land must surely be worthy of an audience.'*

Without waiting for a response, the giant mass moved away from Felicity. It led her down another stony path, flanked by those towering cliffs, and round another bend to a mass of rock columns, all neatly stacked according to height – the tallest closest to the cliff and the smaller stones leading down to the sea's edge. The stones were hexagonal in shape and rimmed with silver, which boomeranged sunlight around them. The sides of each column looked vibrant and alive, even in the mist and overcast colour of the day, winking at her and looking suspiciously as if they were made of solid gold.

As they drew nearer, Felicity saw that the tops of the stones shone like glass and she found it hard to wrench her gaze away from them. The cloud kept leading her onwards, however, past the columns, through another archway, around a bend and a smooth sculpted rock, which looked like a giant chair, up a steep hill and onwards towards a huge stone organ set deep into the cliff-side.

The stone pipes were not cold and silent, but glowed gold and played melancholy music at them as they approached. The notes sounded sad and gloomy and Felicity, reaching out to touch the warm pipes, felt a tremor running through them.

Yet still the cloud moved on, past the organ, up another hill and around a corner until they reached a huge auditorium. From their high vantage point, the auditorium sprawled out in a massive circle below, almost surrounded by vertical cliffs but with the furthest end open to the sea beyond. The vast structure was empty – a crumbling ruin, its base strewn with loose boulders and smaller, jagged rocks.

Her guide had stopped and was hovering over the middle of the space. As Felicity watched, the dark cloudy mass billowed and spread outwards, upwards and downwards, taking on a blurred outline, and within a few seconds had transformed into the very clear shape of a person. A few seconds more and the cloud solidified into flesh and Felicity faced her very first giant.

## Chapter Thirty-Nine

# Secrets

The giant had a low, broad brow, bushy brown hair and eyebrows, a long bulbous nose and a very wide mouth. Huge ears stuck out from tufts of messy hair and two hazelnut eyes looked back at Felicity. He wore dusty, khaki-coloured trousers, a scruffy green shirt missing buttons and a pair of shiny brown boots.

'I can speak freely here, without harm,' he said, in a normal, if gravelly, voice. 'The auditorium was designed and made with magic and allows us giants to converse safely with non-giants. So – no more mind-speak!'

Felicity was glad of that. She hadn't liked having someone speaking in her head. 'Why weren't you in this form when you met me?' she asked.

'Ah, that is because I wanted you to come with me and was afraid that if you saw me outright that you would not follow,' said the giant. 'But with you now up there and me down here, we can speak almost eye to eye

– and without mind-speak! So, what brings you to Giant Land, young girl? We rarely have visitors here.'

Felicity decided the best thing to do was be honest. The giant seemed friendly enough. Perhaps he might help her.

'My name is Felicity and I'm here because I have to solve a riddle.'

The giant raised his bushy eyebrows at her.

'It's the Riddler,' she said. 'He –'

'He sets three riddles for you to solve so you can return from whence you came,' said the giant. 'I know of him and his meddling ways. And so – you have come here in search of something and hope that I will help you.'

Felicity nodded. She asked the giant if he wished to hear the rhyme and he did, so she spoke it three times until he could repeat it back.

'So you're after a secret?' he mused, scratching behind his ear. 'Well, you've found the right giant, for it was I who had "a tiff" as the rhyme says, but, oh, it was long ago and now I'm the only one left in these parts – well, almost the only one – and who knows what this secret is that you need and whether I should give it to you or even have it to give. Why should I help you and, in so doing, help that wretched Riddler, hmm? He's no friend of giants!'

It was a good question and one Felicity didn't immediately know the answer to, but as she thought about what the giant had said, she had an idea.

'The rhyme doesn't specifically say I have to *tell* the Riddler what the secret is,' she said with a grin. '*There you will find a secret untold* … Yes – but it doesn't say anything about passing that secret on! So, if we can work out what the secret is, and if you will only agree to tell it to me, then the riddle is solved and the Riddler will know – he always pops up when I solve one – and that will have to be enough for him!'

The giant frowned in concentration, then a slow smile spread across his furrowed face.

'Outwit the Riddler,' he said. 'I wouldn't mind doing that. He has meddled in our affairs from afar before now and deserves no kindness from me!'

'If you helped, then I could go home as well,' said Felicity anxiously. 'I've been in the Fairy Realm for so long now and I need to get back to my family as soon as possible.'

Her earnest look and heartfelt plea made the giant smile again.

'I will help!' he announced. 'I will search for the secret and you will wait over there, in my guest room.' He pointed to the other side of the auditorium. 'You'll be much more comfortable.'

It looked unreachable, except by giants, and now it was Felicity's turn to frown.

'How will I get over there?'

'I carry you,' said the giant simply and he held out his hand, palm upwards.

Not so long ago Felicity would have balked at the very notion of stepping onto a giant's outstretched palm, but she did so now without hesitation, in the hope that, at last, she was nearing the end of her adventures.

The giant curled his hand inwards a little so Felicity wouldn't fall out and she steadied herself against a thick, grubby finger. It was an odd sensation to be carried by the giant across the auditorium and from this height she didn't even want to think about the option of falling. On the way over, she found out that his name was Facoonlimn, or 'Lim' for short.

When they reached the other side, she stepped off Lim's hand gratefully. This part of the cliff had crumbled away, so there was an impassable gap between her and the remainder of the path heading seaward. The other side meanwhile was blocked off by large boulders. She frowned as she realised her mistake too late.

The giant grinned. 'Now I have a maiden,' he said delightedly. 'A maiden of my own. Someone to talk to and to sing to me and tell me stories. You will have all the jewels you could ever want and, in return, you will entertain me!' Felicity gasped. 'What about my riddle – the Riddler – me getting home?' she sputtered. 'You lied to me!'

'Oh, don't worry about the Riddler. He'll never be able to get at you here, and you'll have much more fun with me.' The giant started to whistle.

'I'm going for a swim now, so you can explore your rooms and think about how you will thank me for my kindness and generosity. I will return at dusk.'

'*Thank* you? No! Wait! Come back here!' Felicity's calls were lost in the empty auditorium as the giant strode out of it in just a few brisk steps. Back by dusk? It was only mid-afternoon now, she thought with despair. She would have *hours* to wait and she *had* to solve that riddle! How could she have been so foolish?

Peeking over the edge of the cliff, Felicity knew there was no way down. The only possible route would have been through or over the boulders, but they stretched high into the sky and when she pulled out a few smaller pieces of rubble from the bottom, the rocks simply rearranged themselves, filling the gaps she had just made. Magic – of course.

She kicked the cliff in frustration and rage, biting back tears. She would *not* be defeated now. She *would* find a way. But in the meantime, she had plenty of time to think – and explore. She walked cautiously to the hole in the cliff which led into her rooms. There was just enough natural light falling in through the entrance and from a couple of low-burning candles to show masses and masses of treasure inside. Coins of all colours, precious stones, silver candelabras, finely woven rugs and glittering jewellery covered the cave, which extended quite far back into the cliff. As much as she explored, however, she couldn't find any gaps or entrances – only cold, solid rock.

Felicity sighed in frustration again and went back to the entrance, gathering up some soft, silky rugs to sit on and pulling her enchanted crockery out of her bag. She ate chicken sandwiches, a squishy tomato and a small slice of rhubarb pie, washing it all down with a nice warm cup of comforting tea.

As she ate and took the time to think through her predicament properly, her mind cleared, and as she chewed her final piece of pie, she realised how stupid she had been. In her panic she had completely forgotten about her ring from the Lagoon of Lost Desires. Of course! She could glamour herself as a crow again and just fly away.

Her elation was dampened, however, as she remembered she had yet to discover the secret she sought from the giants. 'Who will help me?' she whispered to herself. 'There's no one here.'

'*Maybe you are wrong in that,*' a voice murmured in her head.

Someone was using mind-speak on her and it was a different someone than before.

'Who's that? Where are you?' she said.

'*I am Agnethea. I am here,*' said the voice – a female voice.

Felicity still couldn't see anyone. She looked around her in confusion.

'*Back here ...*' prompted the voice.

Felicity turned and walked back into the cave.

'*Further – further yet,*' it encouraged her.

She walked to the very back of the cave, her eyes searching the gloom for something, anything, to indicate a presence.

'*Here ...*' whispered the voice.

Felicity followed it to an old lantern covered with coloured shards of mosaic glass. She couldn't see inside, but it was glowing faintly. She picked it up and the voice congratulated her.

'*Well done! Just don't open it in here, as it's much too small a space in which to release me, as he well knows. I only wanted some company – please.*'

'Everyone wants company,' muttered Felicity in exasperation. 'I just want to go home! Why don't you and the giant out there just speak to each other, instead of him capturing me?' She knew she sounded selfish but she was so disappointed and was worried she would never solve the riddle now.

*'We had an argument long ago,'* said the voice sadly. *'A terrible argument. Rocks were hurled and I was fatally wounded, so I am but a ghost, trapped where he put me because he is unable to cope with his guilt – but too angry to set me free into the spirit world. I am doomed forever.'*

'A tiff …' murmured Felicity. 'So I'm still on the right track then.' The thought filled her with renewed hope. 'Look, I have some magic on me,' she ventured. 'I'm going to leave this cave now – and leave you too – unless you can help me.'

*'Leave? How? No one leaves here,'* said the voice sharply.

'Well, I can and I'm going to,' said Felicity firmly. 'If you help me, though, I'll take you with me and release you once I'm out. You can go to the spirit realm or wherever you want then. So will you help? I have to hurry.'

The lantern was silent for a few excruciating moments.

*'Yes, I will help,'* said the giantess. *'What do you need?'*

Felicity recited the rhyme and briefly explained her predicament in solving it. 'So you see, I've found the land of the giants – and you, who had "the tiff",' she said. 'Now I just need to know the secret. Do you have any idea what it is?'

'*There are many, many secrets hidden here,*' said the giantess. '*To know which one you seek, you must first tell me your story and then I can see which you require.*'

There really wasn't time for all this, Felicity thought, but she reined in her impatience as she realised there was a bit of sense in what Agnethea said. Perhaps her story would make it more obvious which secret the Riddler wanted her to find.

So she quickly recounted her tale to the giantess trapped in the magic lantern, trapped in the magic cave, trapped in the auditorium, and when she had finished, shadows were lengthening at the entrance to her prison. It was almost dusk.

The lamp was silent for quite a while afterwards – the giantess sifting through her secrets, Felicity hoped. When the voice finally spoke again, she jumped.

'*I am sure that the secret you seek is this one and that it is part of this quest and another yet to come,*' said Agnethea. '*It is the secret of the stones. Your pebbles spirit folk away to unknown realms and unknown lands, but the stones from the Causeway of the Giants …*'

She paused.

'They *bring you back again.*'

## Chapter Forty

# Crossing Over

The wind buoyed Felicity onwards as she sped through the sky, quite used to having wings by now. She clutched the lantern with her talons and scanned the ground below for somewhere safe to land. Spying the giant chair, she swooped down towards it, keen to rid herself of her heavy burden. Once back to her own shape again, she studied the lantern. It glowed softly.

'When I let you out, you won't harm me, will you?' she asked.

'Of course not,' purred Agnethea. 'But you must not go back on your word now. I kept my promise so you must keep yours.'

Felicity tugged at the little door of the lantern, and as it swung open, a puff of grey dust sprayed out, followed by a billowing cloud of pale purple. It stretched out into the giantess but, unlike her captor, did not solidify, as she was indeed a ghost.

'Free at last,' she said, yawning widely and no longer using mind-speak. 'It feels wonderful!'

She caught Felicity's anxious look and laughed merrily.

'Fear not child – I'm off to find that cumbersome idiot before I retreat to the spirit realm. I bid you farewell and good luck and I thank you once again.'

She eyed the stone chair. 'That wishing chair might be handy in getting you back to where you want to go,' she said. 'Toodle-oo!'

With that, the giantess soared up and away from Felicity and was soon a distant dot in the darkening sky. Dusk had arrived and Felicity wasted no time in settling herself into the smooth curve of the wishing chair and making her wish, after she changed back from crow to girl.

'I wish I was back at the Mystical Mansion,' she whispered, holding tight to her bag, which was now also carrying some of the magic causeway stones, wrapped up in enchanted silk to shield their power.

She closed her eyes as the organ pipes began to play louder and more furiously in the distance, as the wind picked up and the damp smell of seaweed and salt and moss filled her nostrils. The chair began to rock gently – backwards and forwards, backwards and forwards – lulling her into a light sleep. When she awoke, she was back at the cliff-side where she had first arrived in Fairyland – not far from the gates of the Mystical Mansion, which had returned to its original spot.

Blobs of white fell down around her and Felicity looked up. 'It can't be snowing, surely!' she said in disbelief. She caught some of the white substance on her hand and realised it was foam, floating up from the sea below and drifting down like snow onto the cliff.

'How lovely – what a sight; it's like stardust in the night …' She looked for the Rhyming Riddler immediately and he materialised on a rocky outcrop in front of her, his robe glowing in the gloom.

'So – you've solved your riddle number three. Well, aren't you glad now to see *me*?' he said, grinning.

Felicity glared at him. 'Not really, no – I have to go,' she said, through slightly clenched teeth. 'But I found the secret – you know I did. Now I'm free and of you I'm rid!'

The Riddler's eyes narrowed.

'Aren't you forgetting just one little thing?' he said, smiling a dangerous smile. 'Tell me the secret, for *you* cannot keep it – to *me* you must sing.'

'The riddle says nowhere the secret's to share,' said Felicity, her heart beating wildly. 'But the puzzle's been solved, so my quest is resolved.' She knew she was taking a risk in withholding the secret, but she felt sure in her decision and she was tired and knew that little good would come of telling such a powerful secret to this strange little magic man.

The Riddler jumped off the rock, his face contorted in rage and disbelief. He hopped up and down, trampling the grass, and then began laughing hysterically, pointing an accusing and knobbly finger at Felicity. 'Oh, how clever you are!' he taunted.

*'Clever Felicity – oh, isn't she,*
*As clever as clever as clever can be.*
*She found out the secret and now she will keep it!*
*The riddles are done, there's no more – not a one,*
*So leave here my child, leave the realm and the wild.*
*But mark you my words – and the whisperings of birds –*
*That soon you'll be back and good friends you will lack.*
*Best look out for me – for right here will I be,*
*Waiting and watching for* you *by the sea …*
*You've solved all the riddles, but I tell you this –*
*I won't help you home, you impudent miss!'*

Before Felicity had a chance to take a breath, the Riddler had vanished. She had no idea what his final riddling meant, but she was free – she had solved his rhymes and she was *definitely* going home.

\*\*\*

The heavy door of the Mystical Mansion swung open in welcome and Felicity stepped inside tentatively. A yell from Bob made her turn, as her friend – in brownie form once again – came hurtling from the shadows, followed shortly afterwards by Hatchet, who was grinning from ear to ear. She hugged them.

'You succeeded then?' said Hatchet. 'We knew you would!' And he danced a quick jig around them, making Felicity laugh.

'Yes and I uncovered a very valuable secret, which I think the Enchanter will be extremely keen to hear,' she said. 'Not even the Riddler knows it and he isn't very happy about that!'

Bob frowned. 'It doesn't bode well to make an enemy of the Rhyming Riddler,' he said worriedly. 'An annoyance he may be but his meddling can become much more dangerous than you would believe if you get on the wrong side of him.'

Felicity decided right then and there not to mention the Riddler's parting rhyme.

'Well, I'm here now and I'm OK, so that's the main thing,' she said. 'Let's find the Enchanter and see about getting me home!' She didn't quite feel comfortable calling him 'grandad' just yet.

She followed Bob and Hatchet back the way they had come – into a cheerfully lit banquet room with a table laden with goodies. Felicity's stomach rumbled at the sight of a mouth-watering joint of beef in the centre, surrounded by dishes of vegetables, creamy mashed potato and much more. There was also fresh fruit, a cream-filled sponge cake, chocolate and iced buns and big jugs of chilled orange juice.

'Come, eat,' said the Enchanter. 'And welcome back, Felicitina,' he added with a smile.

During the meal, Felicity recounted her tale, answering all the questions thrown at her by Bob and Hatchet as she did so. The Enchanter, however, simply listened, nodding every now and again at one thing or another.

Finally, all that was left to tell was the secret and all three leaned in closely to hear it. When Felicity revealed what it was, the Enchanter leapt from his chair in astonishment.

'There is a cure!' he exclaimed. 'Why then – that makes the task all the easier!'

He looked at Felicity. 'You *did* bring some stones back with you?' he asked anxiously.

'Of course.' Felicity smiled. 'A whole bagful. The giantess assured me they aren't considered valuable by the giants, so it wasn't like I was stealing their treasure.'

'This means when we find the folk lost to the pebbles, we can simply bring them back with us – including

Seraphina and Aurelia,' said the Enchanter. 'Though we have to find them first … There's so much to do! Your friends can assist you if they wish, or return to their homes –'

'I need to find Butterkin,' said Bob at once. 'I'll certainly help!'

'But first,' interrupted Felicity, 'I'm going home – alone – to speak with my grandmother. I helped the Pebble People, I solved the riddles and I even found out where your wife was,' she said pointedly to the Enchanter. 'But now I need to go back to her and explain everything.'

'Oh, but, my dear, you *are* home,' murmured the Enchanter. 'You *are* home. But yes – you must return to the Human Realm first and tell Aurelia all that has happened. Then I will try to cross over myself and we'll bring her and Seraphina back here with us.'

Felicity didn't want to disappoint her new friends or let anyone down, and she shuddered to think of where some of the fairy folk had ended up after being spirited away by the pebbles, but right now, she knew home was where she needed to be. She also wasn't sure she wanted another adventure so soon and yet … She did wonder, if all this really *was* true – which it certainly seemed to be – what powers might she have and how would she be able to use them?

What on *earth* would Sophie say about all this, and could she even tell her friend what had happened? She'd never be believed! And what about her mother? Could this mean she wasn't ill at all? She had been sent away because of her odd behaviour, but perhaps she had been caught doing *real* magic in an attempt to get back to the Fairy Realm. If she had told Felicity's father her secret, then he must have thought her mad – or, worse, dangerous – and as a result, he'd had her taken away!

She chose her next words very carefully.

'I hope that I might come back,' she said. 'But it all depends on what happens when I go home. Of course I want to help you find Butterkin and the others if I possibly can, but I don't even know how much time has passed in the Human Realm. It could be weeks – or even months!'

'Time is a strange beast and you never know just how fast or slow it will go,' said the Enchanter, 'though one can sometimes hazard a guess.'

Felicity had been in the Fairy Realm for barely a week by her reckoning, so she found it extraordinary to think she could have been missing from her home for much longer – or shorter – than that. She wondered if her grandmother might have an inkling about what had happened.

'So you'll help me then?' she asked the Enchanter.

'You've solved the riddles and you have the power to walk between the realms anyway,' he said. 'You must simply go back to where you crossed over on your way here, close your eyes, think of the Human Realm and then you should be able to go safely back.' He paused. 'We will be waiting for your return.'

'That's all I have to do? Think of home?'

'Think *intently*,' said the Enchanter. 'Banish all thoughts of the Fairy Realm, for forces will conspire to fill your head with magic and mayhem. You must ignore this and shut it out. Picture the other side – the sights, the sounds and the smells, your grandmother's face, her voice … You return in the same way. Just reverse all of this and think only of the Fairy Realm.'

'Thank you,' said Felicity.

'It's late now,' said the Enchanter, glancing at his pocket-watch, a golden antique. 'But no time like the present, eh? Your friends can accompany you. I shall be here when you return.' He looked at her hopefully.

'I'll try my best,' murmured his granddaughter, desperately willing her words to be true.

The Enchanter nodded, then turned on his heel and left the room, his footsteps echoing round the chamber.

\*\*\*

Felicity, Bob and Hatchet made their way down to the little wooden bridge at the foot of the Mystical Mansion, none of them looking forward to the time when they would have to say goodbye. To keep their minds off their imminent farewells, they chattered about their adventures and had long reached the stream and the spot where Felicity had found her original pebble before they finally stopped talking.

Felicity hated goodbyes and they had all agreed not to linger long when the time came for her to go, so, with a smile and a wave, she bid them farewell. Bob had invited Hatchet to stay with him for a while, until he found himself somewhere to live, and the new friends ambled off up the hillside, leaving Felicity behind. She was alone once more. Well – almost.

She was just preparing to cross over when the hillside gave a soft rumble and parted to reveal the little Pebble Leader – Cobble. He was alone this time and looked much more relaxed and happy than he had at their first meeting. Felicity smiled at him a little guiltily. She hadn't even thought about trying to find the Pebble People to tell them she had stopped the thefts, although they'd obviously sensed it anyway.

'My dear girl!' exclaimed the little man. 'You weren't leaving, surely?'

'Oh, well, as a matter of fact –'

Cobble smiled at her. 'We wanted to thank you for fulfilling the prophecy and saving us all from more mayhem,' he said in his gravelly voice. 'I came to invite you to a party in the Rocky Valley in your honour. Will you come?'

'Oh, I'm sorry – I'd love to but, you see, I also solved my three riddles and I really need to get home now,' said Felicity, a little disappointed that she would miss the festivities, as she was intrigued to see where the Pebble People lived.

Cobble looked downcast at her words.

'I *may* be back, though, so perhaps another time? I'm really glad I could help you and I hope you enjoy your party. Please tell the rest of the Pebble People – and Clarity in particular – that I would have loved to come but, right now, I just can't.'

The Pebble Leader bowed.

'I understand,' he said. 'Well, I thank you, human girl, and do not forget us if in fact you do return again. We will be waiting and we would love to welcome you.'

'Will your powers return, now that the pebbles are no longer being taken?' asked Felicity.

'They will strengthen over time, but we must first reclaim the stones and return them to the weeping willows, where their magic will be replenished by the Trees of Enchantment,' said Cobble. 'Thank you again –

Felicity.' The Pebble Leader flashed her a grin, then clicked his pebble shoes and was gone. Felicity smiled to herself – just how did they do that?

She took one last, long look around her and then closed her eyes tight and thought of home – *her* home – without pixies or goblins or fairies or witches. Where crows were just crows and that was that – she hoped.

A jagged moon pierced the sky and she stood still beneath its silver glow. Waves splashed and she breathed in the familiar smells around her – the bramble, the fresh water of the stream mingled with the pungent, salty sea, the rich, earthy aroma of the soil and the grassy scent from the hill. She inhaled deeply and then she heard the wail.

Her eyes were still closed and she was trying to picture her grandmother's kindly face, but instead a young woman appeared in her mind. She was kneeling by the stream, washing a garment and weeping. She looked up and Felicity tried to shut out her image but the young woman's beautiful features melted away before her eyes and an old hag's wrinkled face stared back at her. It opened a sagging, toothless mouth and let out a heart-rending cry and Felicity realised she was once again looking into the eyes of the banshee.

'It's not real, it's not real,' she told herself, although she didn't dare open her eyes to find out.

'Think of *home*,' she ordered herself and pictured the walk back to the cottage, her bicycle, the path she would take, her garden, her grandmother welcoming her at the door … The goblin crouched by the woodshed waiting to get in – the chopped wood, *only* wood – her bedroom and the imp in the wardrobe …

'*No!*' shouted Felicity. '*My* bed, *my* wardrobe – with clothes and *only* clothes inside!'

The imp image vanished and Felicity felt stronger. Next, Silvertoes flitted into her thoughts with a wicked laugh and a flick of her silvery hair.

'*Come dance with me*,' she sang. '*We'll set you free …*'

Felicity erased the elf from her mind's eye and then she was smelling the sweet flowers which grew by her Granny Stone's back door. She was opening the door and catching the full-bodied aroma of freshly baked scones and wheaten bread, her grandmother turning around from the oven with a hot, flushed face and beaming at her with joy, wiping floured hands on her apron and hurrying over for a hug.

Felicity hugged her back. She was home.

# Epilogue

A hard, polished beak preened sleek black feathers as the crow balanced on the branch of a sycamore tree in Felicity's garden. Satisfied it had cleaned effectively, the crow turned its beady eyes back to the cottage and waited.

Something almost always crossed over when the realms were breached, and spying was the crow's forte. One of them anyway.

He would wait.

He would report back and, when the time came, he would play his part.

*So now my dear reader, this tale here is done*
*But will it be – could it be – the only one?*
*Those witches and wizards are watching her still*
*And they'll watch and they'll wait and they'll be there until …*
*Felicity Stone crosses over once more,*
*Takes on the challenge and goes through that door,*
*Into the realm of enchantment and fear,*
*Where magic abounds and strange things lurk near.*
*With mischievous pixies and fairies and elves,*
*The good and the bad and those out for themselves …*
*Goblins and ghouls and giants and ghosts,*
*Which of these folk will frighten the most?*
*Just who is who and just what is what?*
*What there is right and what there is not?*
*Will you be afraid of their tricks and charades?*

*Or take on the next Magical Masquerade?*

# Acknowledgements

It took a few years, but the adventures of Felicity Stone finally made it into print! My thanks goes to everyone who's encouraged me along the way, but to the following people in particular …

To my early readers, who saw the opening chapters of the book (or parts of them) and gave their feedback – Bernie McGill, Damian Gorman, Felicity McCall and Jenny Morris. Also, to my more age-appropriate beta readers who came later on – Jessica and Mia – and to Denise Rosborough for sourcing them. Thanks also to Moira McFadden for her beta reading services and general support.

I would also like to thank my brilliant editor, Emma Dunne, as well as Averill Buchanan – for recommending Emma and for providing general publishing advice and book formatting assistance. Thanks also to Andrew Brown at Design for Writers for the wonderful cover design, and to Laura Crossett for creating the book trailer which came after.

Many thanks also goes to Carlo Gébler and Felicity McCall for taking the time to read and review *Magical Masquerade* pre-publication and provide cover quotes.

Thanks must also go to Kelly Creighton, Anne Caughey, Jane Talbot and Paula Cardwell, who all gave their time to listen, advise and support me along the way. I'd also like to thank Mrs Barbara Crawford, as she encouraged me a lot in my early writing and helped me to develop it, as well as generally inspiring me about literature.

And finally – thanks to my family for being a bookish lot and encouraging me to read from a young age. Thanks particularly to my mum and dad for their support and to my brothers and sister – who all love a good story.

Also … to my nephews in Switzerland – Christos, Alex and Theo – I hope that you'll get to read this book soon and will thoroughly enjoy it!

# About the Author

Claire Savage grew up deep in the countryside around Magherafelt, Northern Ireland, where she spent lots of time reading stories of magic and adventure. Like Felicity, she wanted to enjoy her own exciting escapades, so often went exploring with her brothers and sister – and a fair few cats – in the surrounding fields and lanes.

Holidays were spent on the North Coast, where she now walks every day with her cocker spaniel, Reuben, getting lots of inspiration for her stories.

Claire works as a copywriter and journalist by day, but by night, she can more usually be found conjuring up strange and unusual tales ... A number of her short stories have been published in literary journals, including *The Lonely Crowd*, *The Incubator*, *The Launchpad* and *The Ghastling*, as well as in *SHIFT Lit - Derry* writing magazine, with some poetry also in print.

In July 2014 Claire was awarded a National Lottery grant from the Arts Council NI as part of their Support for Individual Artists Programme, helping her write a collection of short stories and poetry. She was also chosen as one of Lagan Online's 12NOW (New Original Writers) for 2016/17.

*Magical Masquerade* is Claire's first novel.

**Claire blogs at:** *https://clairesavagewriting.wordpress.com/*
**Find Claire on Facebook:** *Claire Savage - Author*
**Follow Claire on Twitter:** *@ClaireLSavage*

Printed in Great Britain
by Amazon